RAINBOW BOYS

Alex Sanchez

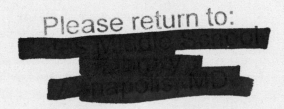
SIMON & SCHUSTER BOOKS FOR YOUNG READERS

New York · London · Toronto · Sydney

SIMON & SCHUSTER BOOKS FOR YOUNG READERS
An imprint of Simon & Schuster Children's Publishing Division
1230 Avenue of the Americas, New York, New York 10020

For information about special discounts for bulk purchases, please contact
Simon & Schuster Special Sales at 1-866-506-1949 or business@simonandschuster.com.
The Simon & Schuster Speakers Bureau can bring authors to your live event. For more
information or to book an event, contact the Simon & Schuster Speakers Bureau at
1-866-248-3049 or visit our website at www.simonspeakers.com.

Also available in a Simon & Schuster Books for Young Readers hardcover edition

Designed by Paula Winicur
The text of this book was set in Mrs. Eaves.

Manufactured in the United States of America
First Simon & Schuster Books for Young Readers paperback edition May 2003

21 23 25 27 29 30 28 26 24 22

The Library of Congress has cataloged the hardcover edition as follows:
Sanchez, Alex, 1957-
Rainbow boys / Alex Sanchez.—1st ed.
p. cm.
Summary: Three high school seniors, a jock with a girlfriend and an alcoholic father, a
closeted gay, and a flamboyant gay rights advocate, struggle with family issues, gay bashers,
first sex, and conflicting feelings about each other.
ISBN 978-0-689-84100-2 (hc)
[1. Homosexuality—Fiction. 2. Coming out (Sexual orientation)—Fiction.
3. High schools—Fiction. 4. Schools—Fiction. 5. Alcoholism—Fiction.
6. Interpersonal relations—Fiction.] I. Title
PZ7.S19475 Rai 2001
[Fic]—dc21
2001020952
ISBN 978-0-689-85770-6 (pbk)

WITH GRATITUDE

to my editor, Kevin Lewis,
my agent, Miriam Altshuler,
and all those who contributed to the creation of
this book with their encouragement and feedback,
including Bill Brockschmidt, Michael Cunningham,
Peter Ho Davies, Sam Dubreville, Barbara Esstman,
Allan Gurganus, Scott Hunter, Chuck Jones,
J. R. Key, Michael Klein, Kate Lesar, Richard
McCann, Patrick Merla, Alex Moe, Elissa Nelson,
Rob Phelps, John Porter, J. Q. Quiñones,
Bob Ripperger, Doug Rose, Sean Sinclair,
Lee Stern, and Michael Walker.
Thank you all.

TO THE COURAGE

of youth—present and past

BE SURE TO CONTINUE ON AFTER THE END
FOR A SPECIAL TEASER CHAPTER OF
RAINBOW HIGH,
THE SEQUEL TO *RAINBOW BOYS*

CHAPTER 1

JASON

KYLE

NELSON

Jason Carrillo walked around the block a third time, working up his courage to go into the brownstone. When he finally stepped off the curb to cross the street, a car swerved past him, blaring its horn. Jason leapt back and caught his breath. Shit. All he needed was to get hit and end up in the emergency room. His parents would discover he'd lied about going to the park to shoot baskets.

He shielded his eyes from the warm afternoon sun and watched a group of teenagers enter the building. He glanced at his watch. If he walked in late, maybe nobody would notice him. Then again, everyone might notice him. Maybe he shouldn't go in at all.

He'd read about the group for teens in his school newspaper the previous spring. He'd torn out the phone number and carried it in his wallet for weeks. Every so often he would unfold it, stare at the numbers, then fold it up again—until one evening, when his parents and sister were out and he was home alone, he uncreased the scrap of paper and dialed the number.

A man answered: "Rainbow Youth Hot Line."

Jason slammed the receiver back into its cradle and jumped up. He couldn't believe he was actually going through with this.

After a while, his breathing slowed and he called again. This time he stayed on the phone.

The voice on the other end of the line was friendly and warm, not at all what he expected.

"Are you gay?" Jason asked, just to be sure.

The man laughed. "Of course."

Jason never imagined that someone could be gay and laugh about it.

He asked questions for more than an hour and phoned the hot line three more times during the summer, speaking with different men and women. Each of them invited him to a Saturday meeting. No way, he thought. He wasn't about to sit in a room full of queers.

He pictured them all looking like the school fag, Nelson Glassman—or Nelly, as everyone called him. Even though a lot of people liked him, Jason couldn't stand the freak—his million earrings, his snapping fingers, his weird haircuts. Why didn't he just announce he was a homo over the school loudspeaker?

No, Jason was *not* like Nelson. That was for sure. He had a girlfriend. They'd gone out for two years, since they were sophomores. He loved Debra. He'd given her a ring. They had sex. How could he possibly be gay?

He remembered the first night he borrowed his best friend Corey's van and he and Debra drove to the secluded lane by the golf course. A little shy at first, they awkwardly clambered in back and lay side by side. The sweat poured off him as he wondered: *Will I be able to go through with it?*

When Debra slid her hand beneath the elastic of his underwear, he panicked. "Are you sure you want to do this?" his voice squeaked. "I mean, what if you get pregnant?"

From her jeans pocket she pulled a condom. His heart raced, as much from fear as from excitement. Excitement won out. That night he made it with her—a girl. Homos couldn't do that. Ergo, he couldn't be a homo.

Ever since, he and Debra had been inseparable. Every day at school they ate lunch together. At basketball practice, she watched him from the bleachers, twirling the ring he gave her on her necklace. Each evening they talked on the phone. Weekends they went to movies. Sometimes they borrowed Corey's van, other times they made love in her parents' basement rec room.

So why'd he continue to have those dreams of naked men—dreams so intense they woke him in a sweat and left him terrified his dad might find out?

On those nights he lay awake, trying to make sense of his feelings. Maybe it had to do with what happened that time with Tommy and how his dad had caught them. But that had been years ago, when he was ten.

He'd turn eighteen in a few months. He needed to concentrate on his future—bring his math grade up, finish senior year, get that basketball scholarship, and go to college. He didn't have time for some stupid Rainbow Youth meeting.

Yet now, on this September Saturday, after six months of carrying the yellowing ad for the group hidden in his wallet, here he was.

He crossed the street toward the brownstone and stopped to

look at himself in a car window. He tried to smooth his hair, but the curls wouldn't cooperate. Shit. Why did he care? After all, it was only a group of queers.

Twenty or more teenagers packed the sweltering fourth-floor room. Some sat on metal folding chairs, fanning themselves. Others lay draped across threadbare couches, grumbling about the heat. A few sat cross-legged on a stained, well-worn rug.

Jason scanned the room for an empty seat. There weren't any. He was thinking he should leave, when suddenly his eyes met those of another boy. Smiling across the crowd was Nelson Glassman.

Jason froze. How could he have been so stupid? That little faggot would spread this all over Whitman.

Nelson fingered a wave, like they were best buds, then leaned toward a boy in a baseball cap and whispered something. The boy looked up, his eyes widening in surprise.

Jason blinked. *Kyle Meeks? What was he doing here?*

"Let's begin, please." A stoop-shouldered man standing in the middle of the room clapped his hands. "Would everyone find a seat? Yes, I know it's hot. Tam and Carla went to get fans. Find a seat, please."

Jason turned to leave, but at that moment Kyle came toward him, extending a hand.

Jason offered a sweaty palm. "Wha's up? I think I'm in the wrong place."

"Can you boys find a seat?" the man shouted over the noise of the group.

"Here," Kyle whispered, and grabbed a folding chair from the stack that leaned against the wall. Without warning, the entire stack started to slide. Jason reached out to stop them, but it was too late. The chairs hit the floor. *Crash.* Then, silence. All eyes turned to stare at him and Kyle. A couple of boys on the rug burst into applause. The rest of the group followed with hoots and whistles. Jason wanted to crawl under the rug and die.

"All right, all right." The facilitator waved his hands, signaling the group to settle down. "Boys, please take a seat."

Kyle turned to Jason, his face red from embarrassment. "I'm sorry." He turned to pick up the fallen chairs.

"Let me do it," Jason said. The last thing he wanted was for Kyle to knock over the rest.

Nelson came over to help. "Way to go, Kyle."

Jason opened chairs for Kyle and himself, then sat down, avoiding Nelson's gaze.

Nelson unfolded a third chair and wedged himself between them. "Well hello, Jason. Imagine seeing you here."

Jason had never spoken to Nelson during their three years at Whitman. He wasn't about to start now.

But Nelson was relentless. "Of course, I always suspected—"

That was too much. Jason turned to him, but the facilitator clapped his hands again, and Nelson looked away, smiling, letting his words hang.

"My name's Archie. I'm today's facilitator. Let's go around the room and introduce ourselves by first name." As he spoke an older girl sitting beside him interpreted his words into sign language for two deaf guys sitting by the radiator. "If this is your first time here," the facilitator continued, "let us know, so we can welcome you. Kyle, you start, and we'll move clockwise."

Jason slid down in his chair, furious. The phone volunteers hadn't mentioned introductions. Kyle introduced himself. Jason still couldn't believe seeing him here. He hung with Nelson at school, but he looked so . . . normal—the shy swimmer kid with glasses who always wore a baseball cap. Everyone kidded him about it, but he just laughed along with that goofy grin of gleaming braces. *He's okay,* Jason thought, *in spite of knocking over the chairs and embarrassing the shit out of me.*

The circle of introductions continued. It was a pretty diverse-looking group. Only a few of the guys looked as faggy as Nelson. There were some geeks. One college-aged guy named Blake could've been a fashion model. A group of blond prep-pies, wearing khakis and loafers, monopolized the cooler side of the room.

There were a *lot* of girls. When a girl with boxy glasses intro-duced herself, Jason could've sworn he'd seen her before. Then he remembered her picture from the *Post*. She was one of six high school seniors nationwide to score perfect SATs. When the paper interviewed her, she'd come out as a lesbian.

Across the room, a black girl and a white girl, Caitlin and Shea, sat on a love seat. Earlier Shea had exchanged glances with Nelson. At first Jason thought her gestures were about him, but he wasn't sure. Now the two girls were all over each other. Both were pretty—not his idea of dykes. It was hard to believe they couldn't find guys to like them. He should get Shea's phone number, he thought. She was probably just confused, like him. Maybe they could help each other.

Then it was Jason's turn to introduce himself. He sat up straight in his chair and felt the tension in his shoulders. "My name's Jason. It's my first time here, but . . . I'm not . . ." His throat felt parched. "I mean, I'm just here to see what it's like. I'm not . . . you know . . ." Everyone stared at him while he tried to finish.

Archie rescued him with, "Welcome, Jason," and moved on.

Jason slid down into his chair again.

Nelson bounced up in his seat. "My name's Nelson, and it's

my first time queer—I mean, here." Everyone laughed, and he continued: "In my case there is no doubt that I most definitely am"—He turned and grinned at Jason—"you know . . ."

Jason wanted to deck him right then and there.

"Seriously," Nelson said, grabbing his backpack, "I want to announce that I have queer visibility buttons, courtesy of my mom and PFLAG." He turned to Jason again. "That's Parents, Families and Friends of Lesbians and Gays. My mom is vice president." He pulled the buttons from his backpack. "Lovely pink triangles, Gertrude Stein pins, and a variety of slogans. Here's one: 'My parents are straight and all *I* got is this lousy button.'"

The group laughed.

"Et cetera, et cetera. If you want one, see me at the break."

"Okay, everyone," Archie said. "Today we're going to talk about 'coming out.' What do we mean by that?"

Caitlin's hand went up. "It's when you stop hiding that you're queer—or bisexual, or whatever."

A boy raised his hand. "I thought coming out meant the first time you do it—you know—with someone your own sex."

"That's when you come," Nelson said. "Not come out."

The group hissed, and the boy threw a pillow at Nelson.

Archie smiled. "Let's keep it clean." He motioned for the group to settle down. "Some people don't come out until after they've had sex for years. Others come out before they've had sex with anyone."

"Coming out means you're no longer ashamed to tell people," said Shea. "It's a question of liking yourself and feeling good about being gay."

One of the blond preppies crossed his arms. "I'm not ready to come out."

"No one says you have to," the facilitator reassured him. "Most people do it gradually. Take your own time, it's up to you."

Nelson turned to Jason and winked. "I've been thinking about starting a group like this at school, to help people who haven't come out yet."

Jason averted his gaze. The thought of a gay group at school was beyond belief.

"I think coming out is hardest with parents," said Blake.

Kyle nodded.

Jason thought about his own mom. She already had enough to handle with his dad. And his dad would surely finish what he'd once started—if he knew where his son was.

Blake continued: "My dad couldn't understand how I'd gone out with girls and then suddenly told him I liked guys. I think it's even harder if you're bi."

Jason stopped jiggling his leg. Bisexual? Maybe that's what he was. Maybe he didn't have to stop going out with Debra. Maybe she would understand. But . . . ? His mind spun with questions.

Before anyone else could speak, two adults stepped into the room carrying fans. Everyone cheered and applauded. Over the roar Archie shouted, "Let's take a break and set up the fans."

Jason sprang to his feet, his chair scraping the floorboards. "I better go," he told Kyle.

"You're leaving?"

Jason heard the disappointment in Kyle's voice and was about to answer, when Nelson broke in. "Don't leave yet. After the meeting we go to Burger Queen." He batted his eyelashes and smiled. "Just us girls."

Jason winced. He saw Kyle jab Nelson in the ribs.

Jason's fingers curled into a fist. He had to get out of there before he punched someone. "I need to go."

Nelson reached into his backpack. "At least take a button." He grinned. "It's a gift."

Jason shook his head, but Nelson shoved the button at him anyway. Kyle started to speak. Jason turned and raced for the door. He bounded down the four flights of stairs and burst from the building, cursing himself.

He'd have to brace himself for Monday. Nelson would no doubt shoot off his queer mouth at school. And if people at school found out . . .

Jason opened his hand and looked at the button the little fag had given him. It read: NOBODY KNOWS I'M GAY.

CHAPTER 2

JASON

KYLE

NELSON

Kyle stared at the empty doorway. "I can't believe I was such a spaz, knocking the damn chairs over." He turned to Nelson. "And *you*! Giving him that stupid button. Why'd you do that?"

Nelson gave a contrite shrug. "I guess I screwed up, didn't I?"

Kyle glanced toward the door. "Maybe I can catch up with him."

In an instant, he raced through the door and down the four flights. When he reached the front stoop, he looked down one end of the street, then the other. Had the man of his dreams really shown up at the meeting? He searched every block around the neighborhood. Only after he was completely convinced Jason was nowhere to be found did he grudgingly board the Metro toward the suburbs. Crestfallen, he cursed Nelson all the way home.

. . . .

"Kyle? Honey, are you okay?"

Deep in thought, Kyle had failed to see his mom kneeling by the front-lawn flower bed.

She grabbed a handful of tulip bulbs. "You look a little troubled."

Kyle watched her plant the bulbs in the newly dug earth, wishing he could tell her about Jason. Of course, first he'd have to tell her he was gay. She'd get upset and tell his dad. He'd make a federal case out of it. Guaranteed.

Kyle handed her some bulbs. "I'm fine. Is there anything to eat?"

"Cookies, in the kitchen. Be careful, I just waxed the floor. By the way, Dad has a surprise for you." She called after him. "Remember to wipe your feet!"

Kyle kicked his shoes off inside the front door and set them on the shelf for shoes. His mom was pretty obsessive about cleanliness. His dad sat in his recliner watching a football game. Kyle grabbed a couple of cookies. "Mom said you have a surprise for me."

His dad reached into his shirt pocket and with a flourish whipped out an envelope. "Ta-dah! Guess. Come on."

Kyle hated when his dad treated him like a kid. He was seventeen now. "I don't want to guess." He bit into a cookie.

His dad's mouth drooped. "You used to love to guess." He sighed and opened the envelope, revealing the contents like he was at the Academy Awards or something. "Tickets to the Redskins, the Sunday after Thanksgiving. Just you and me."

Kyle said, "Great." But his mind was still on Jason.

His dad frowned. "Don't look so excited."

Kyle shrugged and started up the stairs. Didn't his dad realize there were more important things in life than tickets to the Redskins?

He sat down on his bed and took his cap off. He opened his nightstand drawer and pulled out his yearbook. He turned the dog-eared pages to his favorite picture: Jason, number seventy-seven, was racing down the court, intensity on his face, curls flying, muscles taut, sheer power in motion. The crowd was cheering in the background. The digital clock showed six seconds before the final buzzer. His shot had led the team to the state championships.

Kyle had met Jason on his first day of high school as he jostled through the crowded halls, searching for his homeroom.

"Hey, wha's up?" called a voice behind him. "You dropped your schedule."

When Kyle turned, the cutest boy he'd ever seen handed him his schedule and asked, "Know where room one twenty-eight is?"

Kyle's heart wedged in his throat, but he managed to cough up an answer. "I think it's this way." He led the boy down the hall and discovered that their lockers faced each other.

For the rest of his freshman year Kyle arrived at school early enough to greet Jason. His olive-skinned Adonis always waved a friendly "Wha's up?" but Kyle felt too shy to respond with anything beyond, "Okay, how about you?" He contented himself with stealing glimpses in the halls. Before long he'd memorized Jason's schedule, knowing the exact instant when he would turn the corner and pass by.

Since Kyle was little, he'd known he was different, though he couldn't explain exactly how. When other boys began to talk about girls, he never felt interested. But it was another story when they bragged about their erections and first ejaculations.

And while he laughed with classmates at fag and AIDS jokes, on the inside he felt ashamed and frightened. His one source of hope was the nightly news, where he saw images of gay people different from the caricatures of jokes. Gay soldiers battled in court for the right to serve in the military. Lesbian moms fought to keep their children. Protesters picketed Congress for AIDS funding. Even the grown men in high heels and elaborate costumes who laughed and paraded on Pride Day seemed anything but despicable.

Then in eighth grade he got braces. That made him feel even more like an alien. His mom tried to cheer him up. "Don't worry, handsome. Once you get your braces off, you'll have to fight off the girls." Whoopee. The image failed to comfort him.

Meanwhile, his dad nagged him to go out for sports. Kyle couldn't throw a ball to save his life, but he liked watching the Olympic swimmers on TV. So he joined the swim team, where he hid among laps in the pool and stole underwater glances.

He was just getting used to being called Metal Mouth Meeks when disaster struck again. The school nurse said he needed glasses. He came home from the optometrist's with wire frames sliding down his nose, retreated to his bedroom, and stared in the mirror. Between braces and glasses, he felt like the ugliest, most lonely boy in the universe.

Then he met Nelson. From the moment he first saw him in art class, Kyle knew Nelson was different. But when Ms. MacTraugh paired them up to draw each other's portraits, Kyle panicked and asked to be excused to the infirmary.

After school, Nelson tracked him down. "Let's get this out. You know I'm queer, I know you're queer. Get over it." He turned and started to walk away.

Kyle felt a rush, like he'd burst from the water after a high dive. He was no longer alone. "Hey!" he shouted.

Nelson turned back toward him. Kyle wasn't sure what to

say. He'd called out on impulse, without thinking. He pushed his glasses up the bridge of his nose and tugged on his cap, stalling. "Uh, you draw really well. I mean it."

Nelson stared at him. "Thanks. My mom's a graphic designer. She taught me. It's not that hard, really."

Kyle stepped closer, even though he still felt a little nervous. "Really?"

"Yeah." Nelson smiled. "I'll show you."

Soon Kyle was spending every afternoon at Nelson's. They wrestled without dumb rules and did mud facials together. With Nelson, Kyle didn't have to pretend to be anything other than himself.

And Nelson seemed to know *everything* about being gay. He told Kyle about Alexander the Great, Oscar Wilde, and Michelangelo. He explained the Stonewall Riots and defined words like *cruising* and *drag*. He told Kyle about gay youth Web sites and introduced him to out music groups like Size Queen and Indigo Girls.

The most amazing thing was how Nelson talked about all this stuff in front of his own mom. She even subscribed to *XY* magazine for him.

"How did you ever tell her?" Kyle wanted to know.

Nelson lit a cigarette. "You kidding? She knew before I did. I'm her fucking cause."

Kyle thought about it. "And your dad?"

Nelson's face darkened behind a puff of smoke. "Never mind him."

When the subject changed to boys, Kyle confided he had a crush on a boy at school. He even admitted that he kissed his pillow at night pretending it was him.

Nelson took a drag on his cigarette. "What's his name?"

"Promise you won't tell?" Kyle hesitated. "Jason Carrillo."

Nelson burst out coughing. "Carrillo? *Ding-ding-ding!* Gay-dar! Gay-dar! Closet case. Big time. At least bi."

Kyle felt as if Nelson had just smacked him. "Shut up. He is not. How do you know?"

Nelson grinned. "The same way I knew about you."

Now Kyle thought back on it. Maybe Nelson had been right about Jason. But everyone knew Jason had a girlfriend. Last year they'd been voted Cutest Couple. This year Debra was running for homecoming queen.

Jason couldn't be gay. But then why had he shown up at the Rainbow Youth meeting? Maybe he was bi. But even if he was, Jason would never be interested in him. He'd probably walked in by mistake, like he said. But Kyle hoped he hadn't.

His mom tapped on the doorway of his bedroom, smiling. "Honey, are you sure you're feeling all right?" She raised her eyebrows. "I've called you to dinner three times already."

The high point of the meal was a phone call from Nelson. Kyle's dad picked up his knife and cut into his beef. "Doesn't he know not to call at dinnertime?"

His mom extended the receiver to Kyle. Without even saying hello, Nelson started talking. "Where did you go?"

Kyle turned away from his parents. "None of your business."

"Stop being such a drama diva! Come on. What do you want to do tonight?"

Kyle pondered for a moment. "Slit my wrists."

Nelson sighed into the phone. "Yeah, and *after* that?"

"I don't know," Kyle said. "I. Don't. Know." He slammed the receiver down and returned to the table.

"Sounds like you two had a fight," his mom said.

Kyle nodded tentatively and sat down.

His dad stabbed a piece of meat with his fork. "Why does he have to call you every five minutes? Doesn't he have a life?" His dad waved his wrist in the air. "Maybe you should develop some friends that are less, you know, that are more . . ." His hand took a nosedive and thudded onto the table. "Athletic!"

Kyle's mom glared at his dad and tugged on her ear. Kyle had figured out years ago that this was a signal for his dad to lay off. It usually took his dad a while to catch on, and tonight Kyle didn't feel like waiting. He grabbed his cap from the back of his chair. "Can I be excused?"

Back in his bedroom Kyle tried some homework, then scanned Jason's yearbook photo into his computer. He turned off his light and rolled over in bed. His mind drifted to images of Jason in the locker room of tenth-grade gym class—his biceps bulging against his T-shirt sleeves, his butt framed by his jock-strap. Kyle wrapped his arm around his pillow and, smiling, fell asleep.

The following Monday, Kyle arrived at school early, determined to find Jason and apologize about Nelson. But Jason was nowhere to be found. As Kyle watched for him outside the cafeteria at lunch, he heard Nelson's voice come up behind him.

"I made you a tape of the new Pansy Division." Nelson held out a cassette. "Truly gorgeous."

"Thanks." Kyle slipped the tape into his pocket, hoping Nelson would leave before Jason showed up.

Nelson's face brightened. "You going to lunch?"

"Not hungry. You go ahead."

But Nelson didn't budge. He stuck a finger into his blond hair and scratched. "You still upset about Saturday?"

"No," Kyle lied. "Look, just leave me alone."

"I'm sorry, for the thousandth fucking time."

Kyle turned away.

"Fine," Nelson said. "If you're going to be a dick about it." He strode off.

Kyle didn't see Jason at lunch—or for the rest of the afternoon. When the last bell rang, he sulked toward his locker. Maybe Jason was sick or, more likely, too embarrassed to come to school. Kyle tossed his books into his locker, then closed the door.

There stood Jason, clutching his red backpack across his shoulder. "Wha's up?"

Startled, Kyle pushed his glasses up the bridge of his nose. "Uh, hi."

Jason twisted his backpack strap in his hand and looked over his shoulder, taking a sweeping glance of the thinning crowd of students. "I kept stopping by here looking for you today." He cocked his head—a caring look. "I thought maybe you were sick."

Kyle melted beneath Jason's brown eyes. "I'm sorry," he said, though he wasn't certain why he was apologizing. "That's what I thought. I mean . . ." He didn't know what he was saying, only that he was making a fool of himself. He shut his mouth and forced a smile.

"Listen." Jason swallowed and his Adam's apple bobbed in his throat. He looked left, then right, then straight at Kyle. "About last Saturday . . . I wasn't sure what kind of meeting it was."

Kyle knew it was a lie but nodded politely. What else could he do?

Jason continued, his voice low. "You haven't told anyone, have you? I mean, that you saw me there?"

Kyle saw the fear and shame in Jason's face. "Of course not. I wouldn't tell anyone."

Jason let out a sigh but then added, "You don't think Nelly—I mean, Nelson—will tell anyone, do you?"

Kyle didn't think so, but Jason's worry made him worry too. Abruptly Jason drew back, gazing behind Kyle. Kyle turned and saw Debra Wyler, Jason's girlfriend.

"Hi, Kyle." She gave him a sweet smile, and Kyle said hi back.

But Jason looked scared senseless. Kyle realized he'd better leave. "Well, I'll see you later."

"Later," Jason said, and smiled a forced, worried smile.

Kyle stepped down the hall, picking up his pace. He had to find Nelson and make sure he didn't tell anyone about Jason. He hoped it wasn't too late.

CHAPTER 3

JASON

KYLE

NELSON

After school, Nelson went to Shea's for a haircut. In preparation, he spread a linen sheet on her bedroom floor while she finished up on the phone with Caitlin.

"Where's Kyle?" Shea asked when she hung up.

"How the fuck should I know?" The words came harsher than Nelson intended. "Sorry," he mumbled.

Shea placed a chair in the middle of the sheet. "Does this have anything to do with that cute new boy at the meeting Saturday? The one you signaled me about?"

"Oh, gag me!" Nelson couldn't believe that even his best dyke friend thought the basketball slut was cute. "I'm sick of everyone saying how cute Jason is."

Shea stopped tying the towel around Nelson's neck. "Wait a minute! That was *the* Jason? Kyle's every-other-word crush Jason? He's *gay*?"

Nelson shook a cigarette out of his pack. "T.C.J. Tragic closet jock. Budding homo." He flicked his match into the incense bowl. "Oh, he's okay. I just can't stand Kyle going on about him. You saw how he flew over to him? All of a sudden I was history."

Shea picked up a pair of scissors. "So, you and Kyle had a fight because Jason showed up? Hmm . . ." The scissors snipped close to his ear. "Interesting . . ." Her voice took on that therapist's tone.

Nelson hated it. Why did girls always act like they knew everything? "Don't start that again! I'm not in love with Kyle." Wet clumps of hair fell to the floor. "And he's not in love with me."

The phone rang. Shea dropped the scissors and rushed to it. Of course, it was Caitlin.

"You just talked to her," Nelson protested.

You would've thought they hadn't talked in a hundred years. Caitlin was applying to colleges for next year. She and Shea had to discuss the ins and outs of every frigging detail: local or out-of-state, dorm or apartment, blah, blah, blah. It drove Nelson bonkers.

While Shea talked, he stared at himself in the mirror. He couldn't stand how boring he looked: the same blue eyes, as always. And even though Shea gave the most awesome haircuts, he'd grown tired of his blond hair. Dull. He read the hair dye labels on Shea's dresser. KAMIKAZE BLOND. That had crashed and burned. AUBURN. Lame. LUMINESCENT GREEN—GLOWS IN THE DARK. Hmm . . . But would Kyle like it?

"Hey, faggot! Someone spit mouthwash on your head?" The voice belonged to Jack Ransom, school asshole.

Jack had bullied Nelson since middle school—calling him

names, knocking the tray out of his hands in the cafeteria, punching him as he passed in the hall. Nelson fought back but usually got creamed. When his mom complained to the school, Mr. Mueller, the principal, argued that Nelson had to learn to control his temper.

Then last year, Jack and his thugs cornered Nelson in the boys' restroom, kicked him down, and shoved his face into the toilet. Nelson's mom pressed charges. Nelson hoped Jack would get fried in the electric chair. But he only got put on court probation.

Every morning since then, like a broken record, Nelson's mom drummed into him: "If anyone bothers you, you just turn away. Promise?"

So Nelson flipped Jack the finger and quickly turned away, walking smack into Debra and Jason.

"Oh, my God!" Debra said enthusiastically. "I love your hair!" She turned to her so-called boyfriend. "Isn't his hair outrageous?"

Jason was trying his hardest to avoid Nelson's gaze.

The big phony, Nelson thought. He felt sorry for Debra. If she only knew . . . But he wasn't going to be the one to tell her.

Jason tugged her hand. "We better get to class." As he led her down the hall Debra's voice trailed behind her: "He's such a riot! You never know what he'll come up with next."

Nelson smiled. He loved every minute of the attention he received for his new do. Unfortunately, the person whom he most wanted to see it was taking geeky advanced-placement tests all that rainy day. As soon as the final bell rang, Nelson headed toward Kyle's homeroom. He hoped Kyle was over being angry at him.

Kyle closed his locker and grinned. That was a good sign. "I like your hair."

Nelson pouted. "I thought you weren't speaking to me."

. . . .

Outside, the boys stood beneath the overhang of the front entrance. Rain was pouring down. "You really like my hair?" Nelson asked.

Kyle shrugged. "It looks okay." He fidgeted with his umbrella. "Look, I need to ask you something—"

"Just okay?" Nelson interrupted. That was the lamest compliment he'd gotten all day. "Not spectacular? Not fabulous?"

"It's about Jason."

"Jason's more important than my hair?" He shook his head. "I dooon't think sooo."

Kyle adjusted his glasses. "Shut up and listen. Did you tell anyone about him showing up at the meeting?"

Nelson heard the worry in his voice and decided to tease him. "Of course."

Kyle's eyes widened. "You did?"

Nelson strained not to grin. "Didn't you hear the loud-speaker announcement this morning?"

"Very funny. I'm serious."

"Let's see . . ." Nelson tapped his fingertips on his chin. "I phoned Sheila Ledbetter yesterday morning. You know what a mouth she is. Of course I told Maria at lunchtime." He parodied a Spanish accent: *"Jason es un maricón!"*

Kyle crossed his arms. "Damn it, just tell me. Did you tell anyone or didn't you?"

"No, I didn't tell anyone."

"Are you sure?"

Nelson really felt irritated. He hadn't had his after-school smoke, it was pouring rain, he didn't have an umbrella, and Kyle was being an asshole. "Kyle, I should know if I told anyone."

"If you did," Kyle persisted, "you better tell me now."

"Screw you!" Nelson stepped into the torrent and hurried down the wet sidewalk. He bent his head and squinted his eyes as drops pelted his face. The slap of Kyle's footsteps followed him.

"Okay, I believe you." Kyle unfolded his umbrella as he jogged up.

Nelson kept walking, not bothering to look at him.

"You want to share my umbrella? You're getting wet."

Like Nelson hadn't noticed. The sensible thing would be to accept Kyle's offer. But even though he was drenched and cold, he ignored him. By the time they reached the stoplight at Washington Boulevard, his shoes felt heavy as water buckets.

"Sure you don't want to share my umbrella?" Kyle asked.

Rain dripped from Nelson's hair into his eyes. His soaked shirt clung to his skin and he was shivering. "Fine," he relented.

Kyle huddled next to him, shielding him with the umbrella. They walked silently until they reached Lee Highway. Nelson stared at the light. "My toes are swimming. Hold on." He leaned against Kyle and pulled off a shoe, emptied the water, then he did the other.

The light turned green and they continued. By the time they reached Albemarle Street, the rain had tapered to a drizzle.

"Say, listen." Kyle stared at Nelson through rain-spotted glasses. "I'm sorry about . . . you know." He held out his hand. "Shake?"

Nelson extended his hand just as a sneeze escaped him.

"Bless you!" Kyle said. "Your hand is like ice."

"Never mind that. How's my hair? The green isn't running all over me, is it?"

Kyle grinned. "No." He folded up his umbrella.

"So?" Nelson said, trying not to sound eager. "Are you going to tell me what happened with you and Miss Jason?"

Kyle shrugged. "We talked after school yesterday. I think he's pretty scared that someone's going to find out he came to the meeting. I know you said you haven't, but . . . you *won't* tell anyone, will you?"

"Of course not," Nelson said. "You should've seen his face this morning when Debra ran up to see my hair. He looked scared poopless. Afraid I'll tell his sweetheart he's a cock-sucker."

Kyle rubbed his forehead beneath the bill of his cap.

"Stop worrying." Nelson pulled a cigarette out of his pack. "I told you I won't say anything. Look, I know you're obsessed with him. You're powerless. Out of control." He struck a match, but it was too soaked to strike a flame. "Shit."

Kyle tipped his cap back. "Do you really think I'm out of control? I know he's not interested in me, but maybe we could be friends." He grew silent, staring into space.

Nelson recognized the look: glazed eyes, sullen mouth, jaw thrust forward—like a zombie. Kyle had entered "The Jason Zone."

Nelson snapped his fingers. "Hey, you want to come over?"

Kyle continued staring into space.

"Hello!" Nelson shouted. "Anybody home?" He cupped his hands around his mouth. "I said—"

Kyle raised his hand to stop him. "I heard you." He swung the bill of his cap sideways—back and forth across his forehead. "I can't. I have a paper to write."

Nelson sneezed again. "You can write it at my place." He wiped his nose.

Kyle frowned. "You're going to catch cold. Here." He took off his cap, then pulled off his sweatshirt. His T-shirt rode up, exposing his abs. Nelson wished he had abs like Kyle's. He wished he had a body like Kyle's—slender and toned, broad swimmer's shoulders, thin waist. Kyle handed him the sweatshirt, put his cap back on, and pulled his shirt down.

"Come over," Nelson insisted, pulling the sweatshirt over his head. "Just for a little while. Please?"

Kyle smiled. "All right."

Nelson felt the warmth of Kyle's sweatshirt. It smelled like Kyle, a good smell of chlorine swimming pools. Nelson dried his face with the shirtsleeve and breathed it in. Maybe Shea was right, maybe he was in love with Kyle.

CHAPTER 4

JASON

KYLE

NELSON

Friday evening Jason showered and dressed to go out with Debra. He clasped a chrome bead chain around his neck, admired it in the mirror, and headed to the kitchen.

As he walked in, his mom handed him a jar to open. "Honey, can you, please?"

His six year-old sister ran to him, holding a crayon drawing. "Look at my kitty!"

Jason handed the opened jar to his mom and compared Melissa's crayon blob with his cat, Rex, on the windowsill. "Yep, looks just like him."

Melissa giggled and sat down. His mom told him Debra had called while he was in the shower. "She said she's on her way."

"Can I have money for dinner and the movie?" Jason asked, picking up his mom's pocketbook.

His mom spooned some mayonnaise into a bowl. "Take ten."

"Ma!" Jason protested. "You can't even buy a frigging French fry for ten."

His mom rattled the spoon against the bowl. "Okay, twenty. But don't tell your dad."

Jason pulled out the money. As he returned her wallet a pamphlet caught his attention. "Al-Anon?"

His mom looked over at him, then at Melissa, like she was deliberating. "Sue at work gave it to me. It's a group to help people involved with alcoholics."

Jason grabbed the Coke out of the refrigerator. "He's the one who needs help."

"I wish you two would try to get along."

Jason had tried, but there seemed to be no pleasing his father. Even when he did what his dad told him—take out the trash, clean out the truck, turn down the stereo—his dad still called him names: Stupid, Dummy, Fairy-Boy, Pansy. His anger seemed more than just a "Latino temper," as his mom called it. Jason had given up trying to understand what made him so full of rage.

He poured a glass of Coke as headlights flashed in the driveway. His mom grabbed the Al-Anon pamphlet and stuffed it back into her pocketbook. Melissa ran to the door. "Daddy!"

He scooped her into his arms. "Hi, princess."

"Hi, honey," said Jason's mom, trying to be cheerful, as usual. "How was your day?"

"Same crap as always." He put Melissa down and grabbed a beer from the refrigerator. Then his dark eyes locked on Jason. "What's around your neck, pearls?"

Melissa put down her crayon and covered her ears.

Jason sipped his Coke. "No, diamonds."

"Don't mouth off to me. You look queer. Take it off."

"I'm not taking it off. Debra gave it to me."

His dad grabbed for the chain, and his arm knocked Jason's glass. It shattered to the floor.

"Would you both stop?" His mom shoved her hands between them.

His dad backed down, sipping his beer. "Always mothering him. No wonder he's such a pansy." Disgust dripped from his voice.

The doorbell rang. "There's Debra." His mom grabbed a sponge. "Go. I'll clean this up."

Jason pecked her a kiss. "Thanks."

His dad slammed his beer bottle down. "Make him clean it up!"

"Honey, I said I'll do it."

Jason patted his sister and hurried out to Debra. He climbed into the passenger's side and pulled down the visor mirror, checking his neck chain to see if his dad was right.

Debra leaned over and kissed him. "You like it?"

He wanted to tell her what his dad had said. He wished he could share with her all his confusion. Instead he flipped the visor back up and said, "Yeah."

At the mall they met Cindy and Corey and went to the burger place. In front of them in line were two thin guys in polo shirts. Debra dangled her wrist limply, and silently mouthed the word "Homos."

Cindy and Corey burst out laughing. Jason didn't.

Debra's smile sagged. "Jason? What's the matter?"

"Nothing," he lied. "Let's order."

While they sipped their drinks, they talked about school. Eventually the conversation turned to Nelson's green hair. Cindy laughed. "He's such a freak."

Corey shook his head. "It's amazing someone hasn't killed

him. Remember when Jack Ransom tried to flush his head in the toilet? If I hadn't gotten the principal—"

"You were there?" Cindy broke in. Corey nodded, biting into his burger.

"I admire him," Debra said. "He sits next to me in chem class."

Jason felt the cold ice of his drink against the back of his throat. He'd forgotten that Debra had a class with Nelson.

"He wants to start a Gay-Straight Alliance at school," Debra continued. "He asked if I'd join."

The ice slipped into Jason's windpipe and he coughed.

Debra patted him on the back. "Are you all right?"

Jason nodded and fought for breath.

Debra lifted a french fry between her fingers. "I asked him what the group would be like, and he told me about this gay and lesbian group downtown. And you know what he said when I asked him if there was anyone else from Whitman?"

Jason's heart raced as Debra sipped on the straw in her drink. "He said I'd be surprised."

Jason lifted his burger, then set it down. His throat felt like it had a noose around it. If he tried to eat, he'd choke.

Cindy leaned toward Debra. "Did he say who?"

Debra patted her lips with the tip of her napkin before answering. "No. I'm dying to find out, though. I'd be curious to go sometime."

"I'd go with you"—Cindy stopped and laughed—"except they might think we're a couple!"

Debra laughed and turned to Jason. "How about if you go with me?"

Jason's mind reeled. She couldn't be serious.

Corey and Cindy stared at him, waiting for him to say something. But no words would come.

Debra laughed. "I don't know why guys are always so scared about gays. How about you, Corey? Would you go?"

"No way." He crumpled the burger wrapper in his fist. "You won't catch me in a room full of faggots."

Jason forced down the rest of his burger, though he'd lost his appetite.

At the movie all he could think about was the dinner conversation. He imagined Debra going to the queers' meeting and Nelson telling her about him. Why had he ever gone? The meeting had only confused him more, with all the talk about coming out. He wasn't coming out to anyone.

When the movie ended, they said good night to Corey and Cindy. He and Debra drove back to her house. In the basement rec room, she sat beside him on the couch and took hold of his fingertips. "Sweetheart, you've been biting your nails again. I thought you were over that."

He yanked his hand away. "I am." At least he had been, until that stupid meeting.

"Honey, what's the matter?" She put her arm around him, her soft red hair brushing his cheek. "You didn't laugh once through the whole movie."

Could he tell her? After all, she had said she admired Nelson and that she was curious to go to the Rainbow Youth meeting.

He drew a breath. "I was thinking . . . about what we talked about at dinner. You know, about . . . have you ever, like, thought about, you know, doing it with another girl?"

Debra stared at him, then sat up and stared at him some more. "No! Why does the thought of two girls always turn you guys on?"

Jason knew he shouldn't have said anything. It was useless.

She would never understand. "I was just curious," he said, and bit into a fingernail.

Debra gently took his hand away from his mouth. "Well, it's not going to happen, okay?" She kissed him, and her voice softened. "I only want to be with you." She gazed dreamily into his eyes.

He knew she wanted to fool around. That was one of the nice things about her. He felt sorry for his friends who had to coax and cajole their girlfriends just to get a little squeeze. And after worrying about the stupid homos' meeting, Kyle, and Nelson all week, Jason definitely wanted to fool around too. At least it would take his mind off everything—and prove once again he wasn't queer.

He leaned over her. As usual, they would kiss for about fifteen minutes. Then he would slip his hand into her blouse, and she would remove her bra. Her breathing would come in short little bursts. Then he would slide his hand into her pants, and her breathing would become longer and deeper. Once she began to moan, he knew she was ready for him.

But the routine didn't work tonight. As soon as he started to kiss her, the thought of chartreuse-haired Nelson sitting beside her in science class intruded. Jason turned away, frustrated, and buried his face in his hands.

"Did I do something wrong?" Debra said.

Jason looked up at her. "No."

"Then what is it?" Her blue eyes stared at him. "Tell me."

Jason shrugged. "I'm just tired of this routine." He knew that wasn't really it, but it was part of it. "W-why do I always have to make the moves?"

Debra laughed, but she sounded offended. "'Cause I'm the girl. Would you rather have sex with a guy?"

The words stung like a slap on the face. "What do you mean by that?"

Debra folded her arms. "You do *not* make all the moves. I remember when you used to be desperate to be with me. Now half the time you don't even seem interested."

He was interested, if for no other reason than to reassure himself he wasn't queer. But he sure as hell couldn't tell her that.

She shook her head. "Sometimes I feel like you don't really care about me anymore."

He put his arms around her. "I'm sorry," he whispered, kissing her. "I do care about you."

She unfolded her arms and let his tongue in, then rolled her tongue across his. And taking his hand, she gently kissed his fingers. "How about we try something different?"

His pulse quickened. "What do you mean?"

She slid his fingers into her mouth and rolled her tongue around them, between them, making them wet. "Relax, baby."

His heartbeat grew faster. Was she about to do what he thought?

She leaned over him, and her kisses moved down his torso as she unbuttoned his shirt, then unfastened his belt. Although they'd had sex dozens of times, she'd never done this with him. "Too one-sided," she'd protested.

Her head was in his lap. He wanted to ask if she was sure she wanted to do this. But it was making him too wild with excitement to say anything.

He ran his fingers through her hair, feeling like he was about to burst. He watched her through the blur of half-closed eyes, then suddenly it was no longer Debra but Kyle, her red hair transformed into Kyle's cap.

Unsettled by the vision, Jason tried to stop himself but couldn't. Too late.

It was over. He leaned back against the sofa and slowly regained his breath. He couldn't believe what had just happened. He'd wanted to have sex with his girl to feel better. Instead he'd thought about another boy while his girl . . . He didn't want to think about it.

Debra brought her head up from his lap and laid it on his chest. He held her for a while, stroking her hair, all the while wanting to leave.

He needed to talk to someone about his queer confusion— but who? He couldn't go back to the meeting, not with Nelson— or Debra—there. His dad? He shuddered. His dad would kill him. And his mom had enough to deal with. Coach Cameron never talked with him, just bellowed. His counselor only talked about class schedules. His teachers were . . . just teachers. And his friends made fag jokes. Who else was there?

Kyle? No way. He still couldn't believe he'd thought about Kyle while he was with Debra. Now it would feel too weird to talk to Kyle. But Kyle didn't have to know what had happened. Why not Kyle? He could trust him. He hadn't told anyone about his going to the meeting, and apparently he'd persuaded Nelson to keep his mouth shut. Kyle was okay. If Jason ever did make it with another guy—not that he ever would, he assured himself—but if he did, it would be with someone normal, like Kyle.

CHAPTER 5

JASON

KYLE

NELSON

Kyle and Nelson stayed after school on Tuesday to discuss the idea of a Gay-Straight Alliance with Ms. MacTraugh, the art teacher. Everyone suspected she was gay. Students called her Miss Mack Truck or Big Mac. Once in class Jack Ransom tried to embarrass her by asking, "Are you a lesbian?"

Without even looking up from the clay in her hands, she fired back, "Are you?"

No one ever asked again. Students loved her. She was always hauling a carload of kids somewhere—art museums, plays, music festivals. Students voted her Best Teacher every year, until hard-ass Mueller concocted a policy prohibiting anyone from being voted best anything for more than three years.

While Nelson and Kyle helped her clean up the day's supplies, Nelson asked, "Will you be the group's faculty adviser?"

She shook the water off some brushes she'd rinsed. "I have

no doubt students—and faculty—would benefit from the group. But not everyone will agree." She gazed at him from behind round owl glasses. "You realize you're bound to get opposition."

Nelson crossed his arms. "I don't care."

MacTraugh wiped her large hands on her paint-smeared smock. "The group will require Mr. Mueller's approval. It may not be easy. Yes, you can count on me. But it would help to have parents' support too. Kyle? What about your parents?"

"Uh"—he glanced down—"they don't know about me yet."

Nelson rolled his eyes. "Earth to Kyle! Hel-lo! Your best friend's the school fagola. Your mom and dad aren't brainless."

Kyle hated when Nelson talked to him like that in front of other people.

MacTraugh patted Kyle on the shoulder. "Well, consider telling them. Believe me, it's better your family find out from you than from someone else."

Kyle thought about that as he and Nelson cut through the teachers' parking lot toward home. A brisk autumn breeze whipped through his hair as they snaked between cars. He looked down to button his jacket, bumping into Nelson. "What're you—?" He looked up.

Jack Ransom loomed in front of them, obstructing their path. "Hey, faggots."

Kyle's heartbeat quickened. They were sandwiched between two cars. Instinctively he spun around. José Montero blocked them in from behind. They were trapped.

"Yo, Metal Mouth." Jack walked toward Kyle. "Why you hang out with this green-haired faggot?" He knocked Kyle's cap off his head. It spiraled onto the pavement. "You queer too?"

He leaned so close that Kyle could feel the heat of his breath.

Nelson picked up Kyle's cap. "Jack, leave him alone."

Jack slapped the cap out of Nelson's hand. "What're you going to do, scratch me with your pretty blue nails?"

Nelson started for him, but José grabbed him from behind, pinning back his arms.

"Oww!" Nelson yelled. "Let me go, asshole!"

Kyle watched, feeling helpless. Jack turned back to him and shot his arms out, slapping Kyle's chest. The force knocked him against the car. "I said, you queer too?"

The metal jabbed into Kyle's back. His heart raced and he was trembling. He wanted to say something, but nothing came out.

Nelson struggled against José. "Leave him alone." He kicked backward, but José tightened his grip. "Oww!" Nelson shouted. "Cut it out."

"Hey!" a voice called.

"Shit!" José let go of Nelson, as Mr. Mueller rushed up, spreading his arms between the boys.

"What's going on?"

Nelson pointed to Jack. "They jumped us."

"We did not!"

"Break it up," said Mr. Mueller. "It's after school hours. You're supposed to be off the grounds."

Nelson sneered at Jack and José. "Fucking assholes!"

"That's it." Mueller grabbed Nelson by the jacket. "Come with me. You, too, Meeks."

Jack flailed his wrist. "Bye, Nelly. Bye, Kyle." José puckered his lips and laughed.

Mueller whirled around to them. "You want to come too?"

Jack and José practically ran as they hurried away.

Kyle followed Nelson to Mueller's office, angry at both of them—at Nelson for shooting off his stupid mouth and at

Mueller for being so unfair. While Nelson argued that it wasn't their fault, Mueller sat behind his huge desk pulling a rubber band between his fingers. "Nelson, I don't want to hear it. If you'd just stop acting so . . ."

Nelson faked a yawn, making Mueller madder. "Can't you just act *normal!*"

Nelson bit his lip, then blurted out, "We want to start a Gay-Straight Alliance."

Mueller's face went blank. "What?"

Kyle thought Nelson must be crazy. This was totally the wrong time to bring this up. He tried to get his attention, but Nelson persisted: "A club, where gay and straight students can talk."

"About sex? Not in my school."

Kyle racked his brain, trying to think of something to say.

"Not sex!" Nelson shot back at Mueller, almost yelling. "About homophobia. MacTraugh said she'd be our faculty adviser."

Mueller yelled over Nelson: "Ms. MacTraugh doesn't run this school." He stood up. "I said no!"

"Mr. Mueller?" Kyle raised his hand. "Excuse me, are you denying our right to start a club?"

Mueller turned to him. For a moment Kyle doubted his nerve to continue, but somehow he managed. "Because if you are, I think you're in violation of the First Amendment and the, uh, Federal Equal Access Act."

In the silence that followed, he wondered: Had he really said that? Mueller and Nelson both stared at him. Then he saw an ever so slight smile creep across Nelson's face as he turned to Mueller and said, "Can you give us the application for school clubs, please?"

As they crossed the street, Nelson swung his arm around Kyle. "Way to go, dude! Where the hell did you pull that from?"

Kyle shrugged, trying to calm down. "The Internet. We're hardly the first people to start a GSA, you know. Besides, I had to say something with you two yelling at each other."

Nelson pulled out a cigarette. "Now if you could just stand up to Jack and José like that."

Kyle glanced over his shoulder to make sure the goons weren't following. "My heart's still racing. I kept thinking, 'Two days before I'm supposed to get my braces off, and that jerk screws up my teeth again.' Imagine having to wear braces another three years."

Nelson exhaled a stream of smoke. "You can't freeze up like that, Kyle. You've got to be ready to fight them. If they see you're scared, you're dead meat."

"But I've never fought anyone."

Nelson punched the air with his fists. "Fake it. You're bigger than that little fleawart."

Kyle shook his head, unconvinced. "What good would it do? For every Jack Ransom, there's ten more. He's not the problem, homophobia's the problem."

"And you know what your problem is, Kyle? You're too damn rational. I can just see you standing there while Jack punches you out, and you say, 'That's okay, Jack, you're not the problem, homophobia's the problem.'"

Kyle slung his backpack higher onto his shoulder. "I just don't think fighting him is going to change anything. I'm going to call his probation officer."

Nelson tossed his cigarette aside. "What good will that do? You saw what happened with Mueller."

When they got to Kyle's house, Nelson stirred up instant brownie mix.

Kyle pulled out the application for the school group. "Are you sure we should do this? Who's going to come to the group with Jack Ransom around?"

Nelson slid the brownie tray into the oven. "He's not going to stop us, Kyle. Especially after your little speech to Mueller. Now, shut up and write."

Kyle read the application. "Purpose of the group?"

"To meet cute, sexy boys."

"Will you get serious?"

Nelson tickled his ribs. "J.F.K., Kyle. Just fucking kidding. Loosen up. How about: to address the violence and fear gay people experience at school and to help promote tolerance."

Kyle wrote that down. "Excellent! No way can they turn that down."

Nelson peeked in the oven at the brownies. "Bet Mueller finds a way to wuss out."

They carried the brownies and milk to Kyle's room. After they finished the application, Kyle walked over to the mirror and stared at his teeth. "What do you think he'll say when he sees me without braces?"

Nelson peered into Kyle's aquarium. "Who?"

"Jason, who do you think?"

Nelson sprinkled some fish food. "Oh. Him."

"You think he'll notice?" Kyle asked.

Nelson shrugged. "He'll probably just grunt—that's how jocks communicate. One grunt, he likes it. Two grunts—"

"Shut up." Kyle noticed a zit on the left side of his chin. He squeezed some acne cream onto his finger and rubbed it into his face. "He says hi *every* time he sees me now. He didn't before."

"He probably has memory lapses. Sports injuries. Brain damage."

Kyle threw the tube of cream at him. "Shut up, I told you." He ducked as Nelson threw the cream back at him. "I wish I could talk to him more, but he's always with someone."

Nelson nodded. "Herd mentality."

"If you don't shut up," Kyle said, "I'm not telling you any more about him."

Nelson ran to him and knelt down. "Oh, no, not that!" He clasped his hands together in supplication. "Hit me, beat me, call me a queen," he screamed. "But don't stop telling me about Jason!" In a dramatic gesture he pressed the back of his hand to his forehead. "I'd just die." He spread his arms out as though crucified and then flung forward, wrapping himself around Kyle's legs.

Kyle bent over to push him off. "You're really a dick, you know that?"

Nelson clung tightly around Kyle's ankles, tackling him onto the carpet, and they rolled around, each trying to pin the other, until Kyle climbed on top of Nelson and held down his wrists.

Nelson smiled. "See? You could beat up Jack Ransom."

Kyle rolled off of him and retrieved his cap. He didn't want to think about Jack Ransom. He lay back on the carpet, catching his breath and staring at his model of the starship *Enterprise* hanging from the ceiling. "Do you think he'll ever come back to a meeting?"

"Huh?" Nelson rolled onto his side and propped himself up on his elbow. "Oh . . . we're back to him." He shrugged. "Who cares? Invite him. See what happens."

Kyle turned to him as Nelson sat up.

"Don't look at me that way. I'll behave if he comes back."

Kyle returned his gaze to the ceiling. "So, do you think he'd come if I asked him?" He folded his arms behind his head, and his T-shirt rose up across his midriff. He noticed Nelson staring at him. "What are you looking at?" He pulled his shirt down.

Nelson's eyes darted away. "Nothing." He got up and walked over to the mirror. "I'm thinking of getting an eyebrow ring. Only I can't decide which side to get it on." He already had three rings in his right ear and four in his left. As he stared in the mirror he suddenly screeched.

Kyle sat up. "What's wrong?"

Nelson frowned. "My roots are starting to show. Blond and green. Makes my hair look like layered Jell-O."

They studied for a while, until there was a tap on the door. Kyle's mom, who had come home earlier, leaned in the doorway. "Supper's nearly ready. Nelson, you want to join us?"

Nelson shook his head. "Thanks, but I better get home. It's my turn to cook tonight."

At dinner Kyle's dad remarked, "His hair is green."

"So?" Kyle crossed his arms. "Maybe I'll dye my hair *blue!*"

His mom tugged her ear. "Honey"—she passed the potatoes to his dad—"Nelson's a creative boy."

His dad held his hands up in defense. "It was only an observation. Forget I said anything. How was school today?"

"Fine." Kyle thought about the GSA and what MacTraugh had said about telling his parents. But how could he come out to them?

Maybe after dessert. No, better after his calculus homework. Together he and his dad usually breezed through problems, but tonight neither of them could get the answer for one particular problem to jibe with the back of the book.

Kyle suggested they skip over it, but for nearly an hour his dad worked and reworked. Finally he tossed his pencil down. "I've gotten the same answer three times. The book must be wrong."

"Dad, the book can't be wrong."

"Of course it can. The book's wrong."

Kyle sighed to himself. Come out to his dad? Not tonight. Not ever.

Thursday morning Kyle's mom suggested he take the car. "You can drive straight to your orthodontist's appointment after school." She didn't need to persuade him.

After the final bell, he bolted to the car and started down Washington Boulevard. At the third intersection, he spotted a familiar red backpack. His heart began to pound. He adjusted his glasses and slowed down for a better look. Sure enough, it was Jason.

The rational thing would have been to keep driving. He didn't want to be late for his appointment. But this was a chance he might not get again. He tapped the horn, leaned across the passenger's seat, and rolled down the window. "Hi!"

Jason hesitated, then strode over to the car. "Wha's up? I didn't know who you were."

"It's me," Kyle said. *Ugh. Dumb. Try again.* "Want a ride?"

Jason stared at him, raising his hands as if to apologize, then dropping them again. "I live pretty far."

Kyle said, "I know." He had looked up Jason's address in the student directory and walked, biked, and driven by the white ranch-style house at least a million times over the past three years. He knew exactly where it was.

Jason's brow furrowed. "You do?"

Uh-oh. Way to go, Kyle. Get yourself out of this one. "Sure." He pointed in the general direction in which Jason was headed. "That way."

Jason laughed and his curls bounced. "Okay." He peeled off his backpack and climbed into the car, folding his frame into the front seat.

Kyle's heart throbbed against his chest. Jason Carrillo was sitting in his car, right there in the seat beside him! A faint musky essence wafted up Kyle's nose and into his memory.

"Do you live this way?" Jason asked.

"No, the other way." Kyle pointed over his shoulder.

"Oh." Jason gave him a confused look. "Where you going?"

Kyle looked ahead of him and had to think for a moment. "Uh, I have an orthodontist's appointment. I'm getting my braces removed."

"Oh," Jason said.

Kyle drove in silence, trying to come up with a topic of conversation. "It's turned out to be a nice day," he said, motioning out the window.

Jason looked up at the sky and gave a polite smile. "Yeah, sure has."

They passed by the county hospital. Now, that was a handy topic. "I was born there," Kyle said.

"Really?" Jason said. "Me too."

Kyle imagined Jason sleeping in the crib next to him. "When's your birthday?"

"January thirteenth," Jason said. "First day of bad luck in the year."

"Oh," Kyle said, disappointed. "May fifth."

"It sucks being born in January," Jason said. "So close to Christmas, I don't get half as many presents as my sister. She was born in July. Course, she would probably get more presents no matter when she was born."

"Is she older or younger?"

"Younger. Six. She's a pain in the butt. Always getting into my stuff. But she's all right."

Kyle smiled and tried to think of what else to talk about. "So . . . where you going next year?"

Jason shrugged. "I don't care. Anywhere, to get out of the house. Maybe Tech. Coach says I should be able to get a scholarship if I keep my grades up. My math sucks."

Kyle felt his synapses popping. "Really? Math's my favorite subject." His breath came fast. "I could probably help you." He tightened his grip on the steering wheel, trying to calm down. "If you wanted."

Jason gave a noncommittal nod. "Sure."

That didn't offer Kyle much encouragement. They continued for a few blocks. Kyle sneaked a glance at Jason and saw him chew his nails. That surprised him. He didn't think of Jason as nervous. He always seemed so cool and confident. His hands looked strong. Kyle imagined what it might be like to hold one, to feel the calluses and the strong fingers. His grip on the steering wheel relaxed. He turned onto Piedmont Street and pulled up in front of Jason's house.

He half expected Jason to bolt from the car, just as he'd run from the youth group, but instead Jason stared at him curiously until he finally said, "You knew exactly where I live."

Kyle blushed, realizing his mistake. Busted.

The car began to roll. Kyle slammed on the brake and fumbled with the gear shift. "I better put it in park."

"Good idea," Jason agreed. He looked out the window at his house and sat quietly a moment, before turning to Kyle. "Look, can I ask you something? So, are you . . . ?"

Kyle knew what Jason was asking, but he hesitated to come right out and tell him, afraid that Jason might never speak to him again.

"Yeah," he finally said. "Gay."

Jason studied him and remained silent a moment, clutching his backpack close to his chest. "About that group . . ." He bit his lip, then continued. "I never thought I'd see anyone from school there. You know I have a girlfriend. I mean, we have sex and everything."

Kyle nodded. He wanted to say the right thing. "I know," he uttered simply, amazed at how confident and self-assured it sounded. He was enjoying being with Jason, sitting beside him, and didn't want the afternoon to end.

Jason let out a sigh. "Thanks for not saying anything in front of her."

Kyle's new self-confidence gave him the courage to say more. "Well, if you ever want to go back to the meeting, I can give you a ride. You know, go with you."

Jason's face clouded over. "Listen"—his voice quivered—"I told you, I'm not . . ." He grabbed the door handle. "I better go."

Kyle sat up. He'd blown it again. "I'm sorry. I just—"

Jason pushed the door open and climbed out of the car. "Thanks for the ride."

Kyle watched Jason stride up the sidewalk and disappear into the house. He felt like his heart was being ripped out, while his mind swirled with the lingering scent of Jason. He looked at the car clock and saw that he was already fifteen minutes late for the orthodontist. Crap. He took a deep breath, shifted into drive, and floored the accelerator, feeling like the most unlucky boy on Earth. Oh well, at least Jason had sat in his car.

CHAPTER 6

JASON

KYLE

NELSON

The following morning, Nelson rummaged through his closet, searching for his camera.

His mom called out the latest countdown. "Nelson, it's seven thirty-three." She should've been a mission controller for the space program. "You're going to be late for school again."

Nelson yelled back, "Have you seen my Polaroid?"

His mom leaned in the doorway. "Look at the mess you're making!"

"Kyle got his braces off. I've got to take his picture."

His mom raised an eyebrow. "I swear, sometimes I think you're in love with him. Let me check in the den."

Nelson paused his search. Did the whole world think he was in love with Kyle?

His mom yelled, "Here it is!"

Nelson hurried to the den. "Thanks. You're the best." He grabbed the camera and smacked a kiss in her direction.

In order to catch Kyle before homeroom, Nelson ran all the way to school, slowing down only once for his morning cigarette. He arrived just as Kyle closed his locker. Nelson grabbed him by the shoulder and spun him around. "Let me see!"

Kyle cracked a smile. "Was it worth three years of looking like a nerd?"

"You look even more studly than before." Nelson opened his backpack and pulled his camera out. "C'mon. I want to take your picture."

Kyle held up his hand, trying to block the camera. "Not here!"

Before Kyle could protest any further, the Polaroid flashed and spit out the photo.

Kyle leaned toward Nelson, whispering, "You'll never believe what happened yesterday."

Nelson waved the photo, hoping to make it develop faster. "Don't tell me. I know it's a remote possibility since you hardly ever mention him, but by some bizarro chance could it have anything to do with Jason?"

Kyle grinned. "Yep."

"You saw her in the bathroom and caught a glimpse of her pee-pee?"

Kyle shot him a hostile look and pulled his backpack up on his shoulder. "Shut up."

Nelson swatted him with the photo. "The bell's about to ring. Tell me!"

Kyle's lips parted into a tremendous, gleaming grin. "He let me give him a ride home. Can you believe it? He sat in my car, right there beside me."

That was chummy, Nelson thought. He tasted bile at the back of his throat, like he had just burped up something. "So?" he asked cautiously. "He was in your car. B.F.D. What happened?"

Kyle leaned back dreamily. "We talked—"

The brightness of Kyle's teeth suddenly annoyed Nelson. "Did you at least get a little feel?"

Kyle stared at him. "Huh?" Then his smile fell. "You're a real jerk, you know that?"

"Yeah?" Nelson said. "Well, just because you get your braces off and give ultrajock a ride home, don't act like such hot shit all of a sudden."

The bell rang. Nelson turned and stormed off, not sure why he felt so angry. During homeroom he stared at the photo of Kyle's gleaming smile, feeling stupid. Why should it bother him that Kyle and Jason were alone together in a car? He wasn't in love with Kyle. He hated Kyle. Kyle was a dickhead in love with a frizzy-haired jerk.

After school, Nelson walked to Shea's and vented. "I don't know why I got so upset. I always knew he had the hots for Jason. It never used to bother me. I guess I didn't think it would go anywhere. Now suddenly he's giving him rides home." He pulled the Polaroid from his backpack. "Want to see him without braces?"

Shea admired the photo. "He looks great."

Nelson flicked his ashes into the incense bowl. "Maybe I am in love with him. But what's the point? He's not interested in me. Why would he be? Look at me." He slapped his hips. "My butt's big as a beehive. My legs are like sticks. Everything's out of proportion, like a fun-house mirror. It's tragic. I hate my body."

Shea pursed her lips. "Don't be so harsh! You have a nice

body . . . for a guy. You have a cute smile, nice broad shoulders, and a sexy butt." She pinched it, as though to prove her point.

"Hey!" He slapped her wrist.

"Nelson, you're good looking. What's tragic is you don't see it."

He didn't believe her. She was just saying that because she was his friend.

The phone rang. Caitlin. Big surprise. While they talked, Nelson stared in the mirror at himself. He did have nice shoulders, considering he never worked out. Maybe he should take steroids. In the meantime, he needed to ditch the lemon-lime hair. He curled a finger through it and looked at Shea's hair. She had a cute perm. He thought of Jason's hair, with those dark, wild curls—talk about Miss Mess, though it did look sexy.

"How about," he asked Shea when she hung up, "dark brown wild, sexy curls."

She pouted. That was weird, considering she'd just talked with Caitlin. He walked over and put his arm around her. "Something wrong?"

She stared wistfully at the phone. "Caitlin is applying to Smith for next year. It's supposed to have an incredible lesbian community."

"So?" he asked. "Can't you move up with her?"

Shea gave a halfhearted shrug. "I could. I'll have my beauty-school certificate then. I can cut hair anywhere. But . . . I hoped she'd choose a local school. I'm not sure I want to leave Mom, or you and my other friends." Her green eyes twinkled at him.

"All right," he said. "Don't get gooey on me."

Nelson's perm didn't come out exactly like he'd hoped. When he arrived at the meeting Saturday, Kyle took one look at him and shook his head in disbelief.

"Go ahead," Nelson sighed. "Say it—I look like a poodle. Does it really look that bad? No, don't tell me." He sat down beside him. "And before you say anything, I want to apologize. I know I got a little out of line about Jason the other day."

"A little out of line?" Kyle shook his head. "You mean ballistic. I can't believe you sometimes."

Nelson twirled a curl. "Neither can I. It's not easy being me. Imagine what I have to put up with twenty-four / seven. At least you can get away from me occasionally." Kyle smiled and Nelson relaxed. "You really do look great without braces."

After the meeting Kyle asked Nelson to help him pick out perfume at the mall. "Tomorrow's my mom's birthday."

When they got to Kyle's house, his parents were rushing out to dinner. His mom told Nelson she liked his curls.

His dad stared silently at Nelson's hair, probably thinking he'd get reprimanded if he said anything about it. "We're going to the Millers'," he told Kyle. "There's some of my world-famous pot roast in case you boys get hungry."

After eating, Kyle and Nelson went to Kyle's room. Nelson put a CD in the stereo. "Hey, I've got this awesome idea."

Kyle sat on the floor and pulled his mom's perfume from his backpack, sniffing the box. "You're scheming again. I can hear it in your voice."

"I'm not scheming. Just shut up and listen. It's our senior year, right? Homecoming is next week. So why don't you and I go?"

Kyle's eyebrows scrunched together. "Who would I take?"

Nelson smiled and twirled in front of him.

"Are you crazy?" Kyle shook his head. "No way!"

Nelson shushed him with a wave of his hand. "Why not? Those two girls in Richmond went to the prom together. They even made a TV movie about them. It would rule, Kyle! Can you imagine? We'd be media divas."

"But I don't want to be a media diva."

"Come on. At least think about it."

Kyle continued shaking his head. "Nope." He returned his attention to the box of perfume. "Hand me the wrapping paper."

Nelson frowned. "You know, Kyle, I often think what a boring life you'd have if it wasn't for me."

He stood up and looked at himself in Kyle's full-length mirror, stroking his curls. Then he remembered the *Honcho* magazine and pulled it out of his backpack. "Hey, look what I got." He opened the magazine.

Kyle laid aside the wrapping paper and fixed his attention on the photos. "Wow!"

Nelson turned the page. "I'm getting hard."

Kyle said, "That's fascinating."

Nelson wasn't sure if Kyle meant the photo or his comment. "I always get hard looking at men. How about you?"

Kyle wet his lips and swallowed. "None of your business."

"Kyle?" Nelson stood up. "Can I ask you something?" He pulled his shirt off over his head. "What do you think of my body?"

Kyle looked up from the magazine and stared blankly. "Huh?"

Nelson flexed his biceps. "Be honest. I mean, do you think I have a good body? I know I'm fat."

"You're not fat."

"Not fat?" Nelson pinched the flesh surrounding his waist. "What do you call that?"

"Skin."

Nelson stuck his tongue out at him.

"Nelson, you're not fat. You're skinnier than I am."

"Then"—Nelson watched Kyle closely—"you think I have a good body? Schultz said he could get me steroids."

"You don't need steroids. You have a good body."

Nelson danced his hands down along his naked chest, exultantly happy. "You think so? Sometimes I look in the mirror and think I'm really good looking. Then other times I think my body's all wrong. I hate it."

Maybe Shea was right after all. If Kyle liked his body, maybe he stood a chance. He turned to face Kyle. "There's something else I want to ask you." He bit down on his index finger. "No. I'd better not."

Kyle shrugged and returned to the magazine.

"Okay," Nelson said. "I'll ask. When you jack off, who do you think of?"

Kyle looked up at him. "I don't know. I think about a lot of people—guys in magazines . . . Jason."

Nelson waved that idea aside and ventured forth, bracing himself. "Do you ever think of *me*?"

Kyle gave Nelson a mystified look. "Why would I think of you?"

Nelson's heart sank. His whole body sank. It had been a stupid question.

Kyle watched him. "You're serious, aren't you? You're my best friend, Nelson. I mean, you don't think of *me*, do you?"

"No," Nelson lied, and quickly pulled his shirt back on. "It's just that you said you think I have a nice body."

Kyle shrugged. "So? I'm gay. I like guys' bodies." He returned his attention to the *Honcho*.

Nelson sat down and lit a cigarette, studying Kyle and considering the conversation. Kyle wasn't interested in him, but if he liked guys' bodies, maybe they could still have sex. It didn't have to mean anything. After all, he wasn't even convinced that he was in love with Kyle. He was definitely horny, though. No one needed to persuade him of that.

"Well, then," he said cautiously, "if you like guys' bodies . . . maybe we should try it sometime."

Kyle glanced up. "Try what?"

Nelson exhaled a stream of smoke. "You know . . ." He couldn't finish. The whole idea was stupid. If Kyle wanted to have sex with him, they would have done it by now. He flicked his ashes. "Forget it."

Kyle returned to the magazine. "Look at this guy."

Nelson didn't want to look at the guy. He was sorry he'd ever shown Kyle the stupid magazine. He leaned over and grabbed it.

"Hey," Kyle protested. "What are you doing? I was looking at it."

"It's *my* magazine."

"Fine!" Kyle fumed. "You've probably slobbered over it a thousand times anyway."

Nelson ignored him, pretending to study the magazine. Out of corner of his eye he saw Kyle sneak a hand into his crotch and rearrange his underwear.

"What's with you lately? You seem so weird." Kyle glanced at his watch. "Poop, it's almost eleven o'clock."

Nelson knew it was time to leave, even though he didn't want to go. He closed the magazine. "What are you doing tomorrow?"

Kyle yawned. "It's my mom's birthday, remember? We're going to my grandmom's. Want to come?"

"Sure," Nelson replied. Kyle's grandmom had a horse farm,

and they always had a great time there. He tossed the magazine back to Kyle. "Here. It might help take your mind off Mademoiselle Jason."

Kyle caught the magazine, staring in surprise. "You mean it? I better not. What if my mom finds it?"

Nelson laughed. "That would be an original way to come out."

Kyle smirked. "Yeah, right." He dropped the magazine into his nightstand.

When Nelson got home, he walked his dog around the block, then trudged upstairs and undressed for bed. He looked once more at the photo of Kyle's bright, gleaming smile before turning off the light. Wrapping the covers around himself, he imagined slow dancing at homecoming, his arms around Kyle.

CHAPTER 7

JASON

KYLE

NELSON

Jason pinned the homecoming corsage onto Debra's white satin evening dress. In spite of all the confusing shit going on, he still thought she was the most beautiful girl in the world. She patted him on the lapel and pecked him a kiss. "There, you look perfect."

They sat with Corey and Cindy at their usual lunch table and watched couples dance beneath the mirrored ball twirling in the decorated cafeteria. Jason felt the buzz from the vodka and Pepsi they'd drunk in the parking lot. He began to sing to Debra, changing the lyrics of the love song that was playing to include her name. When he finished, Corey and Cindy applauded him. He stood and took a bow. Debra wrapped her arms around his neck and kissed him. "That's the first time you've sung to me since . . ." Her blue eyes drifted up as she thought. "Gosh . . . since last spring?"

Cindy smiled. "This is the best night ever." She paused,

then held Debra's hand. "Of course, it would be better if you'd won."

Debra shifted in her seat. She'd lost homecoming queen by only twenty-three votes, but she was being a good sport.

Corey laughed. "I heard Nelson Glassman was going to run."

Debra flung her wrist in the air. "But he's already a queen!"

Cindy joined in. "He'll probably show up in an evening gown any minute."

Jason sat back in his chair, leaning into the shadows. Why did they have to bring up Nelson just when he was starting to enjoy himself?

"Whoops," Debra said, contritely covering her mouth. "I think we just stepped out of bounds for proper homecoming conversation."

Corey clapped his hand onto Jason's shoulder. "Come on, Jason, what's with you, man?"

"Nothing. I just don't like—forget it."

Debra placed both hands on the table. "It's not like I'm saying anything bad about him," she protested. "He's told the whole school he's gay."

Cindy scowled at Jason. "So, what do you care?"

Jason tugged at his tie and glared back at her. "I don't."

Michelle Phillips, the homecoming queen, waltzed over wearing a smoldering red strapless and a wrist corsage of speckled carnations. Her tin crown sparkled in the light of the mirrored ball. She asked if everyone was having a good time and made dutiful chitchat. Two seconds after she left, Cindy grabbed Debra's hand again. "The bitch. You should have won."

"I really don't care," Debra said. "We're seniors and I'm

going to have a ball this year, no matter what. I'm going to drink, ƒ like a bunny"—She leaned against Jason, laughing—"and have a fantastic time." She lifted her eyes to Jason and extended her hand. "Shake on it?"

But Jason didn't want to shake on it. He didn't like her bringing up their sex life in front of the whole world, either. In fact, he felt irritated by the entire evening. "I wish you wouldn't talk that way."

Debra let her hand fall to the table. "Talk what way?" Her tone turned serious. "I've always talked that way, Jason."

He pulled at his tie again. It was choking him to death. Corey and Cindy stared at him, making him feel like it was his fault he was having such a shitty time. "Well, it makes you sound like a—" He stopped, about to say something terribly hurtful. Corey and Cindy braced against the table, poised for the verbal blow. But Jason backed down. "I—I just don't like it."

The DJ started to play a slow number, and Cindy pulled Corey onto the dance floor. Debra leaned into Jason's shoulder and kissed the tip of his earlobe. "Please, let's not fight anymore," she whispered.

He put his arm around her. He didn't want to fight. He felt bad for being such a downer. "Want to dance?"

She looked up at him, and he knew she wanted him to kiss her.

For the next couple of hours they danced and talked, and then the lights flashed on, the crowd booed, and the DJ thanked everyone. Mr. Mueller got on the mike and told everyone to go home. The dance was over.

In the parking lot, they said good-bye to Corey and Cindy. Debra waltzed toward the car. "Wasn't it beautiful? Mr. Mueller said it was the best homecoming he's ever seen, and you know he's been at Whitman forever."

Jason pulled at his tie. "I've been wanting to take this fucking thing off all night."

"Oh, don't." Debra circled her arm through his. "You look so dashing!"

Jason slipped away from her arm, yanking the tie from his collar, then pulled his jacket off. Debra twirled in a circle beside him. "This has been the happiest night of my life." She gazed up at the sky. "Look at the stars!"

At the car, Jason opened the door for her and climbed in the driver's side, draping his tie over the rearview mirror.

Debra got in and laid her hand on Jason's. "Honey, let's drive out by the golf course."

They parked in the little lane by the fairway. Debra leaned close to Jason. "Can you crack your window and leave the heater on?" She snuggled against him. "It's cold!"

He did as she said, and she sank into his shoulder. "Guess what? It's almost our two-year anniversary. We started going out right after homecoming. Remember?"

"Hm," he said, the radio music drifting in and out of his consciousness. He stared across the golf course at a row of clouds drifting across the sliver of moon. He thought how he hated being angry at Debra and how he hated living at home; he thought about his grades and SATs; he thought about wanting to graduate and get away to college. He thought about the jokes at Nelson's expense. And he remembered Kyle giving him a ride home.

Debra lifted her head from his shoulder. "Are you angry at me?"

The suddenness of her question startled him. "No." He started to kiss her, pressing his lips against hers, but a yawn overpowered him and he had to pull away.

"Honey?" She reached up and ran her fingertips across his face. "What's the matter?"

"I don't know," he said, a little choked. "Maybe it's the heat." He shut the heater off, hoping that was it, but the truth was that he felt no desire for her. Two weeks had passed since the last time they had sex—when he couldn't keep himself from thinking about Kyle.

He leaned back in the seat and stared out the windshield. The wind had blown all the clouds away, but the moon was thin and dim, barely lighting the darkness. He wondered if he should even try having sex. Maybe touching her would rev him up. He leaned over and unzipped the back of her dress.

She helped by peeling off her bra. Her breathing became quicker, but it only reminded him of snoring, like when his little sister fell asleep on the couch watching TV. Before he could contain it, another cavernous yawn escaped his mouth.

Debra laid her hand on his. "Please tell me what's wrong."

Jason looked at her face. The dim moonlight glistening in her eyes made her look like she might cry.

Debra pulled up her gown, covering herself. "There's something you're not telling me."

Jason shuffled his feet. "Nothing's wrong." He bit into the nail of his left thumb.

Debra folded her arms across her chest. "You know, half the time I have no idea what's going on inside that head of yours."

Jason bit off another crescent of fingernail and tried to think what excuse he could give her for not wanting to make love. But he shouldn't have to make excuses. His anger clouded his thinking. Maybe they should just break up.

"It's *my* head," he snapped at her. "I don't have to answer to you. And I don't like the third degree."

Her eyes sank into her face. She blinked, and a tear rolled down her cheek.

He knew he'd hurt her and he felt ashamed for it. He should have left things alone. He took a deep breath. "I think maybe I need some space to think about some things."

She looked up at him, her brow knit up in confusion. She brushed the hair away from her face, but a strand remained stuck to the wet spot on her cheek. "What kind of things? Can you at least give me some idea what this is about?"

He looked out the window again, across the golf course. He wanted to be honest with her, but when he opened his mouth to speak, his throat clenched.

"Is it me?" Debra said, her voice cracking.

He leaned his head onto the steering wheel. "No," he sighed.

From the corner of his eye, he saw her pull a tissue from her pocketbook. She patted her eyes, then crumpled the tissue into a little white ball in her fist. "Jason?" Her voice was stern. "Is there someone else?"

He knew she meant another girl. He wished there were. That would be easier. He considered making up a story, but he'd already been less than honest. "No," he sighed. "I'm just trying to figure things out . . . to decide what I want. That's all."

She studied him for a moment. Mascara smeared her cheeks, giving her eyes a bruised and frightened look. She carefully uncrumpled the tissue from her fist and spread it onto her lap. Then she grew quiet.

He decided to keep talking. "I know I should've said something before now—"

She raised her hand to stop him. The fearful look was gone from her face, replaced by one of bold resolve.

"I'm sorry." He leaned forward to kiss her.

"No!" She blocked him with her arm. "I don't want to be around you while you figure things out!"

The force of her words made him wince.

She must have realized it, because her tone softened. "I don't mean it like that. What I mean is . . ." She shook her head. "Maybe we should take a break for a while."

He hadn't expected that. He'd expected her to get upset—to cry, maybe hit him—but he never thought *she'd* tell *him* to blow off. She was proposing exactly what he wanted—some space apart. Only now he wasn't sure he wanted it.

She crossed her arms and looked out the window. "I want to go home."

"Maybe we should talk some more."

"No! I don't want to. There's nothing else to discuss."

Jason drove her home, angry at himself for the mess he'd made and angry that Debra had told him off. When he parked in her driveway, she got out without kissing him.

The following week, he got back an algebra test with a bold red *F* on the front. Mr. Perez spoke to him after class. "Coach Cameron asked me how you're doing."

Jason collected his books. The last thing he wanted was a lecture, but Perez kept talking. "You're a good kid, Jason. I like you. I want to help you, but you need to decide what you want. You want to study, or you want to screw off?"

Jason slung his backpack over his shoulder. "I'm not screwing off."

"Hold on." Perez put up a hand. "Is there anyone who can help you at home? Your dad?"

What a joke. "We don't get along," he told Perez. "And my mom doesn't understand this stuff."

"Is there anyone else who could help?"

Jason remembered Kyle's offer. But . . . what if Kyle got the wrong idea?

The following afternoon he stopped by Kyle's locker. "Hey, you got your braces off. Looks good." He wished his own teeth looked that good. But his old man would never pinch over a single dime for his teeth.

Kyle flushed red and cracked a shy smile. "Thanks. How's it going with you?"

"Okay. I start basketball practice next week—every afternoon except Wednesdays. It makes it hard to keep up my grades." He waited, hoping that Kyle would get the hint.

Kyle slid his glasses up the bridge of his nose. "I can help you if you want."

Jason knew he should make it clear that he only wanted math help—nothing more. But he didn't know how to say it. Instead he agreed to meet Kyle at the flagpost after school the next day.

All day Wednesday he chewed his nails and debated whether to go through with it. He half hoped Kyle wouldn't show up.

But there he stood by the flagpost, glancing in one direction, then another, nervously playing with the bill of his cap. When he spotted Jason, he broke into a huge smile. "Hi!"

Whoa, Jason thought, *calm down.* "Look, all I want is help with math, okay?"

Kyle's smile disappeared. "Well, sure." He scrunched his eyebrows. "What do you mean?"

Jason kicked the ground. "Never mind."

They didn't talk much on the walk to Jason's house. Every once in a while he glanced over at Kyle. He had never really taken a good look at him before. His eyes were hazel, and his wire-frame glasses gave him a teddy-bear face. His hair was a honey color and hung down in bangs from beneath his cap. His shoulders were broad for such a thin guy. He remembered Kyle telling him he was on the swim team. He had a body like a swimmer—long, firm, and lean.

Once they arrived at Jason's, Kyle stopped at the sideboard in the living room. "Wow, all these trophies are yours?"

Jason nodded. "My mom likes to show them off." He did too, but he didn't want to seem conceited. His dad constantly harped that his ego was too big. He pushed open the kitchen door. Rex greeted them. Jason poured a bowl of Cat Chow, but Rex backed away when Kyle bent down to pet him.

"He's kind of skittish. You hungry?" he said, handing a pack of cupcakes to Kyle. Then he grabbed a couple of Cokes from the refrigerator and led Kyle to his room.

Kyle gazed around, staring at everything. Jason watched him, trying to figure out what he found so interesting. It was an ordinary room, not much to look at—pale blue walls; his bench and barbell set; the stereo system his aunt Claire had given him; posters of basketball stars above his bed; Whitman team pictures; his dresser, lined with his cologne and stuff. "Never seen a bedroom before?" Jason asked.

Kyle blushed. "Just looking." He pointed to the cologne. "I wondered what you wore."

Jason picked up the bottle. "Want some?"

"Sure." Kyle grinned and set the cupcakes down, rubbing the cologne on his wrists. "It smells like you." He glanced at the gold-framed photo on the dresser, of Jason with Debra. "That's a great picture."

Jason didn't want to think about Debra. He sat down on the bed and gestured to the desk chair for Kyle. "We had kind of a fight the other night." He hadn't planned on talking to Kyle about it. In fact, he hadn't told anyone about the fight—not even Corey. "Not really a fight. We decided to take a break for a while. Actually, *she* decided."

"You're not"—Kyle sipped the Coke Jason handed him—"breaking up, are you?"

His concern surprised Jason. "I don't know." He grabbed the cupcakes off the dresser, ripped open the pack, and shoved one into his mouth. "Want one?"

Kyle took one, while Jason kicked off his shoes, not thinking anything of it. Rex had followed them into the room and began circling Kyle, rubbing against his legs.

"Wow," Jason said. "He usually doesn't warm up to new people."

The cat hopped onto Kyle's lap, then bent his head down into Kyle's crotch, tapping his nose on Kyle's zipper as he sniffed.

"Rex!" Jason shouted. He stood up and grabbed the cat. "Sorry about that." He tossed him into the hall. "Come on. Out you go." He closed the bedroom door and suddenly became aware that he was alone in his bedroom with a guy he knew was a homo. His palm slid off the doorknob, clammy with sweat. He turned to see Kyle untying his own shoes.

A feeling Jason couldn't exactly identify—an excited feeling—coursed through him.

Kyle stared at him. "Is it okay if I take them off?"

Jason shrugged, wishing he'd left his own shoes on, and sat down again.

Kyle bent over to untie his laces, and a cassette tape fell out of his shirt pocket.

"What's that?" Jason asked.

Kyle picked it up. "A tape Nelson made. Want to hear it?"

Jason considered for a moment. Did he want to play in his stereo a tape made by Nelly? "Sure. Why not?" He put the tape into the stereo. Almost immediately he liked the music. "Who is it?"

Kyle hesitated, then mumbled something.

"*Who?*" Jason asked, louder this time.

Kyle looked embarrassed and said, slightly louder, "The Butthole Surfers?"

Jason burst out laughing. "No way! That's their name?"

Kyle nodded, cracking a smile. "You like it?"

"Yeah." Jason smiled. "I like it."

They listened to the tape and drank their Cokes. Kyle drummed his palms against his jeans. Jason tried not to notice how the soft denim outlined Kyle's legs and curved over the front of his pants. He rubbed the sweat from his palms. "Can I, like, ask you a question?"

Kyle leaned forward. "Yeah?"

Jason knew what he wanted to ask, but he wasn't sure how to ask it. "Did you always know you were . . ." His voice trailed off.

Fortunately, Kyle seemed to get his drift. He grabbed the bill of his cap and nodded. "Well, yeah. I didn't know what it was called . . . until sixth grade, when I saw this headline in the newspaper." He flipped the bill of his cap up, then back down. "After that, I heard guys talk about, you know, queers. I felt embarrassed. I kept to myself a lot. My mom got pretty worried. She didn't know what was going on. She still doesn't know. It wasn't till I met Nelson that I started coming out."

Jason hadn't expected such an involved answer. "But how did you know for certain?"

Kyle scratched his head beneath his cap and shrugged. "I knew I liked guys."

The simplicity of Kyle's response bothered Jason. His hands

dripped with sweat as he leaned toward Kyle. "Well, you don't look, you know, I mean . . . Like Nelly—I mean, Nelson. You can tell he is. Have you two . . . ?"

Kyle shifted on the bed. "Huh? No! No, we're just friends." He pulled his cap off and ran a hand through his hair. "I've never, you know . . . I've never done anything with anyone, girl or guy."

Jason stared at him, feeling silly for ever worrying that Kyle would make a move on him. He wiped his palms across his pants.

Kyle twirled his cap. "I never know what to say." The cap spun out of his hands and rolled across the carpet.

Jason picked it up and tossed it back to him.

"Thanks." Kyle smiled. "I'm always afraid that, I don't know, if I told a guy I liked him, he'd punch me out or something." He wrung the cap in his hands and looked up at Jason. "But I don't want to bore you with all my problems."

Jason wasn't bored. It was the first time he'd ever talked with another boy about shit like this. Though it made him sweat as much as a workout, it was better than sitting in a room full of people whom he didn't even know.

Kyle pulled his cap back on. "Well, I'd better help you with your math."

Jason nodded. He felt disappointed that Kyle didn't want to talk anymore, but he also knew that if his hands sweated any more, there would be a puddle on the carpet. He took his math book out of his backpack. "I should warn you. I don't get this stuff."

Kyle shrugged, sliding his chair over. "We'll go slow."

Jason opened the book. "I mean it. I really suck."

"That's okay. We can't all be good at everything. My basketball sucks."

Jason laughed, remembering Kyle in tenth-grade gym class. He did suck at hoops—he tensed up too much.

Kyle began explaining the equations. He made a lot more sense than Perez ever did. He explained each step, then stopped and asked a question, like Coach Cameron did when he described plays. And Jason understood it.

In fact, it seemed like they had just started when he heard the front door. He looked at the clock on the nightstand and saw they'd been studying for nearly two hours. He'd never sat through math that long.

Footsteps sounded in the hall. Jason realized how close he and Kyle were sitting. Shit. He stood up just as Melissa burst into the room. "Jay!" She ran to him.

He picked her up and swung her around. "Hey, monkey. Say hi to Kyle."

She waved hello to Kyle as Jason's mom leaned in the doorway.

"Hi, Mom. Kyle's helping me with math."

His mom smiled. "Great. Hi, Kyle." She turned to Jason. "Honey, can you bring in the groceries?"

Kyle helped unload the car, carrying several bags at a time. He was a lot stronger than he looked, Jason thought. It must be the swimmer's muscles. He thanked him for his help with the math.

Kyle beamed, grabbing his backpack. "I can help you again sometime, if you want."

"Yeah?" Jason said. "That'd be great." He meant it.

Kyle waved, "Laters," and walked down the street. Jason watched him for a moment, then carried the two six-packs of his dad's beer into the kitchen, where his mom was putting away the groceries.

"Why do you keep buying beer for him?" Jason asked.

She stared at Jason as if he'd spoken a foreign language. "I guess I never thought about it." She closed the cupboard. "Your friend seems nice."

Jason agreed, though he wondered what she'd say if she knew Kyle was queer.

He returned to his room, turned the stereo on, and bounced onto the bed, feeling happy. He'd enjoyed being with Kyle. He liked hearing what it was like for him to be . . . gay. Who would've thought that one day he'd have a gay guy over and together they'd listen to a tape of a group called The Butthole Surfers?

CHAPTER 8

JASON

KYLE

NELSON

After dinner that evening, Kyle lay in bed, hardly able to believe he'd actually been inside Jason Carrillo's room! He recalled the basketball trophies, the posters, the algebra book on Jason's lap. It had been torture trying to concentrate. He'd had to take one step at a time and keep asking Jason questions just to keep on track. He could still smell the cologne. He pressed his wrists tightly against his nose, taking in the rich Jason aroma, and sighed.

There was a knock on the door, and his mom peeked in to say good night. Kyle wanted to tell her everything that had happened: "He's on the basketball team. I love him!" That would be one way to come out. Maybe he could invite Jason over. "Mom? Dad? This is Jason, my future boyfriend." Right. It would never happen.

Kyle brushed his teeth, undressed, and turned off the

aquarium lamp. He dug his hand into the nightstand drawer and pulled out last year's *Zephyr*. He thumbed through the dog-eared pictures of Jason and felt himself swell up. He would never get to sleep like this. He put the yearbook away and found the *Honcho* magazine Nelson had given him. He turned the pages to a photo of a guy in Kalamazoo, Michigan, draped naked over an electric car he'd built from old automobile parts, solar panels, and a glider wing. Before Kyle knew it, he was asleep.

When he awoke, the bright sunlight of morning shone in his eyes. His mom sat on the edge of the bed and stroked his hair. "What happened?" she said. "Fell asleep reading and forgot to set your alarm?"

He watched groggily as she glanced around. For the past week she'd nagged him to straighten up his room. She reached down, picking something up off the floor.

With a jolt he snapped awake. She'd picked up the *Honcho*.

She stared at the magazine with the sort of bewildered look she got when she worked crossword puzzles. "Kyle, what is this?" Her voice was stiff and formal.

His mind spun. Think fast. What could he say? *Gee, Mom, how did that get there? It's certainly not mine. I don't know where it came from.*

She raised her hand as though to stop him from whatever nonsense he might say. Placing the magazine down on his nightstand, she abruptly smoothed her skirt, and rose. "How about you get ready for school and we'll talk downstairs?" She left the room.

Kyle sprang out of bed and shoved the magazine beneath his sheets. As if that would do any good now. He should never have taken the stupid magazine. He could kill Nelson. He took a deep breath and looked out the window at the driveway. His dad had already left for work. Thank God.

He showered and brushed his teeth, accidentally dropping the toothpaste cap into the toilet. Crap. He pulled the magazine back out from under his sheets and stuffed it into his backpack. Maybe his mom would forget about it. Keep dreaming. She might be too embarrassed to mention it, but she wouldn't forget about it.

He pushed the kitchen door open a crack. His mom was wiping the countertop with one hand. In the other, she held a steaming mug to her lips, blowing into it.

She turned and saw him. "Kyle, we need to talk."

He grabbed a yogurt from the refrigerator. "I'm late, Mom."

She set her mug down. "We need to discuss this." Her tone was deliberate. "Can we agree to talk when I get home?"

He nodded and bolted out the door as fast as he could.

When he arrived at school, he spotted Nelson amid the crowd in front, wearing his black leather jacket. Kyle pulled out the *Honcho* and grabbed him by the shoulder. "Take your stupid magazine."

Nelson glanced at the rolled-up magazine thrust into his hands. "Don't you want it?"

"Would you put it away, please? My mom saw it."

"You're shitting." Nelson stashed the magazine in his backpack. "Well," he sighed. "You wanted to come out to them."

"Correction,"—Kyle jabbed his finger at Nelson—"*You* wanted me to come out to them."

"Yes, 'cause I hate to see you in agony about being in the closet all the time."

"I wasn't in agony. Until now."

"Yeah? Between obsessing about your parents and Jason, I'm surprised your grades haven't suffered."

"What are you talking about? My grades are better than yours."

The homeroom bell rang. "Meet me at lunch," Nelson told him. "In the meantime, try to relax."

But in class Kyle could hardly sit still. Would his mom phone his dad? He kept expecting to hear Mueller call his name over the loudspeaker, ordering him to report to the front office, where his dad would be waiting.

At lunch Nelson waved him over. "How's it going?"

"Crappy," Kyle said, sitting down beside him. "I feel like skipping the rest of the day."

Nelson's eyes lit up. "Yeah? Let's do it!"

"I was kidding, Nelson. I'm not skipping, so drop it."

"At least eat something."

"I can't." Kyle pushed aside his tray.

The second half of the day was even worse than the morning. Ms. Cho asked him if he wanted to go to the infirmary. Kyle almost said yes, but he was afraid the nurse might phone one of his parents.

After school, Kyle and Nelson slowly walked home, leaning against the wind, past the brick box houses. Nelson popped a candy into his mouth. "Your dad will probably think I brainwashed you."

"No, he won't," Kyle said, kicking the leaves beneath his feet. But he knew it was true.

"Well," Nelson said. "If they kick you out"—he jumped up, suddenly excited—"you can come live with me! It would be cool as shit, Kyle. We'd have a blast."

"Whoa, Nelson. Read my lips: One, they are not kicking me out. Two, I am not going to live with you."

"Well, excuse me! You don't have to sound so horrified. I was just trying to help."

Kyle felt guilty and apologized, knocking aside a pile of leaves. "It's my dad I'm worried about. I know he'll lecture me. I can hear it already."

"Yeah, life sucks. You want a Jolly Rancher?"

They reached the corner where their paths separated. "Why don't you come over?" Nelson asked.

Kyle considered the invitation. At least he wouldn't be stuck waiting for his mom. But he decided against it. "I better clean my room up, so at least she can't chew me out about that."

As soon as he got home, Kyle started on his room. He collected his shoes and lined them up neatly in the closet, then vacuumed the carpet and straightened the books and papers on his desk. He tossed the shirt hanging on the back of his chair into the hamper. He changed the bedsheets, tucking in the corners like his mom had taught him and spreading the cover flat, folding it back and over his pillow. All the while he tried to think what to say to her about the magazine.

Downstairs, he decided to make dinner. Unlike Nelson, he wasn't that good a cook, but coming home to a meal would make it harder for his mom and dad to yell. While he cooked, he debated what to say.

He watched the kitchen clock as he shuttled around the kitchen. By the time he heard his mom's car in the driveway, the smell of tuna casserole permeated the air. Canned corn cooked on the stove.

He gripped the counter and tried to smile as the door opened and his mom came in, carrying a grocery bag. "Hi, Mom," he said casually. "I made dinner. I cleaned my room, too." The timer went off, and he pulled an oven mitt onto his hand.

She glanced at him, then at the oven. "Great." She pulled out a carton of chocolate-chip ice cream. His favorite? Uh-oh. Was this her way of softening the blow—a last meal before the execution? Maybe Nelson was right. He suddenly lost his nerve and started out the door. "I'll set the table."

"Kyle?" his mom said, putting the ice cream in the freezer. "Wait a minute. I'd like to talk about this morning."

Crap. He knew what she really meant: She wanted *him* to talk. He turned to face her. "Well," he said. The sweat beaded up on his brow. His glasses slid down his nose. "Uh . . ."

He knew telling her would change everything. He could never again pretend disinterest in girls on the pretense he was a kid. She would no longer pat his head and joke, "Just remember, when you get married . . ." He could imagine her disappointment. The way she saw him from that moment on would be different, forever.

She stared across the kitchen, waiting for him to continue. His stomach churned angrily. The truth of the matter was he wasn't a kid. He had to grow up sometime, whether he liked it or not, and she had to accept it.

"There is something I've wanted to talk to you about." His heart pounded fearfully against his chest. "Uh . . ."

There was another reason he hadn't told her he was gay: It was like bringing up sex. His mom and he never talked about that. The mere thought embarrassed him. Coming out to her meant admitting he longed to make love with a guy someday. He looked down at his shoes, blushing.

"Kyle, what do you want to say?"

He had to tell her. To keep it hidden now that she suspected would be too much like lying. He took a deep breath.

"I think . . . maybe"—he looked up from beneath the bill of his cap—"I'm gay."

His pulse throbbed feverishly. He'd actually spoken the *G* word, out loud, to his mom.

Her face took on a bewildered look.

"I mean," he corrected himself, "I am." He looked down at his sneakers again, trying to calm his spinning thoughts, then leaned back on the counter to steady himself. "I'm gay."

"Kyle, look at me."

Her gaze made him nervous. He shouldn't have told her anything. This whole thing was a mistake.

The corn on the stove started to crackle, and she rushed to shut off the burner. "Kyle," she said, pressing her fingertips to her temples, "I don't understand. Why didn't you tell me sooner?" She sounded angry.

How could he explain all the reasons? Where would he start? "I don't know." He crossed his arms and stared at her. "I figured you'd tell Dad." That was one big reason. Maybe he could convince her not to tell him.

But she returned to his being gay. "Kyle, are you sure? I mean, how do you know?"

Was she serious? "Mom, I *know*."

She ran a hand through her hair, pinning a loose strand behind her ear, then she adjusted her glasses. "How long have you known?" Her tone was softer.

Kyle brought his arms down. "I don't know. Always. I didn't know what it was called, but I knew I was different. I didn't want to be. I used to sit in my room and tell myself, 'I'm not going to let myself feel this way.' I wanted to tell you."

"But what about Cheryl Brooks? You went with her to the Sadie Hawkins—" She stopped herself as if recalling that it was actually Cheryl who invited Kyle to that dance.

Her voice became despondent. "You'll never have kids."

"I might," Kyle said. "I don't *know* if I will—or even . . ." He couldn't believe he was really saying this to his mom. "Or even if I'll ever have a boyfriend. I just hope one day I won't spend every second of my life thinking how I'm different."

She studied him, then opened the cupboard and pulled out a glass. She poured some water, drank it, then set the glass down on the counter, hard. "Well, I wish you had said something."

"I'm telling you now, aren't I?"

She must have sensed how hard it was for him, because she walked over and wrapped her arms around his shoulders. "I'm sorry, sweetie."

He hugged her in return. "You're not going to kick me out?" he asked softly.

She pulled away a little, holding him by the shoulders, and looked over her glasses at him. "Kick you out? Honey, you didn't think . . . ?"

Before he could answer, the kitchen door opened and his dad stepped in. Kyle drew away from his mom, embarrassed to be seen clinging to her.

"Hi," his dad said, hanging his keys on the rack by the door.

His mom arranged her hair and smiled. "Kyle made dinner. Wasn't that thoughtful of him?"

His dad kissed his mom and laughed. "Yeah? What's he trying to make up for this time?" He reached over and spun Kyle's cap around backward. "Let me wash up. Then you can tell me what happened."

As his dad left the room, Kyle turned his cap back around.

"You know you need to tell him," his mom said gently.

"I will."

His mom insisted. "He needs to know. He is your dad."

"I said I'll tell him."

She stirred the corn. "Do you want me to start, and make it easier?"

Kyle shrugged. "If you want."

"Honey, what do *you* want?"

What he wanted was for her to be either angry or worried, but not both. "Mom, I don't know anymore. I don't care." He adjusted his glasses. "What do you think he'll say?"

His mom drew a deep, slow breath. "I don't know."

The tuna turned out a little dry. Kyle could barely swallow, his stomach was so tangled in knots. When his dad finished eating, Kyle looked across the table at his mom. She nodded, her eyes spurring him on, the way they did at swim meets. Except this wasn't some piece-of-cake hundred yard freestyle; this was more like a death-defying reverse three and a half from the ten meter platform. Even with his mom's encouragement, he wasn't sure he could do it. He took a deep breath. "Dad?"

His dad looked up at him. Kyle hesitated, his pulse throbbing in his ears. Was he really going to do this?

His dad leaned forward, waiting. Kyle looked down, drew a breath, and took the plunge. "Dad, I'm gay."

In the silence that followed he could hear the blood pumping through his head. He felt more alone than he ever had in his life. After a moment he recovered his nerve and looked up.

His dad stared back, eyes narrowing in anger. "Nelson got you mixed up in this, didn't he?"

Kyle felt his head burn. Suddenly he was no longer afraid. "No one got me mixed up in anything! I knew before I ever met Nelson."

His mom slid a hand across the tablecloth between them. "Kyle says he's always known."

His dad spun around to her. "When did you find out about this?"

"Well, today."

His dad turned back to Kyle. "I think it's better if you stop spending so much time with that . . . boy."

Kyle tipped his chair forward. "I'm not going to stop spending time with him. You can't tell me who to hang out with. I'm not a little kid anymore."

"Honey," his mom intervened. "We know that. This has just taken us by surprise, that's all."

His dad wrapped his hand around his wine glass. "Before you decide anything, you better think this through a little better."

"Think through what? Being gay? There's nothing to think about." Kyle tossed his napkin onto the table. "It's not a choice. You're either born gay, or you're not."

"I've heard that," his mom interjected.

His dad glared at her. "That hasn't been proved."

Kyle tilted his chair back. "No one has to prove it to me."

"Well, this certainly isn't something I ever expected of you."

"Sorry I haven't lived up to your expectations."

"I don't think that's what your father meant."

Kyle pushed his chair away from the table. "That's what he said."

His mom smoothed the tablecloth with the palm of her hand. "I think what your father means is . . . this isn't easy for us."

Kyle crossed his arms. "What about *me*? How do you think I feel? He makes me feel like I've done something wrong."

"Honey, we're trying to understand."

Kyle grabbed his cap from the back of his chair. "Can I be excused?"

"We're not through talking," his dad said. "You don't just drop a bomb like this and walk away."

Kyle twisted the cap in his hand. "What's there to talk about? You don't want to accept that your son's queer."

His mom chimed her fork against her glass, the family signal for a time-out. His dad pulled out a pack of antacid tablets and popped a couple into his mouth. His mom picked a microscopic crumb off the tablecloth and deposited it onto her empty plate. She glanced at Kyle, then turned to his father, laying a hand on his. "Maybe we should continue talking about this some other time?"

Kyle jumped at his chance to bolt. "Can I be excused now?"

His dad rolled the antacid around his mouth and nodded. "Yes."

Kyle sprang to his feet and carried his plate to the kitchen. He scraped his uneaten dinner into the garbage disposal and took weird pleasure in the grinding noise. As he passed back through the dining room to the hall he caught a glimpse of his mom patting his dad's hand.

"Kyle?" his mom called, but he felt too angry to answer. He had to get away for a while. He yanked his jacket on and slammed out the front door.

The wind blew cold against him, biting his ears. And he'd forgotten his gloves. He stood there, trying to decide what to do. No way was he going back in. But it was too cold to be outdoors. He jammed his fists into his jacket, walked over to his mom's car, and climbed inside.

He stared at the house, his head still burning from the argument. His dad was a jerk, blaming Nelson and telling Kyle he couldn't spend time with him. He wasn't a kid anymore, and no one could tell him what to do. Maybe his dad would finally realize that.

Behind the gauze curtains, his dad crossed the dining room. His arms moved angrily as he paced back and forth. Kyle wondered how long it would take for him to calm down.

His mom pulled back the curtain and peered outside. A moment later she stepped out the front door, pulling on her coat and looking around. She spotted him and hurried over. "Kyle, can I come in?"

Kyle shrugged. What was he going to tell her, no? "It's your car."

She climbed into the seat beside him. "Honey, are you okay?" She patted his arm. "It's freezing out here. Come back inside. Your dad's worried."

"Did he say that?"

"Well"—she sort of nodded—"I know he is. He loves you. We both do. But you can't expect us to . . ." She flapped her hands, agitated.

If she was upset, how'd she expect him not to be upset? "I'm not going in," he said, his throat choking up. He knew he was on the verge of tears.

"Honey," she said, pulling a tissue from the box between the seats and handing it to him. "We're trying to understand." She looked genuinely worried. "But you need to give us time."

He wiped the dampness from his eyes. It had been years since he'd cried in front of his mom. He thought he was over that.

"Please," she said softly, reaching for his hand. "I know this is hard for you. And I'm glad you told us."

"Are you?"

She gave his hand a squeeze. "I know I love you, no matter

what happens. We both do. Nothing you say could ever change that. Come inside."

He stared out the windshield at the brick house, embarrassed to be sobbing and holding hands with his mom. "Can I just—I'll come in a minute."

She studied him. "Okay." She leaned over and kissed him, smelling like lipstick and the perfume he'd given her. "Promise you won't be too long."

As she walked up the front walkway, Kyle wondered if she and his dad would ever really accept his being gay. The house glowed blue inside, which meant his dad was watching TV. He must've calmed down, finally, and was now sitting in the family room, all cozy. Meanwhile, Kyle was out here in the cold, freezing his butt off. Why? He was only hurting himself.

He blew his nose and climbed from the car, slamming the door. Inside the house, he bypassed the family room and hurried upstairs. For a while, he fussed with his homework. Only when he heard his parents' bedroom door close did he come out. Downstairs, he quietly phoned Nelson.

"Way to go!" Nelson said. "I knew you could do it."

After that, Kyle scooped a bowl of the chocolate-chip ice cream his mom had bought. He carried it back to his room, where his thoughts turned to Jason. He climbed into bed and pulled the *Zephyr* out of his nightstand. At least he wouldn't be embarrassed if he woke up to his mom lifting the yearbook off the floor.

CHAPTER 9

JASON

KYLE

NELSON

Nelson waved from his car. "Hi, Mrs. Meeks." He tried not to sound nervous. It was his first time stopping by since Kyle had come out to his parents two weeks previous.

She stopped raking leaves. "Kyle should be out in a minute. He told us about the youth group. I wondered where you boys went every Saturday."

Nelson climbed out of the car. "I wanted Kyle to tell you. I told him you'd understand."

She started raking again. "Well, at least we're talking about it now."

Nelson fidgeted with his keys. "You know, there's a parents' group too. It's called PFLAG. My mom is vice president of the local chapter. She'd be happy to tell you all about it." As he talked, Mr. Meeks walked out from the garage, slapping his garden gloves against his pant leg.

"Hi, honey. The boys are going to that meeting Kyle told us

about. Nelson says there's a group for parents, too. Maybe we should go sometime."

Mr. Meeks remained silent and studied Nelson. He didn't look angry exactly, more perplexed.

The front door opened and Kyle walked out, carrying his cap in his hand, his hair still slick from the shower.

"Honey, you're going to catch cold," his mom said.

"I'm fine," Kyle replied. "See you later."

As soon as he got in Nelson's car, he let out a groan. "They're making me crazy. Dad's giving me the silent treatment—course, I'm giving it back—and Mom won't leave me alone. All last night she kept asking me questions." He leaned his head out the window to dry his hair.

Nelson put a tape in the stereo. "I think your dad doesn't know what to make of me."

Kyle leaned back in the car. "Did he say anything? I told Mom he better not."

"Didn't I tell you he was going to think I brainwashed you?"

When the boys arrived at the meeting, Shea was talking to a cute, college-aged boy whom Nelson had never seen before. *Yummy smile,* Nelson thought. *Definite hottie.* During introductions, he said his name was Jeremy. Nelson liked the name. He didn't realize he was staring at him until Shea wagged her finger at him. She could be such a wiseass.

Tam, the day's facilitator, announced the meeting's topic: "Friends and Lovers."

Nelson sat up. He'd never had a lover, or a boyfriend, or even a date. He thought about it often enough, especially when he was horny, which was pretty much 24/7. But he'd never even been kissed, except by his family—and Atticus, his dog. Too depressing to think about.

"In the straight world," Tam suggested, "friends are usually same sex and lovers are opposite sex. But if you're gay or lesbian, how do you decide if someone of the same sex will be a friend or something more?"

Blake spoke up first. "I knew the moment I first saw Dane that he turned me on. No question about it. Almost overnight we became boyfriends."

Nelson glanced at Kyle and tried to remember if he had felt attracted to him when they first met.

Kyle didn't seem interested in the discussion. He was doodling or writing something on the back of a bright orange flyer.

"I don't think the two have to be separate." Shea put her arm around her girlfriend. "Caitlin and I have been lovers for three years, but we're also best friends."

Damn it, Nelson thought, *if Shea and Caitlin can be lovers, why can't Kyle and I?*

"Yeah," Caitlin said. "But I think it's different for girls than for guys."

"I don't think so," Shea said. The way those two bickered, it amazed Nelson they stayed together.

The new guy, Jeremy, raised his hand. "Do you have to decide right away if a person's going to be a friend or something more? Shouldn't you get to know each other before you make a move?"

Make a move? Nelson asked himself. He'd known Kyle for three years and still didn't have a clue how to make a move.

He wanted to contribute something to the discussion, but the conversation raised more questions for him than anything. He started to get a headache and was glad when the meeting ended.

At Burger King afterward, Caitlin asked Nelson why he'd

been so quiet at the meeting. Shea answered in his place: "He was too busy checking out the cute new guy, Jeremy. And don't deny it." She grinned at Nelson. "I saw you. He was checking you out too."

"Get out! He was not. Was he?"

Shea brushed her blond curls back. "Yep. And I found out he's single."

Caitlin shook a french fry at Nelson. "Better make a move, Mister Man. The boy won't stay single for long in that group!"

Both girls laughed, though Nelson failed to see the humor. He'd been in the group four years and he was still single.

"Scoot over." Kyle walked up, carrying his tray of food. "Aren't you going to eat anything?"

Nelson slid over in the booth and pulled out a pack of diet pills. "I'm trying to slim down."

"You said your legs were too skinny!" Shea said, reading the box label.

"Yeah, but I think I'm getting a gut." He swallowed a pill and nabbed a sip from Shea's Coke.

Caitlin shook her head at him. "You're crazy!"

Nelson turned to Kyle. "What were you writing in there?" He reached for the bright orange flyer sticking out of Kyle's shirt. "Let me see."

Kyle clutched his pocket. "Hey, none of your business!"

Nelson withdrew his hand. "A love letter to Jason?"

"No! Anyone want some fries?"

Caitlin accepted his offer, feeding Shea a fry. "Don't change the subject. We want to hear the latest, most juicy gossip about Jason."

"There's no gossip."

Nelson drummed his knuckles on the table. "There must be something new. Usually you can't stop talking about him."

"Okay." Kyle put down his burger. "I went over to his house the other day to help him with math. Satisfied?"

Nelson stopped drumming. "You went to his house? You never told me that."

"Oops," Caitlin said, covering her mouth. "I think we just opened a can of worms."

"Since when do I have to tell you everything?"

"You *always* tell me everything!"

"You know," Shea told Caitlin, "maybe we should go find that CD you wanted."

"You don't have to go," Kyle said, but they were already up.

As everyone said good-bye, Nelson moved across the booth from Kyle and pulled his leather jacket tight around him, unsure whether to feel angry or hurt by Kyle's omission of Jason information.

Kyle picked up his burger. "Look, I'm sorry I didn't tell you about Jason's. I was going to, but then all the stuff happened with the magazine and my parents. Besides, lately, whenever I tell you something that has to do with Jason, you go nuts."

Nelson knew Kyle was right; he did go nuts at the mention of Jason. As they walked outside, Kyle put his arm around Nelson's shoulder, something he hadn't done for a long time. That reassured him a little. Kyle hadn't totally ditched him—at least not yet.

On the drive home Kyle suggested they rent a video. "How about a comedy? To get you out of your funky mood."

Nelson lit a cigarette. "I'm not in a funky mood." He punched the radio buttons, trying not to think about Kyle and Jason anymore.

Along with the video Kyle bought a jumbo bag of M&M's. "Want some?" he asked, climbing back into the car.

Nelson plunged his hand into the M&M's, thinking: *Fuck losing weight*. "So, what did you and Jason do at his house?"

"Nothing." Kyle's gaze drifted into space, his eyes glazing over. "I helped him with his math. I met his mom and little sister. I wonder if he'll invite me over again. Maybe I should invite him to my house. What would I say?"

"Tell him you want to suck his dick."

"I'm glad you're done sulking."

"I wasn't sulking."

Kyle shook his head. "He's not interested in me like that. I want to be his friend. I want to get to know him."

"So? Get to know him and then suck his dick."

Kyle tapped Nelson lightly on the head. "Can't you think about anything else?"

Nelson thought for a moment. "No."

When they pulled in front of Nelson's house, his mom was coming out the front door with a man she introduced as a dad from PFLAG. Nelson watched as the gray-haired guy opened the car door for her.

"He seems nice," Kyle said.

Nelson watched them. "He's okay."

Atticus, Nelson's black Labrador, barked and jumped as they went inside. Nelson flopped onto the couch. "It seems like everyone's got someone except me. My mom's dating Mr. PFLAG, Shea's got Caitlin, you have Jason—"

Kyle interrupted, "I do not have Jason."

Nelson buried his head in a cushion, lamenting his existence, then rolled over. "Shea thinks that new guy, Jeremy, is interested in me. He is cute. I hope you don't mind me talking this way. Let me know if it bothers you."

"Why would it bother me?"

"Well," Nelson said, "I don't want you to be jealous."

"Jealous?" Kyle said. "Why would I be jealous? If you like him, you should talk to him."

Nelson thought about it. "He probably won't come back."

Together the boys made stir-fry and ate in the family room. They watched the video, a comedy about two guys in New York who wanted to have sex with each other but couldn't find a private place. Nelson wished he had such problems.

After the movie, they watched the cartoon channel, where Pepe Le Pew, the romantic French skunk, smothered a cat with kisses while the cat tried to scramble away.

"You know Jason wants you," Nelson told Kyle as they carried their plates back to the kitchen.

"He does not. He has a girlfriend."

Nelson ignored him, stacking their plates on the counter. "He's confused about being queer, so he expects you to come on to him. You can help him get in touch with his inner queen."

Kyle swatted him with the dish towel. "Would you shut up?" He bent over and loaded the dishwasher.

That was just like Kyle, Nelson mused—helpful, kind, sweet. Nice butt, too.

They went to hang out in Nelson's room. While Kyle put a CD on, Nelson pulled a magazine from his dresser. "Want to see my new *Blueboy*?"

Kyle pushed the magazine away from him. "No way! I never want to see a porno again."

Nelson flipped through the magazine while Kyle rolled around on the floor with Atticus. The Labrador scrambled around the room, and Kyle pretended to chase after him. Then Atticus brought his chew sock from the hall. Kyle tossed it for him to fetch. Atticus brought it back, leapt onto Kyle, and started licking his face.

Kyle tried to hold him down. "Hey, stop that!" But when Kyle let him go, Atticus started to hump his leg.

"Uh-oh," said Nelson. "Jason's got competition."

Kyle pulled his leg away. "Atticus!"

The dog sat down and twisted around, licking himself.

Nelson stood up and stretched. "Come on, Kyle. Let's do something!" The sex scenes in the video, the naked men in the magazine, and watching Kyle roll around on the carpet had worked him up.

"Like what?" Kyle asked.

Nelson tossed the magazine aside. "I don't know. Aren't you dying to find out what sex is like?"

Kyle gave a shrug. "I can wait."

"Wait! Life's too short, Kyle. It's passing us by. I get bashed every day for being queer, and I haven't even kissed a guy yet. That's pretty pathetic." He shook a cigarette from his pack. Then a brilliant idea dawned on him. "Hey, how about if we practice?"

Kyle raised an eyebrow. "Practice what?"

"You know . . ." Nelson lit up a cigarette. "Making out."

Kyle pressed his glasses up the ridge of his nose, looking confused. "With who?"

God, Kyle could be dense.

"You mean—" He suddenly sat upright. "You're crazy!"

"Why not?" Nelson insisted. "It's just practice."

Kyle shook his head. "I can't kiss you. It would feel like . . . kissing my sister."

"So I have tits and pussy now?"

"You're my friend." Kyle crossed his arms. "It would feel too weird."

Nelson cupped his hand over his mouth to test his breath. "You afraid I have AIDS? Rabies?"

Kyle glared at him. "Mad cow disease."

"Screw you!" Nelson puffed on his cigarette. "You'll let my dog lick your face, but you won't kiss me? That makes me feel really special."

A guilty look crossed Kyle's face. "It just doesn't feel right."

Nelson decided to make the most of Kyle's guilt. "I'll put on some mood music." He ran to the stereo and grabbed a Tony Bennett CD. "It'll be fun." He put out his cigarette and walked back toward Kyle, making pucker and smack sounds, like loud kisses. Atticus sat up, ears pricked.

"No way." Kyle shook his head.

Nelson threw his arms around Kyle. Kyle pulled away from him. "Cut it out!" He sounded angry, but he was laughing.

"*Mon chéri!*" Nelson said, imitating the French accent of Pepe Le Pew. "The night is young, the moon is full, and you are so handsome!" He began smacking kisses on Kyle's neck. The downy softness surprised him.

Atticus barked and paced beside them.

"Nelson, stop it!" Kyle pulled away.

Nelson lost his balance and fell, pulling Kyle down with him. As they wrestled on the floor Atticus pawed at them, barking. Nelson laughed as he struggled. Kyle grabbed Nelson's arms and climbed on top of him. "You going to stop it?" His cap fell off and rolled away.

Atticus jumped on Kyle, whining and licking his face. Kyle loosened his grip on Nelson to push the dog away, and Nelson rose up to kiss Kyle on the mouth.

Kyle swung to block him, but instead his hand hit Nelson's chin with a *smack*. Nelson's head flew backward and hit the floor. For a moment, he lay dazed.

Kyle let go of him. "Are you okay? I'm sorry. I didn't mean it."

Nelson's chin throbbed. He felt like crying. He rolled over, burying his face. Even though he'd cried in front of Kyle before, for some reason now he felt ashamed.

He felt Kyle's hand lay gently on his shoulder. "Nelson, you're my best friend. I don't feel that way about you."

"Fuck you! Okay?"

Kyle flinched. "I'm sorry."

Nelson wanted to say something mean. But his jaw hurt too much. "Just leave me alone." He rolled over.

He heard Kyle pad across the carpet and leave the room. Then he heard the front door close. He reached up for his jaw and worked it back and forth. He went to the mirror, expecting to see his face horribly disfigured—or at least bruised. But his jaw didn't look any different.

He noticed the bright orange sheet of paper Kyle had in the youth group meeting lying on the carpet. It must have fallen out of Kyle's pocket when they were wrestling. He unfolded the piece of paper. Kyle must have written JASON CARRILLO, JASON CARRILLO a hundred times.

Nelson tore the paper in half, then ripped it again and again and again.

CHAPTER 10

JASON

KYLE

NELSON

Jason stared at the *88* on his quiz, the highest algebra grade he'd ever gotten.

Perez patted him on the back. "Congratulations. Who's helping you?"

"Kyle Meeks."

Perez nodded. "Good choice. Kyle's a bright guy. Keep it up."

Jason stopped by Kyle's locker and high-fived him. "Can you believe it? Look at this."

Kyle gazed at the paper and smiled. "See? You can do it."

"Yeah, with you. Can you come over this weekend?"

Jason felt someone tug on his arm. He turned to see Corey. "Come on, man. We're going to be late for practice."

"All right," Jason said, turning back to Kyle. "Sunday afternoon?" They agreed on two o'clock as Corey led Jason away.

"Doesn't he hang with Nelly?" Corey whispered.

"So?" Jason shrugged. "He helps me with math. Thanks to him I got an eighty-eight." He waved his quiz to show Corey.

"Yeah?" Corey said. "What's he want in return?"

"Hey. Lay off. He's a friend."

"Take it easy," Corey told him. "All I'm saying is be careful. You know how people talk."

"Doesn't bother me," Jason said, though he knew Corey was right. To be honest, it did bother him. It made him angry that school had to be this way. Couldn't he have a gay friend without people assuming *he* was gay?

Jason wished Corey hadn't seen him with Kyle. During practice he lost the ball twice and missed his foul shots. What was worse, the assistant coach from Penn State was visiting. Each time Jason messed up, Coach Cameron shook his head.

When the sports bus dropped him home, Jason heard his parents arguing all the way from the driveway. His dad's voice had that slur—he'd been drinking.

"You don't like how I treat him? Maybe I should just move out. Then you'd be happy."

Jason knew his dad was talking about him. He bit a fingernail and opened the kitchen door.

His dad leaned against the kitchen counter, a beer bottle in his hand. His mom sat at the table reading one of her self-help books, titled *The Courage to Change.* She looked up as Jason came in. "Hi, honey. How was practice?"

He bent over and kissed her cheek. "Okay."

His dad grabbed a paper bag off the kitchen counter. "You left your trash in my truck." He threw the bag at Jason.

Jason caught it. "Sorry." He tossed the bag into the trash.

His dad pointed his bottle at him. "That's the last time I warn you. Use my truck, then clean it. Hear me?"

"No, I'm deaf."

His dad slammed his bottle down on the counter and raised the back of his hand to smack him.

Jason stepped away. "Keep your hands off me."

His mom stood up, spreading her arms between them. "Would you both stop it!"

Jason stared at his dad and his dad glared back, curling his lip and muttering, "Pansy." He finished his bottle and opened the refrigerator. "There's no more beer?"

His mom glanced at Jason, then at his dad. "I didn't buy any."

"You forgot my beer?"

"I didn't forget." She opened her book again. "I'm not buying you any more beer."

His dad flung the refrigerator door closed and grabbed his truck keys. "Then I'll get my own."

His mom closed her book. "You shouldn't drive."

"I wouldn't have to if you'd bought my beer." He turned and stormed out of the kitchen. The front door slammed, shaking the house. A fork fell off the counter. Jason picked it up.

Outside the kitchen window the truck started and backed out of the driveway.

"Are you okay?" Jason asked.

His mom leaned her head into her hands and nodded silently.

Jason put his hands on her shoulders. "I'm sorry."

"It's not your fault. I keep hoping things will get better. Sometimes they do, then . . ." She trailed off with a shrug.

Things never got better, Jason thought. The fights only got worse. Things would never improve so long as he remained at home. "Maybe if I left—"

Her reaction was instant. "Honey, I've asked you not to talk about that. You don't leave until you go to college."

Jason doubted he could stand his dad that long. He almost said so but didn't want to upset his mom any further.

Sunday afternoon Kyle showed up at 2:00 on the dot. Jason's mom brought them a tray of orange slices and told them to "Study hard," then left for her Al-Anon meeting. While Kyle explained variables, Melissa colored beside them on the carpet.

She proudly handed her drawing to Kyle. "It's for you."

"Wow." Kyle grinned. "It's pretty. Thank you."

Jason couldn't tell what it was. After Melissa went to play in her room, he and Kyle joked about what the drawing might be. Rex came in, and Jason showed Kyle how the cat fetched.

Jason felt relaxed with Kyle. He was so easy to get along with. He seemed so normal. Sometimes he wondered if Kyle was really gay or maybe just afraid to get laid with a girl, like he had been till he met Debra.

When they were between math equations, he asked Kyle, "Did you ever have a girlfriend?"

"No." Kyle gave him a bewildered stare. "Why?"

"Just curious. You never wanted to, like, do it with a girl?"

"No. I guess I'm a Kinsey six."

"A what?"

"A Kinsey six. In the fifties, Dr. Kinsey found that most people aren't exclusively gay or straight. He came up with a scale, zero to six, from totally heterosexual to completely homosexual. I'm pretty sure I'm at the end of the scale. I've kissed girls, but . . ." He made a face like he'd sucked a lemon.

Jason thought about what he said, wondering where he fell on the scale. Again the hours flew, and it seemed his mom had just left when she returned. She invited Kyle to dinner, and Jason encouraged him to stay.

"Sure!" Kyle agreed.

The boys helped prepare the meal. Kyle fixed their beverages and Jason set the table. "How many places?" he asked his mom.

She sighed. "Five, in case your dad comes home."

Jason hoped he wouldn't.

During dinner, his mom asked Kyle if he played basketball.

"I think they'd have to widen the hoop for me to make a basket."

They laughed. It was more than Jason had laughed in months. After dessert Kyle helped him clean up. When they were done, he didn't want Kyle to leave.

"Well," Kyle said, looking at the clock. "I guess I better go home."

"You, uh, want to go to a movie or something?" Jason asked.

Kyle looked surprised. "Well . . . sure."

"Great." Jason knew he'd have to ask his mom for cash, but by the way she'd smiled at dinner, he could tell she liked Kyle and would happily give him movie money.

At the movie theater, Kyle stood in line at the concession stand while Jason got their seats. Jason looked around to see if he knew anyone. Even though he was having a great time with Kyle, he couldn't get what Corey had told him out of his mind. People talked. What if someone from school saw them?

Kyle shuffled into the theater juggling a load of popcorn and drinks. "Here's your Coke. Want some popcorn?"

When Jason reached into the bucket, his thumb accidentally

brushed Kyle's. The touch of skin made him a little uneasy. It was as if a little zap of electricity had sparked through his body. He tried to ignore it, but each time their fingers bumped, he felt himself grow more excited, and when they reached the bottom of the bucket, he felt disappointed.

The lights dimmed, and Kyle pulled a wad of napkins from his pocket and handed some to Jason. Jason wiped the salt and butter from his fingers and started to lay his hand on the armrest between himself and Kyle, but stopped short. Kyle's hand was already there.

Jason straightened his back. Kyle better not try anything funny. They were just friends. Nothing else. Just friends.

The film opened with a barrage of machine-gun fire. Jason tried to focus on the movie, but Kyle's hand irritated him, the way it hung out on the armrest. Jason wanted to lay his own hand down. If someone passed by and saw their hands together . . .

What did he care what anyone thought? He had just as much right to use the armrest. Something was wrong when a guy couldn't simply lay his hand beside another guy's without someone thinking he was queer. It didn't mean anything. Besides, superpolite Kyle would probably realize he was monopolizing the armrest and pull his hand away.

Jason took a deep breath and quickly glanced around the dark theater. No one was watching them. He leisurely extended his arms out in front of him, as though stretching. Then he raised his arm into the air, intending to reach over casually and lay his hand on the armrest beside Kyle's. In the process, Jason, star athlete, miscalculated the trajectory and boxed Kyle squarely in the ribs.

Kyle winced and said, "Oooh, sorry," and removed his hand from the armrest.

Jason felt like a world-class klutz. He slunk down, wanting to crawl beneath the seat. "My fault," he whispered.

At least the armrest was free now. He placed his hand on the soft, warm cushion and began to relax.

But not for long. Kyle raised his arm and rested his own hand back on the armrest, once again brushing Jason's skin. Jason's blood raced in his arteries. He held his breath, staring fixedly at the screen, where the hero blasted some red-haired guy with a flamethrower.

Maybe Kyle thinks I want to hold hands, Jason thought. He recalled the fourth-grade field trip to the Museum of Natural History, when everyone had had to pair up with a buddy. For the whole day, he had held Tommy's hand. And he remembered what that had led to.

Jason tried to clear his head, but the current of electricity buzzing up from Kyle's hand, making the hair on his arms stand at attention, wasn't helping. Maybe Kyle just wanted to share the armrest. Even if he did want to hold hands, he would be too shy to do so. It wasn't going to happen unless Jason took the initiative himself.

That was a weird thought. It lurked in front of him, like someone's fat head blocking the movie screen. What if he did hold Kyle's hand? Yeah, and what if somebody saw them and yelled for the theater manager? The manager would surely phone his house. End of life.

Of course, he could deny everything, say he was simply stretching his fingers. What was the big deal?

One at a time, his fingers stretched out from their resting place. They paused in midair. Then they gently came to rest across the back of Kyle's hand. He held his breath, expecting Kyle to do something—protest or stop him or something. But Kyle didn't move.

Jason's heart thundered like cannon fire. Sweat ran down his forehead. Kyle had to realize what was happening. He was a little goofy, but he wasn't a zero. Was he being polite? Maybe his arm was asleep.

Jason glanced around the theater. His pulse quickened. The longer his hand stayed there, the more significant the fact became, the more difficult it would be to explain away. He should remove his hand now. *Do it. Now.*

But Kyle's hand beneath his own excited him too much. He hadn't expected the skin to feel so tender. The raised veins along the back felt soft and warm.

Suddenly the hand shifted, and Kyle's wrist slowly turned beneath Jason's until the two boys' hands touched palm to palm. There was no mistaking Kyle's hand for an armrest now.

On-screen a mustached guy hung from a cliff. Jason breathed rapidly and heavily. His mind was a whirlwind, while beside him his hand took on a life of its own. Slowly one finger after another fell between Kyle's fingers, until all intertwined. This was surely the climax of his life. Disaster was certain to follow, but he was ready to die happy.

Three rows ahead of him, a man huddled closer to his date. On-screen the hero made love to some mysterious babe on the roof of a hovercraft speeding across the water. Jason turned to look at Kyle.

At that exact moment, Kyle turned to Jason. The light from the movie screen flickered across Kyle's glasses. His eyes were bright and yearning, his mouth slack, his lips glistening in the screen light.

Jason wanted to kiss him. He could practically taste Kyle's sweet, buttery breath, feel the tenderness of Kyle's lips.

Something moved in front of them. A man was walking up

the aisle. Shit! Jason yanked his fingers from Kyle's hand. He sat up stiffly against the back of his chair and fixed his eyes on the screen, wanting to kill himself.

But the man passed without taking notice of them. Jason sighed deeply . . . once more wanting to live. He wiped the sweat from his forehead and swore in his mind he would never do anything so stupid again.

"Are you okay?" Kyle whispered.

"Yeah, I'm okay," Jason mumbled. He tried to concentrate on the rest of the dumb movie but had no idea why the hero tossed the woman he'd made love to off the side of the boat. Several times Kyle turned to look at him, but no matter how much Jason wanted to look back, he couldn't bring himself to do it. He kept his hands safely folded in his lap.

When the credits came up, Jason slid down in his seat. Only after the theater had cleared was he reassured that no one knew what they'd done.

Back in the car, he turned the radio on loud. Maybe if they didn't talk about it, he could forget it ever happened.

Kyle directed him to Sycamore Street and pointed to his house. "That's my room on the second floor, by the oak branch. You want to come over sometime?"

Jason stopped the car and tried to decide what to say. "Look, I . . ." Kyle stared at him, grinning joyously. Jason slunk down in his seat. "I better get home."

"Okay," Kyle said. "I had a great time." He opened the door and got out. As he walked up the sidewalk, he turned to wave, his smile glowing.

Jason shifted into drive and watched Kyle's image recede in the rearview mirror. The farther away he drove, the more calm he felt.

When he got home, he undressed, tossed his clothes onto his desk, and threw himself onto his bed, pounding the pillow with his fist. As much as he fought it, his thoughts remained on Kyle. Not Kyle hunched over some algebra book, but Kyle at the movie theater holding his hand. What would it feel like to kiss him? Disturbed by his thoughts and the uncontrollable stirring beneath his sheets, he rolled onto his stomach and turned off the light.

JASON

KYLE

NELSON

Kyle reached his toothbrush beneath the faucet, being extra careful not to wet the hand that had actually held Jason Carrillo's. He returned to his bedroom and for the millionth time brought the palm to his face, breathing deep the aroma of Jason's cologne; then he gently closed his eyes and imagined Jason's lips. He'd wanted to kiss Jason in the movie theater. Now he even felt like kissing his scented hand, but that was stupid.

Instead he pinned the drawing Melissa had given him onto his bulletin board. Then he undressed and removed his glasses, turned off the light, and climbed into bed. Across the dark room, the aquarium filter hummed. Kyle hesitated an instant, then brought the hallowed hand to his lips and bestowed a soft kiss.

He had done the stupid thing. Now he could sleep. With a contented moan he drifted into dreamland.

. . . .

Later that week, Kyle arrived home from school to find his mom standing in the center of his bedroom—not cleaning or tidying up, just rubbing her brow. She'd been acting weird like that ever since he came out to her four weeks ago. She barraged him with questions like, Should she have done something differently bringing him up? or, What about the ex-gay groups that claimed homosexuals could change?

"Mom," he said, frustrated. "You didn't do anything wrong and I can't change. Those groups are full of fakes. Besides, I wouldn't want to change, even if I could. I'm finally starting to like who I am. Are you sorry with how I turned out?"

"No." Tears puddled in her eyes. "I'm just scared."

With his dad it was even more frustrating. He barely said anything to Kyle anymore, other than a gruff "Good morning," "Good night," or "Take an umbrella, it's raining."

Now Kyle came home to find his mother gazing around his room. He softly cleared his throat. "Hi."

She gasped. "Honey, you startled me."

"Sorry." He dropped his backpack onto his desk and braced himself for whatever new question or concern she might have.

"I was just . . ." She motioned in the air, as if grasping. "I'm trying to understand." Her eyes fixed on Melissa's drawing. "I always thought you'd be a wonderful dad."

"I still might! There are gay men who have kids." He pulled off his cap and gave his head a vigorous scratch. "Mom, don't you understand? I have to be who I am. You always told me that. Or did you mean except for being gay?"

She studied him, trying to comprehend. "I'm sorry, honey. I just want you to be happy."

He felt guilty for snapping at her. He had to give her credit for trying. "That's what I want, too."

. . . .

The traditional family Thanksgiving took place at his grand-mom's. Over sweet-potato pie she asked good-naturedly, "So, Kyle, do you have a girlfriend yet?"

Uncle George, his dad's brother, laughed. "Of course he does! A good-looking boy like him? Probably has a dozen. Don't you, Kyle?"

His dad shot Kyle a panicked, pleading look, so Kyle decided it was best just to say: "No comment."

Everyone laughed, as if it were a joke. On the drive home, his dad told him, "Thanks for not saying anything in front of your grandmother," like it was something shameful. Kyle kicked the floor of the car, wishing he *had* said something.

The rest of Thanksgiving break was boringly lonely for Kyle. Nelson hadn't been returning his phone calls ever since he socked him in the jaw, and his other friends were either out of town or busy doing family stuff. Fortunately the city's indoor pool was open for the long weekend, so he spent hours doing solitary laps and daydreaming about holding Jason's hand.

He avoided his dad as much as possible. A fight between them was building. Kyle could feel it. He was dreading going to the Redskins game with him, since his mom wouldn't be there to referee.

With not a little effort, he managed to keep his temper during the game. When the final quarter ran into overtime, he excused himself to the restroom. By the time he started back to his seat, the game was over and there was no way he could fight against the outpouring throng. He decided to go to the car. His dad would figure it out. Except apparently he didn't.

Almost every parking space was empty before his dad finally

marched across the vast lot. "Do you realize," he yelled, "how long I waited for you to come back?"

"Dad! It was impossible to get back."

His dad yanked the car door open. "It was not impossible. I was worried."

Kyle slid in beside him. "Worried about *what*?" This whole conversation was dumb. He knew a fight had been brewing, so he knew this wasn't really about his not going back to his seat. "I never wanted to come to this stupid game in the first place."

His dad shot him a hurt, angry look. "Then why didn't you say so?"

Kyle crossed his arms, unable to explain it: how he felt guilty when his dad had his hopes up; how he didn't want to disappoint him. That was a big part of why it had taken him so long to come out.

"You never asked, Dad. You think just because you like something, I will too. I never liked football, or hockey, or any of those things you think I should like."

"Then why'd you come to all those games with me?"

Kyle stared out the window. He'd gone to all the games because he wanted to be with his dad. He wished he could say that.

"From now on," his dad said softly, "I won't ask you to come with me anymore."

Kyle should've felt relieved and happy, but he didn't.

They arrived home to his mom's cheery smile. "Hi, guys. How'd it go?"

"Fine," Kyle said, and hurried up to his room, not wanting to talk.

Later that evening he overheard bits of conversation: "Just listen to him," his mom said.

"He doesn't realize what he's setting himself up for." That was his dad, of course. "He's making a foolish decision."

The choice stuff again. Kyle tried to do some homework, but couldn't concentrate.

Someone tapped on the door. "Hi." His father strolled in, trying to force a smile.

"Hi," Kyle said. He hoped and prayed they weren't going to continue the fight.

His dad jingled his pocket change. "Anything you want to talk about?"

Kyle thought, *Why bother? You're not going to change your mind, and neither am I.* So he said, "No."

His dad looked relieved. "Well, there's one other question I need to ask, son. Since you brought all this up. Is there anything else we should know? About your health?"

Kyle knew what he was worried about: HIV. As if Kyle had any reason to worry about that yet. "No, I'm fine."

His dad reached over to spin Kyle's cap around. "Well, that's a relief."

Kyle pulled away. "I don't like when you do that."

His dad withdrew his hand. "Okay. I won't do it anymore." He gave Kyle a forlorn look. "Good night, son."

Kyle watched the door close. That hadn't been so excruciating. Even if his dad never accepted his being gay, at least he might stop treating him like a kid.

He still felt awful about hitting Nelson. He felt even more confused about the conversation that had led up to it. Why had Nelson wanted to make out with him? It almost seemed as if Nelson had a crush on him. But that was crazy. Kyle couldn't figure it out, so he'd decided simply to let Nelson cool off. He bought the new Nancy Boy CD as a peace offering and brought it to school the Monday after Thanksgiving.

"Hi," Kyle said, walking up behind him.

Nelson turned and studied him, as if debating whether to stay angry.

Kyle quickly handed him the CD. "I got you this. I'm sorry about . . . how's your jaw?"

Nelson looked down at the CD. "Okay." He relinquished a slight smile. "I may be queer, but I'm not frail."

Kyle gave a sigh, relieved. "How was your Thanksgiving?"

"Pathetic." Nelson shrugged. "The usual bullshit. My dad promised to call and didn't. My mom bought me some clothes."

"Those are nice," Kyle said, pointing to the jeans hanging off Nelson's hips.

"Thanks. Hey, look!"

Kyle turned. Mueller had finished yelling at some freshman for chewing gum and was talking to MacTraugh.

"Do you think he's talking to her about the GSA?" Kyle asked.

After school, they went to her classroom to find out. She was rearranging students' artwork on the wall.

Nelson helped her take down a painting. "Did Herr Führer say anything about our group?"

MacTraugh handed him a new picture, smiling wryly. "I'm not sure who you mean."

"He means Mr. Mueller," Kyle said, tearing off some masking tape.

"Oh, yes. He said he got a call from Fenner Farley's dad."

"Bible-thumper Fenner?" Nelson asked.

McTraugh nodded. "I told you to expect opposition, didn't I?"

"Well, no one is going to stop us. Kyle found out about this law on the Internet. What's it called, Kyle?"

"The Federal Equal Access Act."

MacTraugh laughed, massaging her fingers. "Yes, you certainly made Mr. Mueller aware of it. I don't think he's against the group on principle. But it's a new idea and so it's presenting some difficulties. We should prepare information for the next PTA meeting. Nelson, can you ask your mom to call me?" She turned to Kyle, and he knew what she was wondering.

He cleared his throat. "I came out to my mom and dad like you suggested."

"Did everything go all right?"

"It went okay. I'm glad I told them . . . I think."

After helping MacTraugh clean up, Kyle and Nelson walked home together, agreeing how glad they were that MacTraugh was on their side. They didn't notice the pickup truck barreling down the street, until a beer bottle flew out its window. Nelson yanked Kyle aside just in time. The bottle hurled past Kyle's head and smashed onto the concrete walk, shattering into little brown pieces.

The pickup squealed past. "Faggots!" yelled a voice.

Kyle's heart thundered against his chest. "Did you see their license plate?"

"I know that truck," Nelson said. "It's José's."

"He could've killed me!"

"Duh!" said Nelson, fumbling for a cigarette.

It took Kyle a while to settle down. As they resumed their walk home, he thought how he and Nelson were in the same boat, and felt close to him again. It made Kyle want to confide in him about holding hands with Jason. But he didn't want Nelson to wig out again. They'd barely made up. Then he remembered how hurt Nelson had felt when he hadn't told him about going to Jason's house.

"I want to tell you something," Kyle said, adjusting his cap. "But I'm afraid you'll get angry."

Nelson stopped and lit a cigarette. "Give me a hint. Could it by any remote chance have to do with someone you think about three hundred sixty-five days a year, twenty-four hours a day?"

"How'd you know?"

"I called the Psychic Friends Hot Line."

Kyle regretted having said anything, but now that he'd started, he decided to go through with it. "We went to the movies."

Nelson stared expectantly at him. "You went on a date?"

"It wasn't a date." Kyle braced himself. "Except we held hands."

Amazement filled Nelson's voice. "You *held hands*?"

Kyle nodded. "But he didn't mean anything by it."

"Oh, right. He was just checking your pulse?"

"No, I just—I don't know. He's not interested in me, I know that."

"Kyle, wake up. Two guys don't hold hands unless they're interested in each other."

Kyle wasn't convinced. "He probably just wanted to see what it felt like."

"An experiment for science class?" Nelson grabbed Kyle's arm. "Read my lips: Jason is queer. And he's stuck on you."

"He is not," Kyle said, pulling his arm away. "He's just confused. He has a girlfriend."

"No, *you*, girlfriend, are the one who's confused." He turned to face Kyle square on. "Kyle, are you trying to protect me?"

Kyle adjusted his glasses. "What?"

"You keep denying what's so obvious between you and Jason, like you're afraid I'm going to be jealous. Well, I'm not. I'm over it. You can do whatever you want. Don't worry about me. I don't care. Okay?" He puffed on his cigarette.

Then it struck Kyle. Of course. Nelson *was* jealous. Suddenly all Nelson's weirdness made sense—his wanting to make out, his digs at Jason.

"Okay?" Nelson repeated.

Kyle nodded silently, unsure how else to respond.

JASON

KYLE

NELSON

Nelson felt like Kyle had punched him in the jaw again. "I can't believe those two little weasels held hands!" He paced back and forth while Shea ordered beauty supplies on-line.

"I thought you said you were over him."

"I am!" Nelson snubbed out his cigarette. "I don't want to talk about it anymore."

Shea shrugged her shoulders. "*You* brought it up. Hey, you just got an instant message from someone named"—she squinted at the screen—"HotLove69? Is that a joke? Who is it?"

Nelson rushed over to the desk. "Uh . . . he's a guy." He often chatted with guys on-line, though he'd never actually met one in person.

Shea gave him a suspicious look. "Where do you know him from?"

Nelson leaned over her shoulder, reluctant to tell her. "On-line."

"On-line!" she said, like she was his mother. "What's his real name?"

"I don't know. What difference does it make?"

"Nelson, how do you know he's not some perv?"

"He's not a perv. He sent me a JPEG. Look." He opened the photo of a muscled young man with blond hair and steel blue eyes leaning on a motorcycle. "Isn't he totally gorgeous?"

Shea examined the screen. "How old is he? Sixty-nine?"

"Ha-ha. *Twenty*-nine."

"So, what's he want with a seventeen-year-old?"

Nelson gave a disappointed sigh. "So far, nothing." He sat down on the bed.

Shea raised an eyebrow. "Are you doing this to get back at Kyle?"

"God! Would you stop analyzing me?"

Shea came over and sat beside him. "I'm sorry. Just promise me you won't do anything stupid?" She took his hand and laced her fingers between his.

"I won't do anything stupid. I promise."

She smiled. "Hey, Caitlin's mom said we could have a party for the group Saturday night. Maybe Jeremy will come. I still think you two would hit if off."

Nelson thought about it. Jeremy was extremely cute and closer to his age. Maybe he should talk with him. But what would he say? He'd never put the make on anyone—except Kyle, and look what that had gotten him.

Parties for the Rainbow group were tame affairs, with parents watchfully hovering upstairs. Alcohol wasn't allowed, though inevitably someone had a bottle in a car. Sometimes the parties were exclusively guys or all girls, other times they were mixed. Occasionally a couple would get busted for sex in a back bedroom, but normally everyone left the party as horny as they'd arrived. Nelson brought some CDs, and Shea accompanied him to the stereo.

"Hey, look who's here." Shea waved across the room. "Hi, Jeremy!"

Nelson looked over. "He's wearing a tie? What kind of geek wears a tie to a party?"

"Shut up." Shea glared at him. "You haven't even met him yet. Be nice. Here he comes."

Shea introduced them, and Jeremy extended his hand to Nelson. "Hi. I remember you from the meeting. You're pretty funny."

"Thanks." Nelson looked more closely at Jeremy's tie—a cool design of red AIDS awareness ribbons. Maybe Jeremy wasn't such a geek.

"Hey, Jeremy!" Caitlin shouted from the fireplace. "Help us with this log."

Jeremy turned to Nelson. "My brother has a fireplace. I guess that makes me an expert. Talk to you later."

Nelson watched him walk away and turned to Shea. "See? He's not interested in me."

"He *said*"—Shea sounded irked—"he'd talk to you—"

"Look!" Nelson interrupted. "There's Blake. He's such a babe. I think God created him just to torture me." He'd always had the hots for Blake, a junior at American University. Unfortunately Blake already had a boyfriend.

Shea handed Nelson a Coke. "Did you hear he broke up with Dane?"

Nelson nearly choked on the drink. "No way! They've been together forever." He felt bad for Blake, but . . . hm . . . "You sure?"

"I just found out about it. Hold on, Caitlin's signaling me. I'll be right back."

Nelson fixed his gaze on Blake, who stood alone by the mirror, stretching his arms. His thick biceps nearly burst his shirt apart. His jeans hugged his butt.

Nelson was thinking how he would give anything to get into those pants, when Blake noticed him looking and smiled. "How's it going?"

Shit! Was Blake really talking to *him?* Nelson swallowed the lump in his throat. "Good. How about you?"

Blake ran a hand through his hair. "I almost didn't come. I felt kind of down, but I didn't want to stay home."

Nelson nodded. "Sorry to hear about you and Dane." Sympathetic. Caring. Horny.

"You heard, huh?"

"You guys were like a model couple for the rest of us."

"Really?" Blake stared at the fire. "We came out together. We were each other's firsts. . . . Together two years . . ." He looked at his watch. "You don't want to hear all this."

Nelson shrugged enthusiastically. "I don't mind."

"It's hard breaking up," Blake sighed. "Especially with your first love. I think the first time you have sex with someone it's, like, really special. You always remember it, you know?" He paused as though expecting agreement.

Nelson wanted to say something, but what? He wasn't about to admit he was a virgin. And he definitely couldn't say what he wanted—that he'd be glad for Blake to be *his* first.

"I need a drink," Blake whispered. "Something stronger

than this." He leaned toward Nelson, squeezing his shoulder. "I have some rum in my car. You want some?"

Nelson's heart leapt into his throat. Blake, who hardly ever even spoke to him, was inviting him to his car? Nelson thought he must be dreaming.

Blake cocked his head toward the door. "You coming?"

Nelson swallowed his heart back down his throat, praying he wouldn't wake up.

He hurried alongside Blake down the cold street, trying not to seem overeager. Blake climbed into the car, popping the lock for Nelson. Nelson took a deep breath and got in. "Nice car," he said agreeably, though he didn't really like stick shifts. He wiped his face. The chill wind had made his eyes water.

Blake turned the heat on and grabbed a bottle from between the seats. "You like rum?"

The only rum Nelson had ever tried was in rum raisin ice cream. "It's my usual," he lied.

Blake squinted an odd look at him. Then, with the agility of a bartender, he poured the rum into a bottle of Coke. Covering the top with his thumb, he swirled the mixture, then took a swig and smacked his lips. "Perfect!" He passed the bottle to Nelson.

The mix tasted sweet to Nelson, though not at all like ice cream, and it burned as it slid down to his stomach.

Blake laughed. "Better take it easy."

Nelson handed the bottle back to him, surprised to see how much he had drunk.

"What school do you go to?" Blake asked.

"Whitman."

Blake put the bottle down. "You're still in high school?"

His tone made Nelson feel like a kid. But it flattered him that Blake had taken him for college-aged. "I'm a senior. I haven't decided where I'll go next year. How do you like AU?"

"It's all right," Blake said, taking another swig from the bottle. He seemed wary to extend it to Nelson again. "You want any more?"

The alcohol had soothed Nelson's nerves. "Okay." He drank some more and leaned back in his seat. He felt great, totally relaxed, and for a moment he forgot how lust-crazed he was.

Suddenly Blake leaned over him and pulled his face close, his lips engulfing Nelson with the warm, sweet taste of Coke. Was this for real? Only a minute ago Nelson had felt doomed to eternal virginity. Fast-forward. Now, for the first time in his life, he felt the tongue of another guy—and not just any guy, but Blake. He could hardly wait to tell Kyle.

Blake leaned away. "You smoke, don't you?"

"Uh, yeah," Nelson said, his brain hazy. What did smoking have to do with anything? Maybe Blake wanted a cigarette. But wasn't that supposed to come afterward?

He was about to grab for his smokes, when Blake's hand reached over. He unzipped Nelson's jacket and slipped his fingers inside his shirt. "You're trembling."

Of course he was trembling. He could hardly control his excitement. He wondered if he should put up some resistance. He didn't want to seem easy. But how could he feign reluctance? "I—I'm still a little cold."

Blake glanced at Nelson's lap and grinned. "You'll warm up."

Nelson blinked, and when he reopened his eyes, Blake's hands had somehow gotten into his pants. An old worry popped into his mind: Would Blake think he was, uh, too small? If he did, it certainly didn't stop him from what he was doing. Nelson breathed fast, his heart pounding. He felt ready to explode.

As if reading his mind, Blake retracted his hand. He leaned back into his seat and grinned expectantly. Nelson wondered what exactly Blake expected him to do.

Fortunately, Blake helped by guiding his hand. Nelson couldn't believe to where. Once he got over his astonishment, he tried to unbuckle Blake's belt, but the rum seeping through his brain made it hard to keep his balance. His fingers slipped. His nose sank into Blake's cheek. The steering wheel jabbed into his ribs.

"Watch the horn," Blake whispered.

Nelson propped his elbow on the stick shift, and the belt buckle snapped open. He tugged open Blake's zipper.

Blake laid a hand behind Nelson's neck, gently directing his head down. A rich, musky smell wafted up.

Uh-oh. Through the murk of his brain Nelson remembered something. What about a condom? He knew from the Saturday lectures that oral sex was not the highest risk for HIV infection, but there was still risk.

Nelson hesitated, wondering what he could say: *Excuse me, don't we need a condom?* What if Blake felt insulted? It was all too much to think about, especially with his brain in a fog and his face in the lap of the best-looking guy in the group.

"What's wrong?" Blake asked.

Nelson's mind was spinning. The damn gearshift jabbed into his ribs. He leaned up, his head bumped the steering wheel, and the horn blared. Outside, a dog started barking.

"Shit! I told you to watch the horn."

Nelson leaned back in his seat, catching his breath. "I'm sorry."

Blake studied Nelson. "You're a virgin, aren't you?"

Nelson's heart sank. If he said yes, Blake might never want to have sex with him. "No," he lied.

Blake raised a skeptical eyebrow.

"Really," Nelson insisted. Blake turned away. It wasn't fair; Nelson hated feeling like a kid. "Okay, I am," he admitted. "But I don't want to be. I'm sorry." He felt like crying.

Blake shrugged. "It's not your fault. Look, we never should've done this. You're not even eighteen, are you?"

"I will be soon." He wanted Blake to give him a chance.

But Blake was already zipping his pants. Then he rested a brotherly hand on Nelson's shoulder. "You don't want your first time to be in some car with a stupid dog barking."

Nelson nodded energetically. Yes, he did. "Why not?"

"'Cause you want it to be with someone special."

But Blake was special. He was the hunkiest guy in the group. Everyone wanted to do him.

Apparently Blake didn't see it that way. "You want it to be with someone you really care about. That's how it was for Dane and me. We were best friends."

Nelson thought of his own best friend, who wouldn't even kiss him. He felt like a failure—still a virgin at seventeen. It was ridiculous. "Couldn't—maybe—you and I go out sometime?" He knew it sounded desperate, but he couldn't stop himself.

Blake zipped up his jacket. "Like I said, Nelson. Find someone special."

Nelson felt like a baby—shamefully immature, and the one thing he hated most in his crappy life was to think he was immature.

Blake patted his shoulder. "Let's go back to the party."

They walked silently down the street. What a totally major bummer to finally get the chance to have wild sex—with the hottest guy, no less—and be disqualified as inexperienced. Nelson ducked his face beneath his coat collar to shield himself from the wind. As they crossed the front lawn, he tripped over a sprinkler head and fell onto the ground. "Fuck!"

Blake extended his hand to help him up. "You okay?"

Nelson wanted to crawl into a hole. "Great," he said.

Once inside, Blake disappeared into a group of guys by the fireplace. Shea came over to Nelson. She glanced at the dirt stains on his pants. "What happened?" she whispered.

"Shit happened," Nelson said, wiping the dirt off.

On the ride home, he smoked and stared out the window, thinking about Kyle losing his virginity with Jason—instead of him.

CHAPTER 13

JASON

KYLE

NELSON

After school on Monday, Jason discovered a note shoved between the slats of his locker.

> Dear Jason—
> I had a really nice time with you at the movie. I'd like to go to a movie with you again sometime if you would like to. I've looked for you, but I seem to keep missing you. Do you need help with your math? You can call me if you want.
>
> Your friend,
> Kyle

At the bottom of the page was Kyle's phone number.

Jason quickly folded up the note and glanced around, hoping no one had seen Kyle stuffing it into his locker.

Since the evening they'd gone to the movies, Jason had

done everything possible to avoid Kyle. He arrived at school late, skipped lunch, changed his route between classes, and dodged him whenever he spotted his black baseball cap bobbing through the crowds in the hall. All the while, he felt guilty. After all, it wasn't like Kyle had forced him to hold hands. But to face him would be too embarrassing. He punched his locker.

When he got home, his mom told him Debra had called. "That's the first time she's called in weeks. Is everything all right with you two?" She peered into his eyes, making him look away. "Jason? Do you want to talk about it?"

He wished he could talk to her about the fight with Debra and everything else. But how? Besides, his mom liked Debra. He still liked her too and hadn't stopped thinking about her every day. That only confused him further. He wanted to talk to her. Some mornings as he dressed for school he thought he should just be honest with her—tell her about his feelings, about going to the Rainbow meeting, about Kyle at the movie theater. But when he caught a glimpse of her at school, he remembered the times he'd started to tell her and quickly chickened out.

At least he had basketball to take his mind off all this stuff. The season started and Whitman won the first game. The following afternoon, Debra stopped by his locker. She carried a stack of books that pulled her shoulders down, making her look older, different. "Congratulations on the game," she said.

He started to smile, stopped, started again. "Thanks."

She shifted the stack of books in her arms. "Jason? It's been almost two months since homecoming. You haven't called me. Not once."

He closed his locker. "I know, I'm sorry. I've been busy, you know, with the season starting. I've been meaning to call."

She gave him a long, stubborn stare. "You've been avoiding me."

"No." He glanced at the floor. "Really."

She propped her books onto a hip. With her free hand she began fidgeting with her gold necklace. On the chain hung the ring Jason had given her. "Jason, I want to know where we stand."

His brow began to sweat. "I can't talk now. I have practice."

"Jason." Her voice was insistent. "I want to talk *now*."

He looked around. A group of guys walked toward them from the end of the hall. He bit into a fingernail. "Can we at least walk toward the gym?"

She sighed and nodded. They walked past the cafeteria and out the back door. "Jason?" she repeated. "What is going on?"

The sun felt warm against his jacket. He laid his fingertips over his eyes, closing them, and rubbed circles while he tried to think. If he told her, she might get angry and tell people. But she was angry already. If he didn't tell her, she'd just get angrier. *What the hell,* he thought. Putting it off was only making things worse. He was tired of it.

"Okay," he said, opening his eyes. "We said we could tell each other anything, right?"

Debra nodded.

Jason glanced away. "There's something . . . it's really hard to say."

"Jason, you're scaring me. Please! What is it?"

He drew a deep breath and looked up. "I think maybe I'm bisexual." He held his breath, waiting for her reaction.

Her mouth fell open. "You think . . ." She stared into his eyes like he was a stranger. "You think you're *gay*?"

He winced. "No!" He wasn't gay. He liked guys but—but he also liked her. "Well, I mean, I don't want to be."

Debra shook her head. "I don't understand."

Jason wanted to explain but felt tongue-tied. "I don't understand either."

Debra glanced around and whispered in a concerned tone, "Did someone do something to you?"

"No! It's not like that."

Debra brushed the hair from her face. "Then what is it?" she said angrily. "What about us? What about all the times we made love?" Her face began to tremble with emotion. "You never said *anything*." She threw her books onto the ground. "How dare you tell me you suddenly think you like guys!"

She was screaming. He'd been stupid to tell her anything. But there was no going back now. He picked up her books and tried to calm her in a steady voice: "I don't suddenly think I like guys. I always have."

Her eyes widened even farther. "Then—all those times—," she snapped at him, "you lied to me?"

Her shouting was confusing him. "I didn't lie," he said furiously.

Then her hands struck out at him. "I hate you!" she yelled.

He jumped back, raising the books to ward off her blows.

"I hate you," she repeated, pummeling his chest.

"Stop it!" He dropped her books and grabbed her wrists. She kicked at him. He leapt back. "Are you crazy?" he shouted.

Her eyes glowed. "You deserve it, you . . . faggot!" She pulled her arms free and buried her face in her hands, sobbing.

He wanted to put his arm around her, like all the other times she cried, but he knew he couldn't. He didn't blame her for hating him, but he never expected this. He should never have told her anything.

She stopped crying and dug into her pocket, pulling out a tissue to wipe her face. "I can't believe it. You put on a great act."

Jason felt his stomach tighten, as though she had hit him again. "It wasn't an act."

She grabbed the gold chain around her neck and unclasped it, her fingers shaking. The ring slid off and into her hand. "Here."

He didn't want the ring; he'd given it to her, as a gift. "You can keep it."

She gave him a scornful look. He decided to take the stupid ring before she went crazy again. When he handed her the books, she nearly yanked them out of his hands. Without another word, she was gone.

He studied the ring in his palm, rolling it back and forth. He had loved her so much. She was right to hate him. He balled the ring into his fist and hurled it into the dumpster. The metal rang as the ring slammed against it.

He took a few deep breaths of the fresh, cold air. He was late for basketball practice. He'd get in trouble, but he didn't care.

As punishment, the coach ordered him to do push-ups and laps around the court. Once Jason started playing, he kept fouling. He was being a dick, but he couldn't help it. The coach called him aside and set a hand on his shoulder. "I don't know what's with you today, Carrillo, but cut it out."

During the next play his elbow slipped into Lenny Spratt's nose. The coach ordered him outside.

After practice, the sports bus dropped him off at home. From the driveway, he heard his dad's voice inside the kitchen, arguing with his mom. That was the last thing he needed. He avoided the kitchen and walked past the family room. His little sister was playing in front of the TV. Upon seeing him, her brown eyes lit up. "Will you play with me?" She ran to him.

Between his fight with Debra and the extra laps at practice, he was wiped. "Sorry, monkey," he said, prying her little hands loose from his pant legs. "Maybe later."

"Please?" she begged. Her eyes looked so lonely.

"Okay," he gave in. "I'll swing you around one time, but that's it—only once."

She clapped her hands. He swung her twice before retreating to his room. Rex followed behind him, meowing, and hopped onto the bed. Jason closed the door.

Through the air vent he heard his parents shout in the kitchen. He turned on the stereo to drown out their voices and lay down on the bed, listening to the music and stroking Rex. He thought about the fight with Debra. She'd probably tell everyone about him. He should've kept his mouth shut, he told himself. Life sucked.

Suddenly the bedroom door flew open. Rex leapt off the bed and ran under the desk. Jason's dad stood in the doorway. "Shut that off," he yelled, pointing at the stereo. "I've told you before. I don't want it that loud."

Jason bolted upright on the bed, swinging his feet to the floor. "I'll turn it down. What's the big deal?"

"Why don't you use your headphones?" his dad barked.

"They're broken."

"Well, I don't want to hear it," his dad growled, and strode out.

Jason closed the door, turned the volume back up a tiny bit, and lay down on the bed again. He heard his dad resume shouting at his mom.

A soft song came on. Jason turned the stereo volume just a little louder, to hear it better. Rex stared at him from under the desk. "Come on," Jason whispered. "Don't be afraid. He's gone."

Rex lifted one paw after another through the frame of the desk chair. His ears pricked as he cautiously watched the door. Then, as if assured the coast was clear, he leapt onto the bed. Jason picked him up and stroked him. The slow song ended and a fast one started.

Within seconds, the door burst open. "I told you to turn that off," his dad shouted. Rex sprang up, scratching Jason's forearm and kicking him in the chest. His dad stormed over to the stereo and ripped out the plug, silencing the music.

Jason sat up. "What're you doing?"

"Teaching you a lesson." He wrapped his arms around the stereo.

Jason leapt to his feet. "But it's mine. You can't do that."

His dad lifted the stereo. "It's my house, and I told you I didn't want to hear it." As he started across the room, the tangle of speaker wires caught on the shelves, knocking several books to the carpet. Rex cowered beneath the desk.

Jason watched, horrified. "You're going to break it!"

"Get out of my way," his dad yelled, yanking the speaker wires from their jacks.

His mom ran into the hall behind him. "Stop it! What's going on?"

Rex darted toward the doorway, stepping between his dad's legs. His dad stumbled off balance and the stereo fell from his hands, banging onto the carpet. Jason stared in disbelief.

"Goddamned cat," his dad cursed, and glanced at the fallen stereo. "That settles that," he said smugly.

"How could you do that?" his mom demanded.

His dad stepped past her. "I told him I didn't want to hear it." His voice trailed down the hall. "He knew what he was doing. Maybe he'll listen to me next time." The front door slammed. Outside, the truck started.

Jason swallowed, choking down his fury. "I hate him." He knelt beside the stereo, wiping his eyes with his hand, refusing to cry.

His mom knelt beside him and put her arm around his shoulder. "We can fix it."

"What for? He'll just break it again."

His mom rubbed his neck.

"I hate him," Jason repeated, pounding the carpet with his fist. "If he ever lays a hand on me again . . ."

His little sister appeared in the doorway. "What happened, Mommy?" She walked over to them and buried her head in her mom's shoulder.

"Shh," his mom said, stroking her hair. "It's over now. You hungry? It's time to eat." She looked at Jason. "You want to go out for pizza? The three of us?"

Jason didn't feel like going anywhere, but he didn't want to stay home and stare at the stereo either.

During dinner Melissa did most of the talking. When they returned home, Jason reattached the speaker wires, but it did no good—the stereo was definitely broken.

"How about if I get you one of those little CD players with the headphones?" his mom said.

Jason shrugged. He tried to do his homework, but he was too upset to figure out the math assignment. From his drawer, he pulled out Kyle's note. Maybe he should call him, just to talk. But what if Kyle brought up the movie theater? He couldn't deal with that tonight, not on top of all the other shit going on. He closed his math book and climbed into bed, exhausted. Within seconds he was asleep.

In algebra the next morning Perez handed him a quiz from earlier in the week. A *D* marked the top of it.

"You were doing great," Perez said. "What happened?"

Jason stared at the wall clock. He couldn't even begin to answer the question. He knew Perez meant well, but he wouldn't understand. The more Jason thought about it, the more he realized that the only person in his life who really understood him was Kyle.

CHAPTER 14

JASON

KYLE

NELSON

One morning during the second week in December, Kyle arrived at school to find a group of students gathered in the hall pointing at his locker. As he got closer, his heart sank. Across the front in prominent letters was scratched the word QUEER.

"Awww," said a familiar voice. Kyle whirled around to face Jack Ransom.

"Tsk, tsk." Jack feigned a sympathetic pout, then shouted, "Too bad, homo!"

José Montero nudged him, and they turned to see Mueller approaching.

Jack snarled at Kyle. "See you, queer."

Mueller ignored the remark and called out, "Meeks! Tell Glassman I've passed the decision about your club to the school board."

He noticed Kyle's locker and quickly glanced in the direction of Jack and José. "Did you report that?" he asked Kyle.

"What for?" Kyle responded. He was becoming as cynical as Nelson. Before this year, he'd never understood the degree of bashing that Nelson experienced. By staying in the closet and keeping to himself at school, he'd managed to avoid things Nelson went through every day. Now homophobia seemed to be confronting him from every direction—his family, school, Jason. . . .

On two occasions Kyle had waved at Jason only to see him spin around and walk in the opposite direction. Kyle thought, *I shouldn't have held his hand at the movie.* Obviously that wasn't what Jason wanted. Or if it was, he clearly wasn't ready for it.

Kyle felt silly to have gotten his hopes up. He should just forget about Jason. From now on, he wouldn't have anything else to do with him.

That Sunday after lunch, Kyle lay in bed trying to resist his desire to stare at Jason's picture in the *Zephyr*, and failing. From downstairs his mom called, "Kyle? You have company."

Kyle rolled out of bed, put his cap on, and jogged down the hall to the stairway, expecting to see Nelson. When he saw the visitor beneath the balustrade, he nearly careened over the side.

From the foyer below, Jason said, "Wha's up?" casual as an apparition.

He gave Kyle a sheepish look. "I was wondering . . . if you could help me with my math? If you're not busy. You said—if I wanted to come over . . ."

Kyle adjusted his cap. Hadn't he sworn not to have anything more to do with Jason? Nope, not him. Must've been someone else. "Of course I can help you."

Kyle's mom offered to take Jason's coat. His dad walked into the foyer and introduced himself. "That's quite a grip," he told Jason. "You look like an athlete. Am I right?"

"He's on the basketball team," Kyle said proudly.

"Guard," Jason clarified. "I'm better at D. I can't score as much, but I can guard."

His dad gave a smile of approval. "I used to play guard. How many points do you average?"

"Last year, sixteen per game. Some guys on the team are a lot better than me. You should see the recruiting mail they get. But I'm only six feet. I get lucky shots sometimes, but I'm not consistent. A couple of coaches are interested in me. I may get into a Division One school if I'm lucky, but never Georgetown or Villanova. I'll probably end up at Tech."

His dad nodded with interest. "I've encouraged Kyle to make new friends who are more athletic." He turned to Kyle. "I'm glad you're taking my advice for once." He was making Kyle feel like a kid again—in front of Jason.

Apparently his mom noticed. "Honey," she interjected. "The boys want to do homework."

"Huh?" he blinked. "Oh, sure."

Kyle seized the opportunity. "Come on up," he told Jason.

As he led Jason into his room, Kyle noticed the *Zephyr* on the bed, still opened to his favorite photo. He quickly grabbed the book and shoved it into his nightstand. Fortunately Jason didn't seem to notice. He looked around the room and lifted a trophy from the dresser.

"I don't have as many as you," Kyle said.

"I don't have *any* swimming trophies," Jason said. "You know how to do those turns?"

"Flip turns? They're not really hard. I can teach you if you want."

Jason put the trophy back and noticed the photo of Kyle taken after winning the hundred-meter breaststroke at regionals the previous year. The picture showed him dripping wet, wearing only his swim briefs. Kyle rushed to turn the frame facedown on the dresser. "Oh, don't look at that."

Jason grinned. "Why not?" He picked up the photo. "It's a good picture of you."

Kyle blushed. "I look so skinny you can count my ribs."

Jason put the photo down and looked up at the model of the starship *Enterprise* hanging from the ceiling. "Wow! Did you make that? How long did that take?"

"About three days. My dad used to buy me models all the time. You a Trekkie?"

"Yeah." Jason nodded. "Especially *Voyager*." He slid his backpack off his shoulder, dropping it onto the floor, and walked over to the aquarium. "Cool fish." He turned to the computer. "Man, you've got your own computer?"

"If you ever want to use it, you're welcome to come over."

"Here." Jason unzipped his backpack and pulled out a poster. "It's from the movie we saw." He blushed and folded his arms. "I, uh, got it the other day when I biked past."

Kyle admired the poster, feeling moved by the sentiment—a memento of the first time they held hands. "Thanks," he whispered.

Jason cleared his throat. He pulled the chair from the desk and sat down. "I . . ." He shuffled his feet on the carpet. "I told Debra."

Kyle slid his glasses up the bridge of his nose. "Told her what?" He sat down on the armchair.

Jason stared at him, as though it was obvious. "You know . . . that I think I'm . . . you know . . . that I think I'm bisexual."

Kyle was surprised, to say the least. First Jason showed up at his house after avoiding him for weeks. Now this? "What did she say?"

Jason hung his head. "That she hates me."

He sounded so sad that Kyle wanted to reach out and hold him. But his parents were downstairs, and there was no telling how Jason might react.

"I'm sorry. It must be hard."

Jason wiped his cheek. "I just wish she didn't hate me." He grabbed his backpack off the floor, zipping it open. "It was over between her and me anyway."

The implication of what Jason said suddenly struck Kyle. Jason was no longer Debra's boyfriend. Kyle's stomach fluttered—from either happiness or nervousness, or both.

Jason pulled out his math book. "I could really use your help. Oh"—he dug a cassette out of his backpack—"and I brought you back your tape."

"Why? You can keep it."

"Uh, I don't have anything to play it on." He placed the cassette on Kyle's desk. "My stereo broke. My dad . . ." He put his fingertips to his forehead.

Obviously something was troubling him. "You all right?" Kyle asked.

Jason removed his hand. "I don't know. Sometimes I think it's okay, then other times . . ." His dark eyes looked pained. "I get really scared, you know?"

"Uh, not really. What do you mean?"

"Never mind." He scooted his chair over to Kyle. "Let's just study, okay?"

But Kyle felt too worried to drop it. "I'd like to understand. I'll listen if you want."

Jason looked him up and down, trying to decide. "If I tell you," he said, running a hand through his hair, "promise you won't tell?"

Kyle nodded.

Jason shifted in his chair, sat up, and then slouched down, starting and stopping, struggling to get the words out. "A long time ago, when I was ten years old, a friend—my best friend—spent the night. We took a bath and afterward clowned around. Dumb kid stuff, you know? Then me and Tommy . . ." He paused and his voice became low. "We . . . you know . . . touched each other." His eyes shifted between the door and Kyle, like he was ready to bolt. "I never told anyone that before."

Apparently he expected a reaction from Kyle. But Kyle wasn't sure what to say.

"My dad caught us," Jason continued. "He made Tommy go home, and he beat the shit out of me, really pounded me, like never before. He told me if he ever caught me again, he'd kill me."

Jason made it sound like a real threat. A shiver ran up Kyle's spine. He wanted to reach out and hold Jason, protect him. "You don't think he really meant it, do you?"

Jason bit a nail. His finger in his mouth gave him a childlike look. "Well, yeah. As a kid I did." He scratched his wrist. "Do you think . . . it's bad?"

"Of course!" Kyle thought of his own dad, who could be stubborn and pigheaded but would never hurt him, not in a million years. "He's got no right to hit you."

"I don't mean that," Jason said. "I mean, you know . . ."

It took Kyle a moment to reverse his train of thought. "Well, I don't think it's bad . . . if two guys . . . you know, like each other. Do you think it's bad?"

Jason wiped his palms across his pants. "I don't know." He looked so hurt and confused.

Kyle felt closer to him than ever, but it scared him to think Jason's dad might seriously go after him. He'd already wounded Jason, and Jason didn't even seem to realize it.

"Thanks." Jason picked up his math book.

Kyle tried to refocus his attention on the logarithms while Jason struggled with the equations, knitting his brow and chewing on his pencil. Kyle scooted his chair closer, explaining the steps. Inadvertently he found himself leaning onto Jason's shoulder. Jason didn't seem to notice, so Kyle stayed there, feeling Jason's warmth.

Jason solved the problem he was working on and triumphantly ripped the scratch page from his notebook. Unfortunately for Kyle, he also moved his shoulder away, wadding the paper into a ball and making a perfect toss across the room into the wastebasket. *Impressive*, Kyle thought.

While Jason struggled with the next problem, Kyle tried to take his mind off everything they'd talked about. He crumpled a sheet of paper and attempted to shoot a basket of his own. He missed by a little short of a mile.

Jason noticed and Kyle blushed.

"Watch. Like this." Jason wrapped his hand around Kyle's forearm and guided Kyle's wrist in a hinge motion. "Try it."

Kyle tried but, in spite of Jason's instruction, missed— though not quite as badly as before. "I've never been able to throw."

Jason crumpled another sheet of paper and handed it to Kyle. "I've never been able to do math." He grinned. "Again!"

A mountain of paper accumulated around the trash can

before Kyle finally made a basket. He jumped up and down, ecstatic, and Jason slapped him a high five. "See, I knew you could do it."

On a roll, Kyle shot another, followed by Jason. The boys jumped around the room, alternating baskets until Kyle stopped, out of breath, his brow sweating. He took his glasses off and wiped them with his shirt.

"Let me see you without your glasses."

Kyle kept them off. "I'm thinking of getting contacts. What do you think?"

Jason's blurry head nodded up and down. "Sure. Why not?"

Kyle put the glasses back on. "I don't think I'll have enough money left after Christmas presents. And I hate to ask my mom for the money. They're still paying off my braces."

Jason turned to Kyle's dresser and stared at himself in the mirror. "I wish I'd gotten braces. My teeth are a disaster."

Kyle glanced at Jason's teeth, wishing he wouldn't put himself down like that. He wanted to tell Jason how much he loved those teeth, how he spent hours staring at his smiling yearbook portrait.

Jason must have noticed him staring, because his lips closed. Then he said, "I wish I had teeth like yours."

They stared at each other's mouth for an awkward moment, then Kyle said, "Well, I like your smile." He couldn't believe he'd actually said it. Surely, there must be a ventriloquist in the room.

Jason looked down at the carpet, blushing, and Kyle squirmed in his socks. He hadn't meant to embarrass Jason. Yet he couldn't help but stare at Jason's mouth. The fullness of the lips reminded him of the movie theater and how he'd come home and kissed the hand Jason had held.

"Well," Jason said, his lip quivering slightly. "I guess I better go." But he didn't move. He just stood there.

Kyle's legs began to tremble. He longed to kiss Jason, right there in his room. Of course, that was nuts. His parents were downstairs. "Can I kiss you?" he asked.

Jason didn't answer. He leaned forward, as if pulled by an unseen force.

That was all Kyle needed. Jason's head cocked to the right, and Kyle felt himself flung toward him like a sled down a calamitous hill.

Except their mouths didn't fit right. Even though they were the same height, Kyle's nose collided with Jason's left upper lip, and he wanted to die from embarrassment. His nose! What was he supposed to do with his nose? There was no convenient place for it.

Then he felt Jason's breath on his cheek. He turned his head a tiny bit more. He closed his eyes and their mouths met perfectly. Jason's lips softly touched his. A thousand nerve cells tingled and spiraled through skin and sinew, blazed through his blood and soared into his heart. His tongue gently slipped between his teeth and for a moment explored the wet warmth of Jason's mouth. He wanted to remain like that the rest of his life.

He whispered, "I love you, Jason."

Jason flinched.

Kyle opened his eyes and saw Jason's face, flushed red as Christmas paper, glancing toward the door. Immediately he said, "I'm sorry."

"I better go," Jason whispered hoarsely. He stepped back from Kyle, grabbed his math book, and slung his backpack onto his shoulder. Before Kyle could say anything more, Jason passed through the doorway into the hall.

Kyle started after him, but his legs were like jelly as he wobbled down the stairs. At the bottom step, his dad reached out to steady him. His mom was already helping Jason with his coat. Jason uttered polite thanks, and before Kyle could stop him, he disappeared—out the front door and into the starless night.

"Are you all right?" his dad asked.

Kyle faltered as his mom closed the front door. "Kyle?" she said. "Can I ask you a question? Is Jason . . ." She shifted her weight from foot to foot, like she wanted to leave. "I don't know how to say . . . is he . . . someone special?"

Kyle caught his breath. Why'd she ask that? "Gee, Mom, can't I just have a friend over anymore?"

His dad's face caved in, as though crushed by the realization that Jason might be anything other than a titanic heterosexual. "You mean Jason is—"

Kyle nearly screamed. "Can we drop it?"

"I'm sorry," his mom said. "I'm just trying to understand. He seems nice." She smiled at the foyer tile. "I mean, I'm glad we got a chance to meet him."

"Yeah," Kyle said. He turned and ran up the stairs, throwing himself onto his bed, where he hated his life and pondered the ceiling. Until it suddenly struck him: He had actually kissed the boy he loved. And that boy had kissed him back.

CHAPTER 15

JASON

KYLE

NELSON

Nelson tore open the Christmas card from his father. As always, it bore no personal greeting, no fond closing, only the perfunctory signature, and a check for a hundred dollars.

"Why's he even bother?"

His mom refused to fuel Nelson's resentment, even though she and his dad could barely talk without shouting. "Your dad has always taken care of anything you needed," she said, then added as an afterthought, "financially."

Nelson didn't feel like arguing. He already knew what he wanted to buy himself with the check: a pair of Doc Marten boots. He'd saved money for everyone else's gifts. For his mom, he'd get perfume or a scarf. He'd get Shea some funky metal jewelry and Caitlin a tie. He knew Kyle wanted a limited edition watch with the glow-in-the-dark hologram of the starship *Enterprise*, but the stupid thing cost too much. He couldn't buy it and still get himself the boots. And why should he spend a hundred dollars on Kyle? Kyle would probably blow all his Christmas money buying Jason a designer jockstrap.

Christmas afternoon, he went to Kyle's to exchange presents. He immediately noticed the movie poster tacked onto the wall. "Hm. That's new."

Kyle glanced at the carpet and shuffled his feet. "Jason gave it to me."

"Oh, how sweet," Nelson said. He stuck his finger down his throat and made a gagging noise. Then he handed Kyle the box he'd carried over. "Here," he said grumpily.

Kyle unwrapped the package. "Wow!" He carefully opened the carrying case for the watch. "I can't believe you got it for me." He looked at Nelson as if debating something. Then he leaned forward. "Thanks." He pecked Nelson a kiss on the cheek.

"Yeah, yeah, yeah," Nelson said. "You going to put it on or save it as a museum piece?"

Kyle strapped the watch onto his wrist. "It looks great. Here"—he handed Nelson a box—"open yours."

Nelson ripped open the package and screamed. "The fucking boots! You don't know how bad I wanted these."

Kyle grinned. "Yes, I do."

Nelson kicked his shoes off and thrust the boots on. "They're beautiful!" His fingers raced to tie the laces. "You rule!"

He jumped up and down, bounding over to Kyle. "I want a real kiss!" Before Kyle could say anything, Nelson pecked him a kiss on the mouth. "There! Your first kiss on the lips from a boy."

Kyle turned red and Nelson stopped bouncing. "Uh-oh, you've got that constipated look." Although he wondered why, he already suspected. "You kissed him, didn't you?"

Kyle responded with a sheepish nod. "Just last week. I still can't believe it." His eyebrows edged up with that contrite puppy look. "Are you angry?"

Nelson glanced down at the boots. "No." That was a lie. "Yes," he admitted, but he wasn't furious. "I don't know." He fell back onto the bed, as if forced down by the weight of his confusion. He should feel happy his best friend made out with the man of his wet dreams, instead of just feeling sorry for himself. He stared at the movie poster Jason had given Kyle.

Kyle fidgeted with the bill of his cap. "Of course, he ran out afterward."

"Oh, he'll be back."

"You think so?" Kyle asked hopefully.

"Well, for your information, I kissed a boy too. You'll never guess who. Blake Randolph!"

"No way!" Kyle sat beside him, obviously impressed.

As well he should be, Nelson thought. "Way!" he told Kyle. "At Caitlin's party. He was so dreamy. I always suspected he lusted after me." He knew it was a lie, but at least he didn't feel like such a loser.

Nelson hung around his house for most of the holiday break. He took Atticus on walks, surfed chat rooms, examined himself in the mirror, binged on sweets his mom brought home from holiday parties, made himself throw up, admired his new boots, and thought about Kyle.

One afternoon he received an E-mail from HotLove69. After thinking about it a little, he answered the message and phoned Shea. "Can you come over? I want you to take some photos of me."

"Sure," she said. "What are they for?"

He didn't want to tell her the real reason. She'd never approve. So he simply said, "'Cause I'm bored out of my freakin' gourd."

When she came over, he told her about Kyle and Jason.

"So, now you feel hurt."

He lit a cigarette. "I don't want to think about it. Here." He handed her the camera and started changing clothes. "I just wish I could find someone—like you found Caitlin."

"You can't just go out and find someone," she told him. "That's not how it works."

He wished he knew how it did work.

Shea snapped some photographs of him in different outfits and some without a shirt on, but then she got suspicious. "What are you going to do with these?"

Fortunately, from beneath a pile of clothes, the phone rang. Nelson scrambled for it and answered: "Stud-Muffins-dot-com."

"Nelson? Turn the music down. I only have a minute."

Nelson recognized the voice immediately. In the background, he heard an airport loudspeaker. He could picture a briefcase, a cell phone, the airplane gate.

Shea whispered, "Who is it?"

Nelson mouthed the word "Father" and grudgingly turned the volume down.

"I'm flying through next week," his dad continued. "I promised your mom I'd try to see you, unless my meeting runs over. Are you listening?"

Nelson made a fist, glancing at his nails. How lucky that his dad could fit him into his tight schedule. "Yeah. I'm listening."

The loudspeaker announced final boarding for a flight. "I've got to go. I'll call back with the details." He hung up without so much as a "Good to hear your voice," certainly no "I've missed you," and definitely no "I love you."

The dial tone rang in Nelson's ear. He tossed the phone across the bed.

Shea sat beside him, looking worried. "What did he say?"

Nelson shook his head. "It's what he didn't say."

The evening his dad was supposed to see him, Nelson donned and doffed one shirt after another. He looked in the mirror, pinched his stomach, and frowned. Why did he agonize so much about what he looked like for his father? Didn't he hate the old fart anyway? He grabbed a clip-on ring from his dresser and pinned it between his nostrils.

His mom leaned in the doorway and pulled a disapproving face. "You know he hates the nose ring."

Nelson shrugged defiantly. "He can deal with it."

His mom gave a sigh and preened in the mirror. "I'm off to the PFLAG get-together. We're going to discuss the school group and the best way to get PTA support." She smoothed her dress, running her palms across the front. "How do I look?"

"You look great." Nelson patted her hair. "Can I go with you?"

She spun around. "No! What about your father?"

"Oh, yeah. Him."

His mom smirked. "He's very eager to see you. Wish me luck." With a wave, she hurried out.

Nelson stared at himself in the mirror. He knew full well his dad wasn't eager to see him. He was doing this out of a sense of guilt or duty. Nevertheless, Nelson pulled out the nose ring.

His dad had phoned the day before to say he'd arrive at 8:00. "Be punctual," he'd told Nelson. But was his dad punctual?

No. Nelson sat stiffly on the living-room sofa, fidgeting with the remote control, channel surfing. He glanced toward the front door and looked at his watch: 8:15. Atticus lay beside him, looking toward the door every time Nelson did.

A car drove up outside. Nelson stood and walked to the window. Atticus followed. The car passed by. Nelson sat down again, patting Atticus. "False alarm, boy." He looked at his watch, then walked to the kitchen and ripped open a package of Oreos. He dialed his dad's cell phone but got an "out of service area" message. He paced, devouring Oreos, and sat down. He looked at his watch: 9:06. Atticus put his head in his lap. Nelson petted him. The dog sniffed his crotch. Nelson nudged him away.

The phone rang. Nelson jumped for it. "Hello?"

"Hey, fag," said an unfamiliar voice. "Want to suck my dick?"

"I'm busy. You'll have to make an appointment." Such calls were too commonplace to faze him. He hung up and stared at the TV a moment, then he called Kyle. "Hey, it's me."

"Hi. Aren't you supposed to be with your dad?"

"He hasn't showed. Big surprise."

"I'm sorry. Bummer."

"Yeah." Nelson ran a hand through his hair. "Whatever. Want to come over?"

"I can't. My grandmom's here, remember?"

"Shit, I forgot." He grabbed the last Oreo.

"Are you okay?" Kyle asked. "I'll come over if you really need me."

"That's okay. I'm not going to slit my wrists over that jerk. Give Grams a tongue kiss."

"Shut up."

Nelson hung up and tried calling Shea, but she was out, probably with Caitlin. He threw the remote control onto the couch. He glanced at his watch again, debating what to do. Then an idea dawned on him.

He ran upstairs to his bedroom and turned on his computer, slapping it to hurry up. He impatiently clicked onto the Internet. Yes! There, on-line, was HotLove69.

Nelson immediately typed an instant message: "Hi. It's me. Did you get my photo?" He hit "Send" and tapped his foot, waiting for a response. Atticus paced beside him.

On the computer screen an instant message popped up: "Yeah. Sweet picture. What are you up to?"

Nelson leapt up from his seat, his pulse quickening. Atticus watched him and barked. "Calm down," Nelson said, not sure if he was talking to the dog or himself.

He leaned over the keyboard, his fingers trembling a little, and typed back, "Nothing. What about you?" He sent the message and waited for a response, gripping his chair.

A response popped back: "Nada right now. Want to hook up?"

"Shit!" Nelson said aloud. "I can't believe this." He circled the chair, trying to think clearly, without much success. He sat back down and took a breath, tapping on the wrist pad, uncertain what to do.

Atticus sniffed his leg, imploring. Nelson glanced down, feeling like a total loser. That decided it. His life was way too pathetic. He pushed Atticus away. "OK," he typed, and hit "Send."

They had agreed to meet at the Starbucks on Lee Highway. Nelson anxiously waited out front, watching couples stroll in and out, wondering if he'd recognize HotLove69 from his photo. Then a motorcycle roared up. Nelson had forgotten about that.

The broad-shouldered man pulled his helmet off. He was even more handsome than in his photo. "How's it going?" His voice was smooth, magnetic. "My name's Brick." His muscular hand extended a powerful shake. "And your name is . . . ?"

Nelson stared at him, speechless. His name? Shit, why was he nerding up like this? "Uh, Nelson."

"Nice smile," Brick said. "How old are you?"

Nelson wanted to be honest. But he recalled his fiasco with Blake. "Eighteen," he lied.

Brick grinned. "Eighteen, huh?" He slid a confident hand across the handlebars. "So, you want to come to my place?"

Nelson hesitated. After all, he hardly knew this guy. But Brick definitely didn't look like some skanky molester. And Nelson certainly wasn't a kid anymore. He was old enough to take care of himself.

Brick waited for a response. "I won't bite. Unless you want me to." He patted the seat behind him. "Hop on."

Brick's apartment reminded Nelson of the homes in his mom's glossy design magazines. Each wall was a different color. Track lighting shone onto chrome-framed prints. Plush rugs covered the floor. A big-screen TV took up half of one wall, and about a thousand CDs and a stereo system took up the other half. *Totally cool,* Nelson thought.

"Put on some music you like," Brick told him. "You want a beer?"

"Okay," Nelson answered. He didn't really want one, but he didn't want to seem immature. Besides, he thought it might relax his nerves.

While Brick rattled around the kitchen, Nelson started to worry. He really should let someone know what was happening. But who? Kyle was with Granny. Shea was out with Caitlin. His mom? She'd have a conniption. Besides, she was at the PFLAG meeting. And anyway, he'd turn eighteen soon. He didn't need to report his every move.

He flipped through the CDs. Most of the stuff was classical, jazz, or show tunes. Brick didn't seem that type of guy. Nelson turned on the radio to his favorite station. Then he sat down amid the million cushions on the love seat and thought about Kyle. Wait till he told him about Brick. Maybe the three of them could hang out sometime. It would be fun to have Kyle over, sit on the plush rugs, and listen to music.

"Here you go," Brick said, handing Nelson a beer. He sat so close their knees touched. If Brick's hands roamed all over him, Nelson couldn't feel more excited. He gulped the beer.

Brick laughed. "Thirsty?"

Nelson laughed along with him. Nerves. When a huge burp exploded from his mouth, he said, "Excuse me," and set the beer down before spilling any.

Then Brick's face was in front of him—his cheek warm, his lips pressing against Nelson's neck, bestowing wet kisses. It felt different from Blake—passionate.

Nelson grabbed the sofa to steady himself. "I like your apartment," he said, struggling to catch his breath.

Brick ran his hands across Nelson's chest. "Yeah?" He took Nelson's hand. "Let me show you around." He promptly led Nelson down the thickly carpeted hallway. It was all happening so fast.

In the bedroom, tiny lights glowed from behind potted palms, casting shadows on the walls. Above the headboard hung a huge print of a guy in his underwear. Brick guided Nelson onto the bed and pressed him down onto the satin comforter. His warm hands slipped beneath Nelson's shirt, sliding across his skin. Nelson shivered with excitement and closed his eyes. The rush of blood made him dizzy. Nothing had ever thrilled him so much.

Brick slid on top of him, as if wanting more of him, like he was somehow trying to get inside him. He kissed so hard that Nelson's head reeled back. He opened his eyes and found himself looking up at the underwear poster.

"I want you," Brick said, his hands rushing frantically across Nelson's naked chest.

Nelson wasn't sure exactly what Brick meant, though he had a pretty good idea. He wanted to say that he hadn't ever done that—or anything else.

"Okay," Nelson managed as Brick de-pantsed him. "I guess so."

Then he remembered: *Wait. A condom!*

But before he could say anything, Brick was on top of him, pressed against him, touching every part of him, as though needing more, looking for Nelson's very core.

A voice screamed inside Nelson: *Stop! Tell him. He needs to use a condom.*

But if he did say something, Brick might reject him, the same as Blake, the same as Kyle. A wave of despair swept over Nelson, until it seemed he was totally lost to himself. He no longer knew where he was or what was happening, only that he wanted Brick. He clutched at him, soaked with sweat. His heart thundered faster and harder, till it seemed to burst.

Then, just as quickly, it was over. Brick lay on top of him, head cradled in Nelson's shoulder, his breath puffing lightly across Nelson's chest. Nelson looked down at the soft blond hair and broad shoulders of the man he'd let inside him. He'd never felt anything so incredible in his life.

Then he remembered the condom, or lack thereof. A new tide of gloom flooded him. He couldn't believe he'd been so stupid. He knew he'd just done—or, more accurately, let be done to him—the riskiest thing possible. But everything had happened so fast. He stared at Brick, resting so calmly. He wanted to shake him and . . . And what? Say, "Excuse me, what's your HIV status?"

Surely if Brick were HIV positive, he would've warned Nelson. He hadn't said anything, so he must not be. Unless he didn't know. Maybe he'd never been tested. And what if Brick admitted he *was* HIV positive? Nelson would freak.

Better not to know.

Brick stirred. Nelson raised his arm to hide his face.

"You were great," Brick whispered, and pecked him a kiss.

The gesture touched Nelson, and for a moment he felt better. No one as nice as Brick would have unsafe sex if he was HIV positive. And maybe Brick had indeed put on a condom, and in the heat of passion Nelson simply hadn't noticed. That must be what happened. He recalled Brick grabbing something from the nightstand. He looked over. But all he saw was a tube of lubricant.

Brick rolled to the side of the bed and stood up. Nelson casually peeked over. Nope, no condom. Shit. He darted frantic glances across the carpet, searching for a wrapper. Nothing.

Brick walked across the room and brought a towel to Nelson, wiping it across his stomach; it tickled like when he was a little kid and his mom dried him after a bath. For a moment, Nelson came out of his panic and thought, even if Brick was

HIV positive, they could take care of each other. Wasn't that what lovers were for?

Brick tossed the towel aside and pulled his pants on. Nelson glanced past him at the clock on the dresser. Now he wished he'd phoned his mom. She'd be home by now and worried. He sat up and climbed off the bed. "I better go." He searched through the jumble of clothes strewn across the floor and told Brick, "I'd like to see you again."

Brick avoided his eyes. After a long moment, he said, "Sure." He didn't sound very enthusiastic.

While Nelson pulled his pants on, Brick set out a pen and paper. Nelson leaned over the dresser and wrote down his number. "Can I have yours, too?"

"Well . . . ," Brick said, looking away again. "That's probably not a good idea. I have a lover. Right now he's away on a trip."

Huh? Whoa! Did Brick say "lover"? He hadn't mentioned any lover. If he had a lover, then why . . . ? Nelson felt light-headed, like he was going to pass out. He reached out to grab hold of the bed.

"Are you okay?" Brick said. "Sit down. I'll get you some water."

Nelson sat on the bed, suppressing a wave of nausea, and looked around the room. He'd just lost his virginity to some guy who already had a lover, who probably didn't care if he saw Nelson again, and who might even be HIV positive. How could he have been so stupid?

Brick brought him the water and Nelson gulped it down.

"I should've told you earlier," Brick said, resting a hand on Nelson's shoulder. "This is his apartment. I kept thinking you'd ask if I had a boyfriend. Since you didn't ask, I figured you didn't care."

Nelson stared at him, feeling like a dumb kid. Yeah, he should've asked. But how was he supposed to know? He stood up. "I want to go."

Brick offered him a ride. Nelson didn't want a ride. He wanted to walk and clear his mind. But Brick insisted, and Nelson felt too depressed to argue. He climbed onto the motorcycle. As they rode, he recalled how Blake had told him to save himself for someone special.

The wind flicked through Nelson's hair. He wrapped his arms tightly around Brick's waist and thought: *I should've let Kyle come over when he'd offered.*

CHAPTER 16

JASON

KYLE

NELSON

After Jason bolted from Kyle's house the night they kissed, he sprinted crazily down the dark suburban streets past barking dogs, dodging cars like a fugitive fleeing some crime. Once home, he sneaked past the living room, terrified his dad might see him and somehow realize what he had just done.

He silently closed his bedroom door and bent over, his heart racing. After catching his breath, he stepped toward the dresser mirror. A little fearfully, he slid his fingertips across his lips, still in disbelief.

He abruptly whirled around and ripped his jacket off, flinging it to the floor. This was all Kyle's fault. Jason never should've trusted him. He knew Kyle would try something funny. He lifted his math book, filled with Kyle's notes, and started to throw it against the wall, except—

He had to admit Kyle hadn't exactly forced him to kiss. It

would've been easy to stop him. So why hadn't he?

He bit into a nail, or what was left of it, hurting his finger. It was all too overwhelming. He needed to put this whole thing out of his mind. As far as he was concerned, the kiss had never happened. Thank God it was December break from school. At least he'd have two weeks not to see or think about Kyle.

As usual, his Uncle Ramiro, Aunt Ana, and their two little girls drove from New Jersey for the holidays. Melissa giggled with her cousins, while Jason's mom and aunt lugged home shopping bags stuffed with purchases.

Meantime, his dad couched out with Ramiro, swigging beers and arguing stupid crap, like which rum was better—Cuban or Puerto Rican—or whether a certain corporal during their Vietnam service was a *maricón*. They whined about promotions they should've received but were instead given to undeserving blacks or whites. Then their snipes turned to relatives who'd slighted them countless ways.

The arguments gave Jason different clues to his dad's rage— his drinking, the war, career disappointments, family resentments. But just because his dad had suffered a hard life, did he have to make everyone else miserable?

Jason knew from prior years that the bitterness of his dad and uncle would inevitably ignite toward each other. Sure enough, it came after their traditional Christmas Eve dinner of roast pork and plantains. Jason was playing Old Maid with Melissa and their cousins when his mom screamed for him: "Quick! Jason!"

He ran to the living room. His uncle was gripping one of Jason's trophies, about to bash it over the head of his dad, who staggered to shake free. Petite Aunt Ana was slapping Uncle Ramiro, trying to stop him, while his mom grabbed his dad.

Jason hesitated, tempted to let his uncle thwack his old man. But his mom screamed, "Stop them!" Reluctantly Jason helped pry them apart.

Then, as if nothing unusual had happened, everyone but he and his dad dressed up for midnight mass. Jason felt too upset to sit in church, but neither did he desire to stay home with his drunken father. Instead he walked to the park to shoot baskets.

Only the streetlamps lit the court, but he didn't care. The cold night air felt fresh and cleansing after his crazy family. It never ceased to amaze him how much his life sucked. As he dribbled across the concrete, he prayed that somehow he'd get through. After several shots he remembered something a priest had taught him during First Communion classes: During bad times, think of just one person or thing to be grateful for. That would lead to another and another, until he no longer felt so bad.

First on his list was his mom, second was his little sister, then Corey, then his stuff, then . . . Kyle?

He gripped the basketball in mid-throw, surprised by the thought. In spite of the kiss, Kyle had helped him out a lot, not just with math, but with helping him to realize it was okay to be bisexual or whatever and not be a total flamer like Nelson. He didn't want to lose Kyle's friendship. He'd just have to make it clear to Kyle he only wanted to be friends, nothing more.

Satisfied with that idea, Jason shot one last basket and headed home.

The first day back to school, Jason had barely gotten to his locker when Corey rushed up to him. Gauging by the look on his face, something had happened.

"Man, I've got to talk to you." Corey pulled him aside. "Debra told Cindy something you should know."

Jason bristled. But had he really expected Debra to keep what he'd said to herself? He knew the risk he was taking when he came out to her, and he'd done it anyway.

Corey glanced around and lowered his voice. "She said you're . . ."

Was it so shameful that Corey couldn't even say it? Jason said it for him. "Queer?"

Corey nodded.

Jason braced himself. "What if I am?"

"Whoa, whoa!" Corey raised his hands to stop him from going any further. "No, you're not. Settle down. Stop bullshitting. I know you're not."

Jason tried to calm down. It unnerved him that they were having this conversation in the middle of the crowded hallway their first hour back to school. "Believe what you want," he told Corey, and pulled his books from his locker.

Corey stepped around to face him. "But what about you and Debra?" he protested. "I mean, didn't you like it?"

Jason closed his locker, frustrated. "Did I like sex with her? Yeah!"

Corey looked puzzled. "Then why would you . . . ?"

Jason leaned back against his locker and glanced up at the wall behind Corey. "I don't know. I just have these feelings. I wish I didn't, but I do."

Corey brought a hand to his forehead, like he'd suddenly developed a headache. "Look, man." He narrowed his eyes at Jason. "I don't care who you do it with. But you're up for your scholarship letter. You want to mess that up?"

Of course Jason didn't. It wasn't like he'd been eager to come out to Debra, and he hadn't intended for her to tell Cindy, or for Cindy to tell Corey. It was snowballing out of control. He started chewing a fingernail, scared that his dream of a scholarship and escape from home was evaporating. "What am I supposed to do?"

"Man, I don't know."

"You won't tell anyone, will you?" Jason knew he sounded desperate.

Corey shook his head. "Of course not. You're my best friend. I doubt Cindy will either. She thinks it's cool."

Jason felt his shoulders relax a little. "Does it bother you? About me?"

"Well, no," Corey said. He didn't sound very certain, but at least he didn't hate him, like Debra. That was a relief. He wished he'd told Corey sooner. Maybe he could've avoided this mess. Now he wanted to tell him more, about all the feelings he was having. But he wasn't sure how to talk about it. "Are you surprised?" he asked.

"Yeah," Corey said. "Though"—his voice became stern—"you better stop hanging out with Meeks."

Jason stopped cold. "What do you mean?"

"Look, if you don't want people to find out, then don't give them cause. Like I told you, people talk."

The bell rang but Jason didn't move. He stood paralyzed, uncertain what to do. He'd returned to school resolved to continue his friendship with Kyle. Now his best friend was telling him not to.

Corey grabbed Jason's arm. "Come on, man." He pulled him down the hall. "You'll be late for homeroom."

At basketball practice that afternoon, Jason felt his timing was off. He started to think teammates were whispering about him. Then Dwayne fouled him, and he tripped, landing hard.

Coach Cameron blew his whistle. "Hey! What was that?"

Dwayne gave the coach an innocent look. "Sorry, Coach."

Corey extended a hand to help Jason up.

"Carrillo," Coach said. "Take a break."

Jason hobbled off the court onto the bench. He studied Dwayne, trying to figure out if he'd done it on purpose.

After practice, Coach Cameron told Jason the Tech coach had called and asked more about him. "Don't get your hopes too high, but it sounds like he's interested."

That evening Jason tried studying but kept thinking about what Corey had said. It felt like he was being forced to make a decision. He didn't want to keep hiding, but he didn't want to lose his chance at a scholarship, either.

In the kitchen, his mom and dad were arguing. "Al-Anon?" his dad yelled. "What the hell's that?" Apparently his dad had found out about his mom's group—or she'd finally told him.

"It's a twelve-step recovery program."

At his desk, Jason sensed someone watching him. He turned to see Melissa in the doorway, wearing her pajamas, covering her ears. She whispered in a scared voice, "Can I come in?"

Jason stretched out his arms. She ran to him and tightly grabbed hold.

His dad yelled, "It's a *what* program?"

Jason could feel Melissa's heart racing. "It's okay," he told her.

"It's a group for people in a relationship with an alcoholic," his mom said, her voice quivering slightly.

"A couple beers makes me an alcoholic? You don't need to go to any group."

Melissa let go of Jason and climbed into his bed, covering her ears.

"I'm not going to argue," said his mom. Her tone was firm. "I'll be home by ten."

His dad didn't say anything. Suddenly Jason heard his mom shout, "Let go of me!"

Jason jumped up, nearly knocking over his chair. But a moment later he heard the front door open and close.

"You're abandoning your family!" His dad screamed after her.

His mom had defied his dad.

Melissa flinched. Jason walked over to her and smoothed her hair, trying to soothe her. He sat beside her till she was asleep, then he carried her to her room. He returned to his attempts to study, but his worries continued to intrude on his thoughts. If he didn't get the scholarship, what would he do? Stay here with his dad? No way. Maybe Corey was right. He had to break it off with Kyle.

To Jason's relief, the following morning no one else confronted him at his locker—nor in or between classes. He talked and joked with friends about Christmas vacation. By third period he'd decided his fears were mostly paranoia. His secret was safe. Now he just had to explain to Kyle they couldn't be friends.

At lunch, he sat with Corey and several teammates. Abruptly Corey motioned to him. "Heads up."

Kyle approached their table, tray in hand. "Hi!" His face was bright and smiling, with an innocent grin that made Jason forget all his resolve. He smiled back, glad to see Kyle after what seemed like years.

Corey cleared his throat, bringing Jason back to Earth. "Wha's up?" he asked Kyle, as if he didn't recognize him. He hoped Kyle would take the hint and leave quietly.

But Kyle didn't go away. "Mind if I sit with you?"

Corey coughed, and Jason glanced over at him. Corey was

shaking his head almost imperceptibly. A darted look at their teammates said the guys were watching. His message to Jason was clear: Don't do it.

Kyle stood patiently, waiting.

Dwayne laughed. Out of the corner of his eye, Jason saw him flip his wrist toward his teammates. Jason could guess what he was laughing at: limp-wrist Kyle—or maybe him.

Kyle saw it too. His smile faded. "Are you going to answer me?" The last trace of his cheer had transformed into a stricken look. "'Cause people are staring and I'm starting to feel really uncomfortable."

It was killing Jason to treat the one person in the world who understood him like this, but he glanced down at the empty seat beside him. "Uh . . . someone's sitting there."

Kyle winced, his eyes turning wet. He exhaled loudly, then without another word he turned and walked away. Jason watched him cross the room and slide his tray through the return window.

"So, Jason," Dwayne said in an effeminate voice. "Is he your new girlfriend?"

In an instant, Jason leapt at him, fists clenched. Corey held him back. "Take it easy, man. He's just joking. Aren't you, Dwayne?"

Dwayne nodded vigorously, shocked by Jason's reaction. "Of course, man."

Jason took a deep breath to calm himself. He sat down again, glancing at the door through which Kyle had left. There was no way could he just sit there. He stood up, abandoning his tray, and walked out of the cafeteria.

Kyle was almost out of sight down the hall. Jason raced to catch up with him. "Kyle!"

Kyle kept walking.

"Kyle, wait!" Jason grabbed his shoulder and spun him around.

"Hey, look, I'm sorry." He caught his breath. "I just don't want people to think I'm . . ." He waited for a couple of students to pass.

"Well," Kyle shot back, not caring who heard him. "You *are*, aren't you?"

The students turned around, glanced at them, and walked away whispering.

"How about if we talk about this later?" Jason pleaded.

"At my house?" Kyle snapped at him. "Where no one can see you?"

Jason knew he was losing his temper. "Look, all I wanted was help with math."

"Yeah, sure. Is that what you call it?"

Corey shouted from the cafeteria doorway, "Yo, Jason!"

Jason glanced at him, then to Kyle. "I'll call you later."

"No!" Kyle said in the same tone Debra had used.

A familiar twinge gripped Jason's stomach. He knew he was about to get dumped. Again. He desperately wanted to stop it and was utterly incapable of doing so. If only he could make Kyle understand how difficult this was. Didn't Kyle realize how much he'd opened up to him? How much he'd trusted him?

Kyle adjusted his glasses. "Jason, I don't get what's going on here. I want to help you, but"—his voice got a little mean with exasperation—"you're acting like a creep." He stared at Jason a moment, his jaw tight. Then he turned and left.

Jason gulped, wondering, *Why do I always end up the bad guy?*

That evening while he studied at his desk, Melissa sat on the floor and played with her dolls. Out of nowhere she asked, "What does 'gay' mean?"

Jason stopped writing. Had he heard correctly? He turned to see her brown eyes peering up at him, waiting for an answer. He knew she trusted him. He didn't want to lie to her.

"Well . . . uh, what do you think it means?"

Melissa peeked down at her dolls. "I think it's like when you're really happy."

Jason breathed a sigh of relief. "Yeah, that's what it means."

Melissa continued to play. But Jason had barely wiped the sweat from his brow when she said, "I think it also means when one boy loves another boy." She stared at him, hard this time—not like a child.

Jason cleared his throat. "Uh, yeah, well, it can mean that, too."

He wondered where she'd heard the word. And why did she ask about it now of all times? He remembered the drawing she'd given Kyle, and how they had joked about it. He wondered if she suspected Kyle was gay. Several times she'd asked when he was coming over again. Jason hated to tell her, "Never."

As if sensing his sadness, Melissa climbed onto his lap. "I know! It means when two boys are really happy 'cause they love each other." She laughed.

He wasn't certain whether to laugh along with her—or cry.

CHAPTER 17

JASON

KYLE

NELSON

Kyle plunged into the swimming pool, trying to cool his anger. Water sealed around him, momentarily soothing his rage. He and Jason were supposed to be friends. So how could he have snubbed him like that?

Kyle furiously kicked forward, breaking the surface of the water. Of course, he hadn't taken into account how after their pre-Christmas kiss Jason had run out. Maybe Jason hadn't liked kissing. Maybe he was angry about it.

Kyle reached the end of the swim lane and turned. Pushing off the side, he recalled how Jason had kissed him back. There could be no mistake, Jason had liked it. Then why did he disappear after that and why brush him off at lunch?

The water sliced between his arms. Approaching Jason in the cafeteria in front of his teammates probably wasn't the wisest move. But he was so eager to see him again after Christmas break. It wasn't fair that Jason let him get so close and then pushed him away. It made him feel like some sort of leper.

Kyle pounded the water, cursing Jason with one stroke, himself with the other. He'd been stupid to think that it would ever work out with Jason—and a jerk to tell Jason he loved him.

He swam up to the wall, pulled off his goggles, and squinted at the clock. Hours had passed since he dived in. No wonder he was exhausted.

For the third day in a row Nelson failed to show at school. Kyle had phoned him and left messages, but Nelson hadn't called back. Kyle decided to stop by his house on the way home. He rang the doorbell and waited, listening to Atticus bark inside. He rang the bell again and heard Nelson telling the dog to calm down.

The door opened and Nelson peered out, squinting as he shielded his eyes from the light. His eyes were puffy, and a black wool cap rolled low over his eyebrows. A stained T-shirt hung over his rumpled jeans, and a lit cigarette dangled between his nicotine-yellowed fingers.

"Are you okay?" Kyle said. "You look terrible."

Nelson exhaled a stream of cigarette smoke. "I feel like dog shit." He flicked his cigarette into the yard and grabbed Atticus by the collar. "Come on in."

Kyle followed Nelson to his room, Atticus bounding along-side. The room was a mess—strewn with junk-food wrappers. Obviously Nelson had been bingeing. An ashtray overflowed with cigarette butts, and a cloud of smoke hung in the air.

"How can you breathe in here?" Kyle coughed. "Mind if I open a window?"

Nelson shrugged and coughed. He sat down on the carpet and grabbed a fresh cigarette.

Kyle opened the window. "It's supposed to snow later." He picked up some of the wrappers and tossed them into the wastebasket. "How come you haven't come to school?"

Nelson blew smoke out his nose. "Too depressed."

Kyle sat down across from him. "About what?" Atticus lay down beside him. "You haven't called me back. Did I do something wrong?"

Nelson peered out from under his wool cap. "No. It's not you." He looked down at the carpet and brushed his hand across it. "So, what's new with Jason?"

Kyle realized it was an attempt to change the subject. Nelson was avoiding something. "It's over," Kyle told him. "He's a creep. I don't want anything else to do with him."

Nelson looked up from the carpet. "What happened?"

Kyle wanted to talk about it but didn't know where to start. "I told you we kissed, right?"

Nelson nodded and Kyle paused. He knew he hadn't said anything to Nelson about telling Jason he loved him. Now didn't seem like the right time either. Instead he told Nelson what happened in the cafeteria.

"You asked to sit at the B-ball table? That was brazen."

Kyle shook his head. "It was dumb."

Nelson nearly rolled over laughing. "I wish I'd seen their jockstrap faces when little mild-mannered you asked to sit at their table. Did you really expect him to say yes?"

He made it sound so comical that even Kyle had to laugh. "I was excited to see him! I didn't think." He felt foolish now. "There's something else: I told him he's a creep."

Nelson stopped laughing and sat up. "In front of everyone?"

"No. I wouldn't do that."

"Oh, well," Nelson said philosophically. "So, now he'll disappear for a while. Then he'll get over it."

"He can disappear forever, as far as I'm concerned. I'm sick of it."

"You'll get over it," Nelson said, studying his cigarette.

"No, I won't." Kyle folded his arms. "I don't want any more to do with him. He's too scared."

"Scared?" Nelson raised his eyebrows, so that they went up beneath his cap. "Kyle, you're the one who's scared."

"Me? Scared of what?"

Nelson gave an exasperated shrug. "I don't know. Scared that you're in love with him and he doesn't love you, even though it's so obvious he does." Suddenly his tone turned somber. He crushed his cigarette, adding the butt to the pile in the ashtray. "You can't just dump him like garbage."

His reaction baffled Kyle. "I'm not dumping him like garbage. He's the one who keeps running away. I'm not going to force myself on him. What's gotten into you? You don't even like him."

Nelson shook another cigarette from his pack. "I never said I didn't like him. I just thought he was way fucked up. But that's no reason for you to give up on him."

Now Kyle was sure something was up. "How come you haven't come to school?"

Nelson shrugged evasively. "Didn't feel like it." He took a sudden interest in his nicotine-stained fingernails.

Kyle stared at him, waiting. He knew Nelson hated silence. Wait long enough and eventually Nelson would talk.

"Okay," Nelson sighed. "I'll tell you what happened." He tapped his cigarette on the ashtray rim. "I met a guy on-line."

Kyle sat up. "You mean you physically met him? When?"

Nelson took a drag and exhaled. "The night my dad didn't show. This guy I.M.'d me. We hooked up. And I went home with him."

Kyle leaned back, shocked. This wasn't the story he expected. "Just like that?"

Nelson made a sputtering sound. "You make me sound like a slut."

"That's not what I meant. I mean: Who is he?"

"His name's Brick. You should see his apartment. It's so fucking cool." He drummed his cigarette. "He's got a million CDs. Anyway, one thing led to another. God, Kyle, it was so intense! Like nothing you can imagine. Fuck, it was fantastic!"

Kyle sat mesmerized, trying to absorb everything Nelson was saying.

"Anyway," Nelson continued. "I didn't call my mom. She came back from PFLAG to an angry message from my dad, even though he's the one who blew me off. When I got home, she wanted to know where I'd been."

"Did you tell her?"

"Of course not! She totally overreacted, said how she'd trusted me, blah, blah, blah, and just 'cause I'm turning eighteen, yadda, yadda, yadda . . . all that bullshit." He shook his head. "I couldn't believe how stressed she got. I'm grounded for the next month. I can't use the car. I can't go out at night."

Kyle watched the cigarette smoke curl into the air. "So, what's that have to do with you not being in school?"

Nelson wiped his hand across the carpet again. "Kyle?" His voice quivered. "I need to tell you something. I have to tell someone." His hand trembled as he flicked the ashes from his cigarette. "I let him . . . you know." He gazed up at Kyle. "And I didn't use a condom."

Kyle stared back at him, considering what he'd just heard. Did Nelson mean what he thought he meant? "You mean, you let him . . . ?"

Nelson nodded.

"Without a condom?"

Nelson averted his eyes. "I guess I forgot."

"Forgot?"

Nelson tossed aside a piece of carpet lint. "I'm stupid. Okay?"

"After all the lectures we had in the group?"

Nelson pursed his lips. You could tell he was trying to think what to say. "Okay. The truth is . . ." His jaw relaxed. "I didn't forget, okay?"

Kyle listened carefully, trying to understand. As Nelson explained, his voice grew more excited. "It all happened so fast! I knew we should use a condom, but it was too intense. Kyle, I'm so confused. I feel like an idiot. Please don't yell at me."

Kyle sat still, overwhelmed. He wanted to shake Nelson. But what good would that do? He finally said, "You're not an idiot. We all do stupid things."

Nelson slid back against the bed. "What if I got it? My first time with a guy. Shit! I keep going over it—over and over, as if that will change anything. I don't want to die. . . ."

Kyle shuddered. He tried to think what to say, but no words came.

Nelson looked up at him, and his voice came out small, like a child's. "I'm scared, Kyle. Could you just hold me? I promise I won't try to kiss you or anything."

Kyle leaned forward, scooting alongside him. He reached his arm around, accidentally grazing Nelson's cap. Nelson reached up to grab it, but the cap fell off.

His head was totally shaved. He was bald, down to the ridges of his skull.

Kyle stared at him, stunned. "What did you do to your hair?"

Nelson shrugged sheepishly. "Shaved it off."

"I can see that." Kyle ran his fingers across the bare scalp. It felt soft like a peach. "Why?"

"Kyle, I don't know. It looks stupid as shit, doesn't it?" He groaned. "I hate my life, I hate my hair—my head, rather—and my butt hurts." He folded himself into Kyle's shoulder and started to sob.

It wasn't the first time Kyle had seen him cry, but that didn't make it any easier. And the thought of Nelson getting HIV was more than Kyle could bear. His throat choked up as he leaned over to kiss Nelson's tearstained cheek.

Nelson sniffled. He turned to him, his face only a few inches away. "*Now* you kiss me. I should've gotten sick earlier."

"Shut up," Kyle told him, and wiped his cheek. He wished he'd come over when Nelson had called him. Maybe then none of this would've happened.

They sat together. Kyle couldn't tell for how long, but it turned dark outside.

Finally, a car pulled into the driveway. Atticus, who lay quietly all this time, sprang up and ran out of the room, barking and wagging his tail. Nelson's mom called from the living room. "Nelson?"

Nelson wiped his nose and shouted back, "Yeah?"

His mom stepped in the doorway and switched the light on. "Why are you sitting in the dark? Hi, Kyle." She shot Nelson a hard look. "School called. They said you didn't go again today. Why?"

Nelson shielded his eyes from the sudden light. "It slipped my mind."

"You're really pushing it," she said through her teeth. "Come help with dinner."

"I'm not hungry."

"I don't care! You're eating." She stormed out and Nelson sneered at her.

Kyle pulled away from Nelson's shoulder. "I guess I better go. Ooh, my arm fell asleep." He propped himself up on the bed, his legs sore from sitting in the same position for so long.

Nelson offered a weak smile. "Kyle? Thanks."

Kyle tried to smile back. "For what?"

"For not freaking out."

Kyle gave him a reassuring squeeze and told him, "You'll be okay," though he really wasn't sure at all.

The snow had started when Kyle left Nelson's. He loved snow and how it blanketed everything. It usually cheered him up, but not tonight.

When he arrived home, his mom was in the kitchen peeling potatoes. "You don't look well." She pressed her hand against his forehead. "Is everything okay?"

What could he say? How could he tell her that nothing in his life was okay—Nelson having sex with some guy he met on-line and not using a condom; Jason dissing him in front of the whole cafeteria; Jack Ransom threatening him; being called "homo" every day, having bottles thrown at him, finding QUEER scratched across his locker. It was all too much. He was sick and tired of dealing with it.

At dinner, his dad was serving steak and mashed potatoes when the phone rang.

His mom got up to answer it. "Hello?" Her tone suddenly

turned cross. "Who is this?" After a moment, she hung up.

Returning to the table, she glanced at Kyle. The worry lines in her forehead revealed that she was upset. Kyle could guess what had happened.

His dad studied his mom. "Who was it?"

"They said something pretty ugly." She turned to Kyle. "Has someone been bothering you at school?"

"A crank call?" his dad asked. "Kyle? You know what this is about?"

Kyle tried to shrug it off. "It's probably because of the group I told you we're starting. It's no big deal."

"No big deal?" his dad demanded. The phone rang again. His dad sprang up and grabbed the receiver. "Hello? Who is this?"

Right, thought Kyle. *Like the guy's going to tell you his name. Maybe he'll give you his address, too, in hopes you'll send a Christmas card next year.*

His dad slammed the receiver down. "I'm going to report this. Have you told the school authorities?"

"Dad, they're not going to do anything. It's been since before Christmas and they still haven't painted my locker."

"What about your locker?" his mom asked.

Oops, that had slipped out. "Uh, someone scratched 'queer' on it."

"Kyle!" his mom wailed. The lines dug deeper into her forehead. "What else has happened?"

Kyle scooped out a crater in his mashed potatoes. "Nothing. Someone threw a bottle at me, but it missed. That's all."

"That's all!" His dad stared at him. "Why haven't you told us this before?"

"I don't know." Kyle swirled his fork. "I figured you'd tell me that's what I got for choosing to be gay."

His dad cut into his steak and chewed in silence for a moment. "I'm calling Miller in the morning."

"Mueller," Kyle corrected.

His dad shook his fork. "Mueller! I don't like this at all."

Kyle felt relieved that his dad didn't blame him for the harassment. In fact, it almost sounded like he was taking up for Kyle. That was a shift.

The following morning, Kyle opened his eyes before the alarm sounded, wide awake. For some reason, he felt bold, new. Outside his window the sun blazed bright off the melting snow. He had an idea. On his way out of the house he stopped by the garage. He rummaged through his dad's workbench until he found what he needed.

It was still early when he arrived at school and marched down the hall. The few students stared at him as he passed. He probably looked crazed to them. He reached his desecrated locker and stood before the word QUEER. He reached into his backpack. With one long sweep he spray-painted AND PROUD!

CHAPTER 18

JASON

KYLE

NELSON

Saturday morning Nelson stayed in bed for yet another day, avoiding the universe and obsessing. He looked over at his computer and thought of e-mailing Brick. Would Brick even remember him? What should he say? He got out of bed and crossed the room. His hand trembled a little as he turned the computer on. The monitor stared back at him. He clicked on "New Message" and typed, "Hi. How's it going? What are you up to? Nelson."

He took a deep breath, hit "Send," and reached for a cigarette. Before he could light up, the message bounced back—blocked. He couldn't believe his eyes.

He tried resending the message, but it bounced back again. Obviously Brick didn't want to hear from him.

"Asshole!" Nelson slammed the mouse down and set up a block of his own. That would show the prick, assuming he ever tried to e-mail him.

Nelson puffed on his cigarette and recalled Shea's warning. He'd put off returning her calls all week, knowing she'd be angry. Now he picked up the phone and dialed. On the first ring she answered. "Hello?"

"Hi, it's not Caitlin. It's me."

"Finally! Why haven't you called me back?"

He took a drag off his a cigarette. "You sure you want to hear it?"

"Nelson, I'm really pissed at you."

"I'm sorry," he told her. "I meant to call you back. I was just so depressed."

"You think you're the only one with problems?"

He knew from her messages that she'd had a fight with Caitlin. "I know you have—," he tried to interject.

But she went on: "Whenever you need someone to listen, you always expect me to be there. But this week when I really needed you—no calls back."

"Well, I'm calling you now, aren't I?"

"To tell me you were too depressed? Oh, please! You bitch and moan about how your father abandoned you, but you do the same thing to your friends. You're just like him."

Youch. He'd told her about his dad in confidence, not for her to use it against him. "Shea, I think that's really unfair."

"Get off your pity pot, Nelson. Take some responsibility."

That really pissed him off. "You know what, Shea? Forget I called." He hung up on her, for the first time in their friendship.

Why was everyone being so mean to him? Was this Shit-on-Nelson Week or something?

He reached for the bag of cookies on the nightstand, but the pack was empty. He shook the crumbs into his palm and glanced at the clock—almost noon. No wonder his stomach was rumbling.

The phone rang and his mom answered downstairs. Good time to snatch some food.

At the kitchen table his mom stuffed PFLAG envelopes, phone cupped to her ear. "My son is organizing a Gay-Straight Alliance at school." She frowned at him and tapped her watch. "Yes, he is quite an activist. Like mother, like son."

He ignored her, pulling a box of Pop-Tarts from the cupboard. The only activism of interest to him lately was eating. He grabbed the carton of orange juice from the refrigerator. Once back in his cozy bed, he devoured the Pop-Tarts. The juice made him need to pee.

"Nelson!" his mom yelled from downstairs. "It's past noon. I want to talk to you."

He closed the bathroom door, peed, flushed, and stepped on the scale. Looking at his weight made him even more depressed. He'd gained eight pounds lying around the house all week. He turned the shower radio on full blast so his mom wouldn't hear him, then he leaned over the toilet and stuck his finger down his throat.

After he finished, he sprayed deodorizer and stumbled back to bed, pulling the bed covers over him.

"Nelson!" his mom shouted again. "Do I have to come up there?"

All the past week she'd tried to get him to talk to her. He wanted to confide in her, but after all the safe sex lectures she'd drummed into him, he could only imagine her disappointment. Each morning he placated her by promising to get up and go to school. But once she left for work, the thought of facing the world overwhelmed him too much. The next day the whole scenario repeated.

Her footsteps sounded on the stairs. He clutched his pillow

over his head. The door opened. "Nelson!" She yanked the pillow off him. "You can't go on this way!"

Nelson grabbed the pillow back over him. "I don't want to
talk about it."

The bed shook as his mom sat down beside him. "Nelson, I
can't deal with this. You want me to call your father?

"Good luck," Nelson mumbled beneath his pillow.

"Nelson?" Her voice trembled. "Would you please just look
at me?"

He grudgingly pulled the pillow off his head. Her face
strained with concern. "Honey, you and I have always talked
about everything, haven't we?"

Yes, he nodded. But he'd never screwed up this badly before.

"What could be so bad that you'd stay cooped up like this a
whole week?"

The phone rang, to his relief. But she didn't budge. "Aren't
you going to get it?" he asked.

"Nope. I'm not leaving here till you talk to me."

Resistance was futile, he decided. Time to face the music.
He sat up in his bed, gripping his pillow for courage. "It's about
the night Dad didn't show up."

She nodded her head, as if she already suspected that.
Nelson continued: "You asked where I went? Well, I went over
to someone's."

Her eyebrows rose up, questioning.

"I . . . met this guy and . . ." His stomach churned as he
spoke. "We . . . went over to his place."

Her gaze traced his face. "You mean, you had sex?"

He bit into his lip and nodded.

"You had *sex*!" Her chest rose and fell. She was totally over-
reacting.

He clutched the pillow in front of him. "You see why I haven't told you anything?"

"Nelson!" She folded her arms. "You need to tell me what happened. This person hurt you, didn't he?"

"No!"

"Then what happened? I'm your mother. I have a right to know. What did he do to you?"

How could he tell her that? "He didn't hurt me. We had sex, that's all. It's just . . ." He forced the words out: "We didn't use a condom."

Her face froze, and he continued talking out of nervousness. "I know we were supposed to, but we didn't. I know you and I talked about safe sex a million times. I don't know why I did it, so don't ask me. It's done. I was stupid. There's nothing I can do about it now."

His mom stared blankly at him. "But *why*?"

A hollow pang of hopelessness echoed through him. "I just told you, I don't know why!"

"But . . . I trusted you."

He winced and covered his face. That was the worst thing she could've said. He heard her inhale a deep breath.

"Why didn't you tell me?"

He removed his hand from his face. "I figured you'd be angry."

She wiped her eyes. "I am angry. But we could've done something! Oh, God, honey. We could've taken you to the emergency room."

"Huh? What for?"

His mom stood up and started pacing, pulling at her hair. "For AZT—or whatever drugs they give people who suspect they've been infected."

Nelson vaguely recalled a discussion at the Rainbow group of new "morning-after" treatments. In his distress, he'd forgotten about that.

His mom kept pacing. "Never mind. It's too late now. I'm really, really angry. You know that? Why didn't you tell me?"

He wished he had. He felt even more stupid than before.

"I'm taking you to the doctor first thing Monday. And your dad needs to know about this."

"Why? If he'd shown up that night, maybe this never would've happened."

His mom pursed her lips. Apparently she didn't buy that. He really didn't either. He remembered what Shea had said about taking responsibility. And he knew he'd been irresponsible.

After dinner, he buried himself beneath the covers again, curling himself into a little ball. He was glad he'd told his mom about Brick, but he still felt rotten.

The phone rang and his mother called from downstairs. "It's Kyle!"

Nelson poked a hand out from under the covers, fumbled for the phone, and snaked it back underneath. "Yeah?"

"Hi. You feel any better?"

"I told my mom what happened. She said if I'd told her sooner, she could've taken me to get some morning-after drugs. I feel so stupid. I want to die." He waited for a reaction.

Kyle gave a nervous cough. "Can I come over first?"

Nelson almost laughed. He brushed his cheek, remembering the afternoon Kyle cradled him in his arms. Maybe if he just said what he'd always wanted to say and never had, he'd feel better.

"Kyle? I want to tell you something. As friends, like you said." He sniffled a deep breath. "I love you." He gripped the phone in the darkness, waiting.

After a pause Kyle said, "I love you, too."

"You do?" Nelson said. For some reason, he hadn't expected Kyle to say it back.

"Of course."

Nelson sat up, throwing off the covers. "I mean it, Kyle," he said more forcefully. "I love you. I really do."

Kyle laughed, still sounding nervous. "Nelson, you're my best friend. Of course I love you. Now, shut up. What are you doing tonight? Can I come over?"

Nelson sprang out of bed. "Yeah." For the first time all week, he wanted to get on with his life.

With Kyle's help, Nelson caught up on the classwork he'd missed and returned to school actually happy to be back. Secretly he'd missed his friends, MacTraugh, even old Nazi Mueller. And he'd missed giving Kyle a hard time.

"You'll never guess where I saw Jason," he told Kyle at lunch. "In the library! What did you do to the poor jock? He looked like he was actually studying."

"Nelson, he's always studied."

"Well, he doesn't look good. He seems so, I don't know, lost. Besides, it's boring without you two lusting after each other."

Kyle sipped his milk. "Look, I don't care about him. Would you just shut up and eat?"

"You just want to see me fat and ugly. And admit it, you do care about him."

"I do not. I told you, I'm over him."

Nelson sighed. "I don't know who looks worse, him or you."

Kyle slammed his milk carton down. "Can we please change the subject?"

"Well, that's a switch."

After school, they walked home together. Nelson had missed that, too.

"By the way," he told Kyle, "Mom said the GSA school board meeting's scheduled for next Tuesday. You and I need to think what to say."

Kyle nodded. "Okay," he said, then stopped in his tracks. "Oh, no! I have a swimming invitational that night."

"Shit." Nelson lit up a cigarette. "I was really hoping you'd go with me." Although he'd looked forward to the meeting for weeks, the incident with Brick and telling his mom about it had rattled his confidence. "Well, at least help me think what to say."

Kyle grinned. "I'm sure you'll come up with something."

The night of the meeting, Nelson's mom pulled out a photo of him at six years old. The image showed him in crisp, new clothes his first day of kindergarten, wearing an excited smile, his gaze aimed eagerly toward the brick school.

"What are you taking that picture for?" Nelson asked.

She glanced evasively out the car window. "You'll see."

The meeting was packed with people. Mueller sat in the front row. Fenner Farley's dad clenched a placard that read: DICK & JANE, NOT DICK & WAYNE. Fenner sat in his shadow.

Ms. MacTraugh waved to Nelson. She'd saved seats for him and his mom. The board president called the meeting to order and explained that each person who wished to speak would be assigned a number and allotted one minute. Both Nelson and his mom signed up. "You go first," Nelson told her, still not sure what he was going to say.

The first several people who spoke were civil—until Fenner's dad. "This so-called alliance is stirring things up to the detriment of the entire community, just so a few sick individuals can prey on our children and recruit them into a life of sin. They want to promote a homosexual agenda and contaminate our young people with vile diseases like AIDS." He spewed on about family values till the president banged her gavel.

He sounds as stupid as Fenner, Nelson thought.

MacTraugh's number was called. "Massachusetts is a pioneer in this area," she said. "State education policy bans antigay discrimination, making schools safe for gay and lesbian students."

Fenner's dad yelled, "Then move to Massachusetts!"

The president banged her gavel, and MacTraugh continued: "As parents and teachers, we have a responsibility to ensure our children are safe from antigay harassment, intimidation, and violence. As a community we should promote understanding between individuals of any sexual orientation. The alliance will adhere to the same guidelines as any other extracurricular group. Such groups are sanctioned under federal law, which prohibits a school club from being banned because of its religious, political, or philosophical views. If we single out the proposed group, we fuel the fires of ignorance, fear, intolerance, and hatred. Is that the message we want to give our young people?"

Nelson's mom was called next. She walked to the front and sat at the microphone. "It's said a picture is worth a thousand words. Since I only have one minute . . ." She opened her pocketbook and passed the photo of six year-old Nelson to the board president.

Nelson squirmed with embarrassment as his mom continued: "That's my son, taken his first morning of kindergarten. Smiling. Happy. When I picked him up that afternoon, however, you would see a very different picture of him. Crying.

Hurt. Sad. You see, his very first day of school he learned a new word: 'sissy.' The next morning he begged me not to make him go back."

Nelson had forgotten all that. Now he understood why she'd brought the photo.

"I promised him school would get better. I believed it then. Now I realize I lied. For the past twelve years, every single school day he's been called names and obscenities, while most teachers have stood by silently. Some school officials even told him he brought it upon himself."

She looked at Mr. Mueller, who turned away from her gaze.

"Simply because he walks and talks differently from other boys, he's been hit, kicked, beat up, spit upon, and received death threats."

Nelson slid down in his seat, wishing she hadn't told everyone he'd been spit upon.

She looked straight at him. "There have been days when I wished my son hadn't been born gay. Not because I love him less for it," she said emphatically, "but so he wouldn't have to endure so much suffering."

She looked at Fenner's dad. "Some here talk about family values while in the same breath they disparage a group that would foster values of tolerance and understanding. I don't know what those families have as their values. But I know students should be able to attend school without being abused. I believe this group will help achieve that. Thank you."

School board members passed the photograph back, looked at one another, and nodded.

Nelson sat thinking. In spite of his embarrassment, he sensed his mom had made the best point of anyone yet.

The next number was called, but no one stood up. "That's

your number!" MacTraugh whispered. Nelson rushed to the front and sat down. The school board members stared at him. He shifted in the hard wooden seat, still without a clue what to say. "Uh, in case you don't recognize me from the photo, that was me." He meant it as a joke, except no one laughed.

But his mom smiled. He cleared his throat, a little reassured. "Not every gay teenager has a mom like mine. Most teens don't. Most aren't even out to their parents, or anyone else. There's a reason for that. As you just heard, it's dangerous being gay."

As he spoke, he felt increasingly confident. "Some people ask: Why do we need a Gay-Straight Alliance? Why do you have to make such a big issue out of being gay? Well, we wouldn't need a GSA if everyone accepted and respected—or at least tolerated— people who are different."

He narrowed his eyes at Fenner's dad. "Some people talk about a homosexual threat. Excuse me, but who's really being threatened in this situation? The purpose of our club isn't to 'recruit' anyone. What we hope to do is change attitudes and build understanding."

He stared out at the sea of faces and wondered whether his message was getting through. "Look, whether or not this group is approved won't affect me. I graduate this year. I'm doing this for those who come after me. Do you really want to make them go through the . . ." He was about to say "shit" but caught himself. He realized he was getting angry and took a breath to calm down. "Don't put them through what I've been through. You can make school a safer place for everyone. You have the power. It's up to you."

As he returned to his seat, MacTraugh whispered, "Bravo!"

When he sat down, his mom grabbed hold of his hand. "I'm proud of you."

"Yeah, yeah." He let her squeeze his palm a moment. "Can I just ask you a favor? Next time, can you use a better picture of me? I really hate that one."

Mueller spoke next, proclaiming some wussy crap about how he wanted to keep an open mind. "I have nothing against students who consider themselves gay. My concern is the club would distract others from learning."

Oh, please, Nelson thought, and turned away. The meeting lasted until after ten.

That Saturday Kyle had another swim meet, so Nelson went by himself to the Rainbow group. When he walked in, Jeremy waved and motioned to the seat beside him. "Wow! When did you buzz your head? It looks cool."

"Thanks." Nelson grinned. "A couple of weeks ago."

Carla, the day's facilitator, led introductions and opened the meeting. "Today we're going to talk about HIV."

Several people moaned, and Nelson chimed in, "Again?"

"Yes." Carla gave a patient frown. "Again."

Nelson whispered to Jeremy, "I'm so tired of AIDS shit. The last thing I want is a lecture from some bozo."

Carla overheard him. "It's not a lecture. We're going to hear a personal story from one of our members." She glanced beside him. "Jeremy?"

Nelson instantly flushed with embarrassment. Oh, God. He slid down in his seat, hiding his face behind his hand.

"Wish bozo luck!" Jeremy whispered, and walked to the front of the group. Nelson slid down in his seat, hiding his face behind his hand.

"I asked to speak to you today to tell you my story. I'm a little nervous, since most of you don't know, but . . ." He hesitated and took a deep breath. "Two years ago I tested HIV positive."

Nelson uncovered his face and sat up in his seat. Jeremy was HIV positive.

Jeremy tapped the stool he leaned against. "One night I went home with a guy. I didn't have the self-esteem to say I wanted to have safer sex. I thought, 'God, if I bring it up, he may not want to have sex with me. He doesn't look HIV positive. What's one time?'"

Nelson listened attentively. *That's my story,* he thought. *He's telling my story.*

"Well," Jeremy continued. "That's all it took: one time. I've felt too ashamed to talk about it. But now I hope that by talking with you, you can learn from my stupidity." He paused for a moment. "No. Not stupidity. Lack of self-esteem. I didn't think I was worth it. Maybe by telling you about me, you won't make the same mistake I did."

He went on to talk more about how he decided to get tested, how depressed he became, and how he got to the point of thinking about suicide, before he finally reached out for help.

Others in the room leaned forward, listening. During the entire half hour Jeremy spoke, no one interrupted or gave him a hard time, like they did with other speakers. Nelson felt ashamed for having judged Jeremy like he had. It wasn't fair that anyone should have to go through HIV. It amazed him that Jeremy could talk so truthfully. *He has guts,* Nelson thought, *more than I do.*

When Jeremy finished speaking, the room was more quiet than Nelson had ever experienced it. Carla broke the silence. "Would you mind if people ask questions?"

Jeremy nodded. "Sure."

A boy wearing a jean jacket spoke up. "Don't you feel angry at the guy? I'd kill him."

Jeremy glanced down for a moment, then met the boy's eyes. "Yeah, I'm angry. But it's not like he twisted my arm—or anything else, for that matter."

It impressed Nelson that Jeremy could joke about it like that.

"Seriously, I'm trying to do something good with the anger, you know?"

A girl raised her hand. "What did your parents say?"

Jeremy sighed. "Well, when I found out, I knew I had to tell them, but I hadn't come out to them yet. I was too afraid. When I finally told my dad, he actually hugged me. That was a shock. My mom took it badly. She still cries every once in a while, when I have a doctor's appointment or something. It's been hard on them to find out I'm gay and HIV positive all at once."

"Do you ever wish you hadn't gotten tested?" another girl asked.

Jeremy scratched his chin. "Sometimes. But I figure it's better, so I won't infect others."

Nelson raised his hand tentatively. "Did you ever see the guy again?"

Jeremy shook his head. "Nope. I'm kind of glad. I wouldn't know what to say."

Nelson nodded and thought of Brick.

A few more people asked questions, then it was time for the break. After the meeting, a group of boys surrounded Jeremy, asking questions and shaking his hand. Nelson waited till they cleared out, hoping he could invite Jeremy for a Coke and talk.

"Hey, I'm sorry about the 'bozo' comment."

Jeremy smiled. "You should have seen your face when I got up to speak."

Nelson felt himself blush. "Uh, do you want to go for a Coke or something?"

To his relief and astonishment, Jeremy said yes.

In the restaurant, Nelson fidgeted with his cup and glanced around to make sure no one was listening. "A few weeks ago," he whispered confidentially, "I went home with a guy." He paused to check Jeremy's reaction.

"Yeah?" Jeremy nodded.

Nelson took a deep breath, then rushed the words out. "I didn't use a condom. There, I said it." He smashed his straw between his fingers. "What if I got infected? Just my luck! The first time I get laid." He tossed his straw aside.

"I hope not," Jeremy said. "But if you did, it's not the end of the world."

That wasn't much consolation. "Oh, great," Nelson said.

"Look," Jeremy told him. "I remember when I got my test results. I stopped going to school. I didn't eat. I thought, 'Why bother? I'll never go to college. I'll never have sex again. Life's over.'" He sighed. "But it wasn't."

He pulled out a pill case, taking out an orange capsule and a white, diamond-shaped pill and swallowing them. "The meds are a pain, but like they say, it's better than the alternative."

"So that's what I have to look forward to?"

"Nelson, I wouldn't wish this on anyone. If I could go back, I'd do things differently. But in many ways this has helped me grow up. I see things a lot more clearly now. I know what's important."

Nelson pondered everything Jeremy had said, both at the meeting and now. Out of all of it, there was one thing he remained curious about. "So, do you still . . ." He hesitated. Could he really ask it? He steadied himself with the table and finished his question: ". . . have sex?"

As soon as he said it, he realized it sounded like a come-on. He hadn't meant it that way—or had he?

Jeremy grinned. "Yeah, though not often enough." He laughed. "I just make sure I tell the person I'm positive. And I insist on being safe."

Later Nelson stared at Jeremy's scribbled phone number. He couldn't believe he'd actually had the nerve to ask for it—and that Jeremy had asked for his in return.

CHAPTER 19

JASON

KYLE

NELSON

Jason regretted what had happened with Kyle in the cafeteria. He felt bad for the way he'd put Kyle off, but at the same time it hurt that Kyle had called him a creep.

In the days following, he spent hours closed up in his room thinking about his future and what Corey had said about his career. He needed to forget about Kyle and this whole coming-out thing. He wanted no more to do with Kyle. Then why couldn't he get his mind off him? His restlessness drove him out of the house and into the night. He pounded the basketball court till his mom drove up, insisting he come home.

At school he pretended everything was fine. He tried to pay attention in class, studied in the library, stayed close to the team, and trained to exhaustion at basketball practice. He thought he'd have to avoid Kyle but found he didn't need to. When they crossed in the hall, Kyle turned away as if he didn't see him. Jason did too, ignoring the ache he felt inside.

One cold mid-winter day, Jason's SAT scores came in the mail, lower than his earlier ones. If a school didn't sign him soon, he worried, he might never get a scholarship. Then one afternoon the coach from Tech returned. Following practice, he offered to sign Jason. Without hesitation, Jason agreed. His future was set. He phoned his mom but could hardly say the words. When he got home, he swung her in a circle and twirled his sister in the air. His dad opened a beer and sneered, "You would've made a Division One school if you had any brains." But not even his dad could dampen Jason's euphoria.

Saturday afternoon, he biked to Corey's. Together they shot hoops and celebrated. Jason dunked one basket after another as he flew through the air with exhilaration. He felt like he could do anything.

As he biked homeward, a pickup truck passed so close it nearly sideswiped him. A familiar face leaned out the window and flipped him the bird—Jack Ransom.

A few blocks later Jason approached Bluemont Park. In the distance he saw the truck pulled over beside two guys on the sidewalk. Jack and the pickup driver got out, gesturing at the guys. Suddenly Jack swung.

Jason cautiously biked closer. He now recognized the driver. José Montero swung at one of the two boys. Jason realized it was Nelson. His heart leapt as he recognized the other boy, being knocked to the ground by Jack. It was Kyle.

In an instant, Jason sprang from the bike and threw it aside. He ran toward Jack, burning with anger. "Leave him alone!" He pushed Jack away, grabbing his shoulder.

Jack shook him off. "Stay out of this!"

Kyle scrambled up off the ground, his chest rising and falling as he breathed.

Jason's heart pounded. "I said leave him alone."

"What are you," Jack scoffed, "a fag lover?"

Jason hit Jack in the face. Jack stumbled backward, falling with a stunned expression.

Kyle shouted, "Nelson!" Jason spun around to see José pinning Nelson to the ground, beating the crap out of him.

Kyle ran toward them, and Jack yelled, "Watch out!"

José jumped up, fists raised. Jason ran over and José swung. But Jason moved back in time to avoid the blow. He jabbed José in the stomach, causing him to double up.

Jack staggered over and grabbed José by the shoulder. "Let's go." He gave Jason a scornful look as he led José to the truck. Once they were safely inside, he leaned out the window and yelled, "Faggots!"

Jason ignored him and leaned over Nelson, who seemed dazed. "Hey, you all right?" When Nelson didn't answer, Jason shook his shoulder. "Hey!"

"Quit shaking me," Nelson mumbled. "I'm okay."

He didn't look it. His face was swollen and his lip gashed. Blood dripped down his chin.

Jason turned to Kyle. His right eye looked badly bruised. He held his wrist out, wincing as he tried to rotate it. "I think something happened to my wrist when I hit Jack."

"You may have sprained it," Jason said, standing up. "Let me see." He took Kyle's wrist and tenderly probed it. "I don't think it's broken." They were standing very close. He could hear Kyle's breathing, still heavy. His sweat smelled like his own cologne. He glanced at Kyle's discolored eye. "Your eye looks pretty bad. Where are your glasses?"

Kyle looked around helplessly. "I don't know."

Jason spotted them a few feet away and picked them up. One of the side arms had broken off. "Here. Can you see without them?"

Kyle pointed to his good eye. "Out of this one I can. At least he didn't hit me in the mouth."

"You lost your cap, too," Jason said, handing it to Kyle. He felt like he was picking up after his little sister. "How'd it start?"

Kyle pointed his chin in Nelson's direction. "He can't keep his mouth shut."

Nelson still lay on the ground, patting his lip with his fingertips. "Don't blame me. They started it."

Jason bent over him. "Need help getting up?"

Nelson rolled over onto his side. "I'm fine." He tried to push himself up, but when he tried to stand, he winced and fell back down again. "I think my ankle's twisted."

Jason grabbed him under the arms. "Easy."

"I can do it," Nelson protested, but Jason ignored him, lifting him up.

Nelson tried to stand but cringed when he put any weight on his left foot. "I might've sprained it."

Jason shook his head. "You two don't get in many fights, do you?"

Kyle pulled out his handkerchief and pressed it against Nelson's lip. "You're bleeding."

"I am?"

"Put your arm around my shoulder," Jason told him. Nelson stared at him, surprised, and Jason realized this was probably the first time he'd ever spoken to Nelson. He draped his arm over his shoulder. "Come on. We're not far from my house. You can clean up there."

Kyle didn't budge. "That's okay. We'll be all right. I can help Nelson."

"Kyle," Nelson said. "Stop being a turd."

Kyle adjusted his cap, shooting a stubborn glance at Nelson. "All right," he agreed.

"Can you get my bike?" Jason asked.

Kyle picked up Jason's bike with his good hand, and they proceeded slowly toward Jason's house.

Jason considered the situation. Here he was with his arm around someone everybody at school knew was gay. Meanwhile, Kyle, whom he'd decided not to have anything more to do with, pushed his bike alongside. And now he was taking both home. Did he really want to do that? "So?" he asked. "What happened?"

Kyle wiped his nose. "We were walking to Nelson's, when the pickup pulls alongside us. Jack yells, 'Hey, faggots!' I say to Nelson, 'Keep your mouth shut.' But Nelson flips them the finger and yells, 'Breeders!' I yank his arm down, but sure enough the truck stops, and Jack and José get out."

Nelson shifted his weight on Jason's shoulder. "I tried to keep quiet. Really, I did."

Kyle sighed, holding his hurt wrist in the air while guiding the bike with his good hand. "Anyway, Jack grabs his crotch and says, 'Hey, queers, you want to suck on this?' And Nelson says to him, 'I don't suck on anything that small.'"

Jason smiled at the image of Nelson standing up to Jack Ransom. "You said that?"

Nelson cracked a grin and his lip started bleeding again. "You should've seen his face."

"Yeah?" Kyle shook his head. "Well, wait till you see *your* face now."

"Kyle, whether I said anything or not, they were going to beat us up anyway."

Kyle turned to Jason. "Then you showed up."

As they approached his house, Jason spotted his dad's truck. *Oh, crap,* he thought. *What if he's been drinking?* Would he make a scene about Nelson? With his earrings and nail polish, he looked so . . . gay. There was no way his dad wouldn't notice.

A familiar car was parked beside his dad's truck—friends of his mom and dad's. That was good. Maybe his dad wouldn't get too out of line with somebody visiting.

"I'd better warn you," Jason said, leading Kyle and Nelson toward the garage. "My dad's kind of crazy. If he says some things, don't pay attention." He opened the kitchen door, trying not to be nervous.

His mom came in from the dining room. "I thought I heard . . ." She gaped at the sight of Kyle and Nelson. "What happened?"

"We got in a fight," Jason said. "You remember Kyle, and this is Nelson."

She lifted Nelson's chin in her hand. "You'd better put some alcohol on that lip." She turned to Kyle. "And some ice on that eye. It hurts just to look at it." She opened the freezer and pulled out the ice trays. "I'll make a couple of ice packs." She turned to Jason. "Honey, why don't you take them to get washed up."

"What about Dad?"

She glanced at Nelson. "I doubt he'll say anything right now. If he does, just ignore him."

Right, like ignoring a rhinoceros in your living room. "Ready?" He started for the door, and Nelson hopped after him on his good leg. *Oh, shit.* Jason had forgotten about Nelson's ankle. "Come on," he told Nelson, and put his arm under his shoulder.

In the living room the Espinozas sat on the couch, drinks in hand, Melissa asleep beside them. Jason's dad sat in a chair with his back to the boys. Jason stepped as quickly as he could, considering Nelson's ankle.

"Hey!" His dad turned around. "Whassa matter with you?" His words slurred. "Don' you have any manners?" He stood up and wavered—drunk, obviously, but not out of control. He blinked at the sight of his son with his arm around Nelson.

Jason's throat tightened. "This is Nelson and Kyle. We were in a fight. Nelson twisted his ankle."

His dad's face contorted as his gaze descended from Nelson's earrings, across the handkerchief pressed to his bleeding lip, to his black and gold fingernails. He pinched the bridge of his nose and gave his head a quick, sobering shake.

"A fight?" said Mr. Espinoza. "I hope you won." He smiled, revealing a gold-capped tooth.

"Your mother told us you got a scholarship," said Mrs. Espinoza.

"Yeah, I signed with Tech."

His dad jabbed his finger in the air. "Tech ain' nothin'. You would'a been accepted to Georgetown if you weren't such a dummy."

A stab of anger plunged through Jason. How could his dad talk like that in front of everyone? His head grew hot, but he bit down on the impulse to fight back.

His mom walked in from the kitchen. "Boys, I fixed you a couple of ice packs in the kitchen." She patted his dad's hand. "Honey, let the boys clean up." Behind his back, she motioned Jason to hurry on.

He took the cue and led Kyle and Nelson down the hall to the guest bathroom.

"I didn't know you'd signed with Tech," Nelson said. "Congrats. I mean it."

"Yeah," Kyle said. "Congratulations."

Jason smiled. "Thanks. I signed this week." He turned the bathroom light on. "Here." He brought out some cotton and alcohol. "I'll clean up in the other one."

After splashing some cool water on his face, he stared with disbelief into the mirror. He had actually brought Nelly the faggot to his house—to his father. There would surely be hell to pay later.

Returning to the guest bathroom, he overheard Nelson. "Can you believe he carried me all that way?" Then he heard Kyle grumble, "Hurry up. I want to go. He doesn't want any more to do with me, and I don't want anything to do with him." The words stung, but Jason couldn't blame him.

Nelson said, "I'll take him if you don't want him."

Jason stepped into the doorway. "How's it look?"

Kyle frowned. "I think we'll have to amputate his mouth."

For a minute Jason thought maybe Kyle wasn't really so mad. But as soon as they got to the kitchen, Kyle asked, "Can Nelson use the phone?"

"Sure," Jason said. "Here are your ice packs."

The three of them sat at the kitchen table. Nelson crossed his legs, resting the ice pack on his ankle, and dialed his mom. While he told her what had happened, Kyle picked up the other pack. "I don't know whether to put it on my eye or my wrist."

"Which hurts more?" Jason asked.

"My wrist."

Jason reached for it. Kyle held back at first, giving him a wary look, then he hesitantly let him take his arm.

Nelson, still talking with his mom, noticed them and made a big show of turning away.

Jason ignored him, gently placing the ice pack on top of Kyle's forearm. Cradling the soft wrist reminded him of the movie theater and holding Kyle's hand. He couldn't believe he was now actually doing this in his own house with his dad in the next room. "How's that feel?" he asked.

"Uh, fine," Kyle said, his voice quivering. Their eyes met and held for an instant before Kyle anxiously glanced away. "Do you think your dad will say anything about Nelson?"

Jason shrugged. "I don't care." He glanced toward the living room. "I wish he'd just leave." He didn't want to think about his dad right now. In spite of everything, he was enjoying the moment with Kyle. He carefully adjusted the ice pack on Kyle's wrist and thought about what he wanted to say next. "Listen." He cleared his throat. "I'm sorry about, uh, you know, the cafeteria."

Kyle gave him a hard look and then relaxed. "I guess I'm sorry too. That I called you a creep."

"No, you were right. I'm pretty screwed up."

"Well, you were brave this afternoon. Nelson and I would be in a lot worse shape if you hadn't come along."

Jason shrugged off the praise. "I never liked Jack Ransom anyway. I think what you did with your locker—now *that* took guts."

They both laughed and their eyes met again. Jason felt a familiar stirring in his heart. Given that he and Kyle had kissed the last time they were together, it was a no-brainer what might happen next.

Just then Nelson hung up the phone. He cleared his throat extremely loudly and turned back to face them. "My mom's pretty upset. She'll be here in two minutes."

Jason's cat sauntered in, tail in the air, sniffing toward Nelson. Nelson stretched his palm out, cooing softly to him.

"You must be the cat that fetches. Kyle told me about you."

Jason laughed. "That's right. Watch." He crumpled a paper napkin and tossed it across the room. Rex ran after it, batted it around the carpet, then bit into it and brought it to Nelson.

Nelson laughed. "I love it." He tossed the paper napkin again.

The cat's ears pricked up. The Espinozas were saying good-bye in the living room. Nelson turned to Jason, as if he wanted to say something. "Hey, thanks for rescuing us this afternoon. I feel like I owe you an apology."

"For what?" Jason asked.

"Well, for being such a jerk to you all this time."

Jason thought about it. "I'm the one who should apologize to you."

Nelson extended his hand across the table. "Shake?"

Without hesitation, Jason shook hands. Nelson smiled. "I hope I didn't freak your dad out too much."

Jason bit a fingernail. "He'll get over it."

A horn beeped outside. Nelson glanced out the window. "There's my mom."

Kyle helped Nelson up. "Thanks again," he told Jason.

Jason nodded, not sure what to say. He walked them outside and waved as they drove off. Once the car had disappeared down the street, he turned to face the house. Flexing his knuckles, he guardedly stepped back into the kitchen.

His mom was loading the dishwasher. His little sister stood beside her, wiping her eyes. "Hey, sleepy noggin," Jason said.

The swinging door slammed open. Jason edged back as his dad barged into the room, swaying from side to side. His gaze bore into Jason. "Why'd you bring that boy here? He looked queer."

Jason felt his pulse pumping with anticipation. "They're my friends."

"Don't bring them here again," his dad sneered. "Hear me? I don' wan' any faggots in my house."

Jason squared his shoulders. Later he would try to determine how he'd gotten the nerve for what he said next. "Well"— he took a deep breath—"you've got one."

His dad's thick eyebrows knitted up and his jaw shook. "What?"

Jason swallowed hard. There was no backing off now. Like Coach always said, the best defense was a good offense. "You heard me."

His dad swaggered toward him, growling. "You disgusting . . ." His fists slammed against Jason's chest.

Jason stumbled back against the counter. "Keep your hands off me!"

His mom shoved her arms between them. "Stop it, he doesn't mean it," she told Jason. "He's been drinking."

His dad pushed her aside. "Stay out of this."

Jason's head burned with rage. "Leave her alone!" He reached out to help his mom.

"Oh, yeah?" his dad bellowed. "Big man! Just because your faggot coach gets you into some school . . ." He shoved Jason.

Jason could barely control his anger. "Stop it! I'm not afraid of you anymore." He clenched his fists but kept them down.

His dad stared at him, rocking from side to side. "Yeah? Wha' you gonna do?" Without warning, his dad swung a fist toward him. Jason blocked the punch, but his dad came back at him with his other arm.

"Stop it!" his mom shouted. His sister grabbed his mom's dress, screaming.

Unable to restrain himself any longer, Jason jabbed his fist into his father's jaw. His dad stumbled backward against the wall, his shoulder hitting with a thud. He grabbed hold of the counter, dazed.

Jason stared at his fist, disbelieving what he'd done. He immediately glanced up, expecting to ward off a new pummeling from his father, but instead he saw a pathetic, insecure man gaping back at him.

In that image, all the events of the past few months connected for Jason: going to the Rainbow Youth meeting; coming out to Debra; finding the confidence to tell Kyle about Tommy. Jason had feared where the experience would lead him, not sure he'd survive. But now the culminating moment had arrived, and miraculously, he was still standing.

Across the stillness, he and his father each waited for the other to act.

Finally his dad rolled his shoulders, edging sideways. "I'm not staying here with no faggot." He slammed the back door open so hard that a cup rattled off the shelf, and staggered outside.

Jason became aware of Melissa's sobbing. Her face was buried in his mom's dress. His mom bent down, gently shushing her, and handed her over to Jason. "I can't imagine he's going to drive." She ran out the door.

Jason patted Melissa on the back. "Don't cry, Missy. It's over."

A moment later, his mom came back in from the garage. "He's gone. I can't believe he's driving." She extended her arms, and Melissa reached out for her. "Oh, sweetie." She carried Melissa into the living room.

A car approached in the street. Jason quickly glanced out the kitchen window. It was only a neighbor. He poured a glass of water and thought about what had happened—and what he'd done. He was glad he'd said what he did. At least he didn't have to carry it around anymore. He examined his fist again and felt glad he'd finally hit back.

His mom returned. "I put her to bed." She started to load the dishwasher again.

Jason helped her and asked, "What do you think he'll do when he comes back?"

She gave a weary shrug, letting the dishwasher door slam. Jason wondered if she was angry at him for causing the fight. She turned the dishwasher on. "I don't know what he'll do. Did you mean what you said to him?"

Jason assumed she meant his saying he was . . . a faggot. He nodded, ashamed.

She sat down and rubbed her forehead, studying him. "What about Debra?"

Jason sighed, unsure how to explain it all. Fortunately his mom didn't wait for an answer. "Did he ever do anything to you?"

Jason knew she meant his dad. He thought of reminding her about what happened with Tommy, but then he thought better.

She let out her breath. "Do you want to talk to someone? A psychologist?"

"I'm not crazy, Ma."

"I know you're not. It's just . . ." Her eyes became damp, and she dabbed a hand across them.

"I'm okay." He wanted to tell her about going to the youth group and about Kyle; about how he felt relieved and excited to be finally accepting himself. He put his arms around her, a little afraid she might not hug him back after everything that had transpired.

To his relief, she held him firmly.

They talked awhile, then he went to his room. He thought about how Kyle had had the guts to paint AND PROUD! on his locker; how Nelson had stood up to Jack Ransom; how Kyle and Nelson had the nerve to try and start a gay-straight club. He regretted it had taken him so long to stand up to his dad, but he was glad he finally did. Maybe some of Kyle and Nelson was rubbing off on him.

CHAPTER 20

JASON

KYLE

NELSON

Kyle fidgeted with the safety-belt buckle in the backseat of Mrs. Glassman's car, worrying what his parents would say about his swollen wrist and black eye.

Mrs. Glassman's fevered rant didn't soothe his anxiety any. "We're pressing charges, against both Jack and José. It's ridiculous they got probation last time. They should've been sent to juvenile detention."

Kyle was glad when she turned onto his street. But then he saw his dad's car in the driveway. *Please don't let him start the "choice" crud again,* he prayed. That was the last thing he needed.

He thanked Mrs. Glassman for the ride, said bye to Nelson, and carried his throbbing wrist into the house. His dad was sitting in his recliner. He stopped reading his *Sports Illustrated* and looked up.

"What happened?" He quickly stood and examined the bruised eye. "Talk about a shiner! What's wrong with your wrist?"

Kyle held it out. "I think it might be sprained."

"Come into the kitchen. Let's get some ice on it. Better get it x-rayed. How did it happen?"

Kyle hesitated at first, afraid his dad would blame Nelson and him for bringing this upon themselves. But as he told the story his dad nodded eagerly, seeming almost proud of him. He grinned as he examined Kyle's eye more closely. "I hope you got at least one good lick in."

"I think so," Kyle said, though it was all a blur now. "I guess that's how I hurt my wrist. Good thing Jason showed up. He clobbered them."

His dad gave an impressed nod and handed Kyle the ice pack. "I think he's someone you should spend more time with."

Kyle tried not to grin.

His dad called the insurance people, beaming as he told them his son had been in a fight. When he finally got off the phone, he patted Kyle on the shoulder. "Come on. We're taking you to the doctor."

Just then his mom opened the door. "Oh, my God!" She dropped her keys on the counter and leaned into Kyle's face. "What on earth?"

His dad puffed out his chest. "He got into a fight."

"You're happy about that?"

"No." He gave Kyle's neck a gentle squeeze. "But I like knowing he can defend himself."

The remark seemed to annoy his mom. "I hope you're taking him to the hospital." She examined the ice pack. "Does it hurt?" she asked Kyle. "I'll go with you."

His dad raised his hand to calm her down. "We've got it under control. Relax."

"Oh, is this some guy thing? Your son's first fight?"

His dad laughed. "Yeah. Why don't you make a victory dinner for us?"

His mom folded her arms. "I don't think this is funny."

"Mom!" Kyle pleaded. "I'm okay." He had to admit he was kind of enjoying the attention.

His dad leaned over and kissed his mom. "Honey, we'll be home before you know it. I'll call you as soon as we see the doctor. Promise."

She pouted and handed him her cell phone. "I want to hear from you within a half hour, or I'm coming after you."

The X-rays revealed only a sprain, no fracture. Nevertheless, the physician said no swimming or diving for two weeks. She wrapped the wrist in a bandage and sling, telling Kyle to keep putting ice on it. For his eye, she gave him a prescription.

Later that evening in his room, Kyle fumbled with his good hand to tape his eyeglass frames together. His mom had said she'd take him to the optician tomorrow, but he had to make do for now.

His dad knocked on the door. "How are you feeling?"

Kyle looked up from the frames. "Better. Still sore, but not as bad."

"That's good." His dad leaned over him, admiring Kyle's eye. "It's a beauty!" He started to smile but stopped himself. "Of course I don't condone it. Like your mom pointed out at dinner, the boys could've had a gun. You never know nowadays."

"I know." Kyle nodded. "But you always told me to stand up for myself."

His dad gazed down at the bandaged wrist. "Well, I'm sorry if I've been hard on you about all this—I mean, your saying you're gay."

Kyle sat up. Was his dad starting to take him seriously?

"I just don't want to see you do something that you'll regret later. I mean, are you sure about this?"

Oh, God, Kyle prayed, *please don't let him start in again.* "Dad, I told you before, it's not a choice. I can't change and I won't hide. Even if it means getting beat up or getting crank calls."

His dad rubbed his forehead and sighed. "I phoned Mueller, when you told us about the incidents at school. He told me the same thing your mother said at dinner: He thinks you're very brave. He said I should be proud to have you as a son."

Kyle thought he was hearing things. Mueller had said that? He must've been sucking up to his dad big time.

His dad cleared his throat. "I'm proud of you too, son. I'm sorry I haven't told you that more often."

"It's okay, Dad."

His dad sat down beside him. "Your mom says there's a group for parents, PFAG?"

"FLAG!" Kyle corrected. "PFLAG."

His dad nodded. "She thinks we should go." Kyle stared at him in disbelief. His dad glanced at the broken eyeglass frames. "She also mentioned you want to get contact lenses."

Kyle felt a surge of exhilaration. "Yeah?"

His dad patted him on the shoulder. "We'll see how we can budget it." He stood up to leave. "Good night, son. Get some sleep. Love you."

"Love you," Kyle said.

Contact lenses. Wow. What a day.

At school, everyone wanted to hear what had happened to him. The more people asked about the fight, the more proud Kyle felt to have survived his first scuffle. But in spite of the attention, he hoped the clash would be his last.

Nelson showed up smiling, jovially hopping on crutches for his sprained ankle. "Watch this!" He twirled a crutch in the air.

They met with the school police officer to file a report on the fight. Nelson requested pressing charges, and Kyle agreed. The officer called Jason in to hear his account.

Jason said hi but seemed kind of somber.

After hearing Jason's version, the officer sent for Jack and José, but they hadn't come to school that day. "I'll request a detention order for them." He didn't seem to like Jack and José either.

After the meeting, Kyle walked down the hall with Jason. "Is something wrong?" Kyle asked.

Jason glanced down at the floor. "After you left on Saturday, I told my dad."

Kyle immediately knew what he meant. "How did he take it?"

Jason bit into a fingernail. "We got into a fight. Two fights in one day. He tried to hit me. I hit him back." He glanced at Kyle, raising his eyebrows. "First time in my life, I hit him."

Kyle wasn't sure what to think of that. It made him a little uneasy that Jason had fought with his dad, but he couldn't really blame him. "Are you okay?" he asked.

Jason gave a shrug. "Yeah. He walked out and never came home last night. We don't know where he is."

Kyle wasn't sure how to respond to Jason, but he wanted to say something. "If you want to talk, let me know."

Jason nodded. "Thanks."

Kyle wasn't sure if it was the fight with Jack Ransom that changed his friendship with Jason, or the fact that Jason came out to his dad. But in the days that followed, Jason often stopped by Kyle's locker.

"My dad came back," he said with a grimace one afternoon. "He says as far as he's concerned, I'm not his son anymore. He didn't try to hit me, but he started throwing things. Mom had to call the police."

It scared Kyle to hear about it. "Maybe you should talk to, you know, a professional."

"I don't know. I went with my mom to Al-Anon. There's a group called Alateen. I might go to that. I wish I could leave home, but she won't let me."

Kyle sparked on a thought. "Maybe one of the counselors at the Rainbow group could help."

Jason cracked a smile. "Maybe I'll come to the school group you're starting."

Kyle couldn't tell if he was sarcastic or serious. In any case, the school board still hadn't announced its decision. Nevertheless, Kyle noticed that when Jason stopped to talk to him in the hall, he no longer glanced over his shoulder to see who was watching them. One day he even asked Kyle to come watch the school basketball game.

"Sure!" Kyle said immediately, though he didn't know with whom to go. None of his friends were into basketball. Certainly not Nelson. Then a brilliant idea dawned on him. In the middle of calculus homework that night, he asked his dad if he wanted to go.

His dad pulled the reading glasses from his nose, giving Kyle a cautious, inquisitive look—as if Kyle were one of the more complex theorems he'd ever come across. Then he broke into a huge smile. You would've thought the prodigal son had come home.

Kyle loved watching Jason play—striding across the court, shimmering in his nylon uniform. Best of all was the moment when Jason spotted him in the audience. With a tilt of his head, he gave Kyle a quick, secret, glorious smile, just between them.

Kyle couldn't help gushing the next day. "What a game! You played really great. I mean it."

"Thanks," Jason said simply. "I'm glad you came." They stopped outside Kyle's classroom. "I was thinking," Jason said. "You want to hang out this Saturday? Go see a movie or something?"

In the past, the word "Yes!" would've sprung from Kyle's mouth quicker than a leap off the diving board. But not anymore. He fidgeted with his book bag, wanting to ask, "If we get together, are you going to freak out again afterward, like the other times?" But instead he merely said, "You mean it?"

Jason took a breath. "Yeah, I mean it."

"Okay," Kyle said, stepping off the high dive.

That Saturday, Kyle got a haircut and picked up his contact lenses. He phoned Nelson, full of excitement. All afternoon he kept startling himself in the mirror—no more braces, no more glasses. For the first time in his life, he actually thought he was good-looking. He straightened his shoulders and grinned unabashedly, eager for Jason to see him.

At dinner, he could hardly contain himself. But as he hurried toward Jason's house, his anxiety returned. What if he said something stupid or did something wrong and Jason ran away again? *Please, God,* he prayed, *don't let that happen.*

As he approached Jason's house, he stepped more slowly. Something seemed out of whack. The driveway was empty. The windows were dark.

Kyle pushed the doorbell and heard it ring inside. No one answered. His heart plummeted. Jason had blown him off, he was sure of it.

He jammed his thumb against the bell one last time and

turned to leave, but something nagged him. The house felt sad and lonely somehow. Maybe he should just look around, make sure everything was okay. He cupped his hands against the little rectangle of glass on the front door. Inside he saw only darkness.

He tried the doorknob, certain the door would be locked. It wasn't. He glanced over his shoulder, drew a deep breath, and opened the door. "Hello?" he said softly. His timid voice fell flat in the dark room. "Hello?" he repeated. Not a sound. What the heck was he doing? What if Jason's father caught him?

Through the dark, he saw a dim light in the hall beyond the living room. He inched around the furniture toward it. "Hello?" he whispered again.

He crept softly down the hall, ready to run if necessary. The door to Jason's parents' room hung open. The moonlight through the window revealed closet doors gaping wide. The dresser drawers were overturned on the bed.

Kyle's heart pounded in his chest. As he continued down the hall, he saw the glow of light coming from the outline of Jason's door, slightly open. Kyle pushed it gently.

Jason sat on the bed, leaning against the headboard. His eyes were closed, his cheeks wet. Headphones from a pocket CD player blared tinny music into his ears.

Kyle attempted to make sense of the dark, empty house and Jason alone in his room crying. He nudged the door a little farther and called softly, "Jason? Jason?"

The damp eyes slowly drew open.

"Hi," Kyle ventured.

Jason raised the back of his hand, wiped his swollen eyes, and pulled the headphones off. Music surged out.

Kyle awkwardly motioned behind him. "The front door was unlocked."

Jason stared at him a moment, then cleared his throat. "Finally happened," he explained. "He left for good. All because of me. I always thought I wanted him to leave, but . . . I should never have gotten into it with him." He buried his face in his hands. "I fucked up big time."

Kyle now understood the empty driveway, the overturned dresser drawers, the sad, lonely feel of the place. "It's not your fault . . ." he started to protest, but he sensed it was better just to listen—just be there. "Where's your mom?"

Jason looked up, his brown eyes misting up again. "My aunt's."

Kyle wished he knew what to do, but he'd never seen Jason like this. He sat down on the bed beside him. "I'm really sorry."

Jason shook his head, then leaned into Kyle's shoulder.

Kyle realized there were tears on his own face now. Trembling, he reached out and cradled his arm around Jason. He felt so sad for him, quivering beneath his touch, crying softly. At the same time, it felt good to hold him, the boy he loved.

Jason looked up at Kyle. His soft, damp cheek brushed his own, and their lips touched. Kyle's body melted beneath the kiss, but his mind flooded with anxiety. This wasn't the right time.

"We better not," he said, drawing away. "You're upset. You may feel different tomorrow."

Jason stared back with a look so hurt it broke Kyle's heart.

"What about your mom?" Kyle insisted.

Jason ran a hand through his curls, as if considering. When he looked again at Kyle, his face was changed, looking calm like Kyle had never seen it. "She won't be back till late. Please, stay?"

The song from the headphones drifted beside them, dispersing Kyle's resolve. If this was what Jason wanted, he would give it to him. He might die from pain if Jason ditched him after, but he'd get through somehow. "I want to," Kyle said, and Jason's arms, strong and determined, pulled him close.

They kissed more boldly now, followed by a tug of Kyle's jacket. The cap slipped from his head, and he started to reach for it but then let it fall. His shirt came off next, momentarily cloaking him in darkness, the air cool against his bare chest.

Jason reappeared, the T-shirt tossed aside, his dark eyes intent. In between kisses Kyle fumbled to unbutton Jason's shirt. He shifted angles, propped himself up, and still couldn't get his fingers to work the buttonholes. "I'm sorry. I feel so stupid."

"Shh," Jason whispered, reaching down to undo the buttons. The shirt miraculously opened with a burst of cologne. Kyle stared in quiet awe at Jason's chest.

Jason said, "What's the matter?"

"Nothing," Kyle lied, and quivering, touched him.

He let his hands go everywhere, wanting to feel every part of Jason—tracing his face and exploring every muscle. Jason reached for the lamp, veiling them in darkness. When their mouths reunited, they kissed with an urgency from which there was no turning back.

Kyle held Jason's face in his hands, kissing him more deeply. He moved his hands down his back and felt how hard his body was. Their movements hastened as they groped and bumped. And Kyle's excitement mounted, till he feared he couldn't contain it.

"I love you, Jason. I really mean it . . . I love you."

As soon as he said it, Jason's hands slid away. Kyle wanted to die. *How stupid could I be,* he thought. *I should just shoot myself and end my misery.*

Then Jason gripped him again, with renewed passion, and in a barely audible voice he answered Kyle: "I love you back."

When Kyle awoke in the dark, it seemed almost as if it had been a dream. But he turned on the pillow and saw Jason beside him, traced by moonlight, entwined in his arm.

Kyle studied him, marveling in silence at the boy with whom he'd made love. A trickle of saliva glistened from his barely open mouth. His breath came in sleepy puffs. Kyle wanted to stay in the room with Jason forever, just as they were. The future seemed clear: help Jason with math so he wouldn't lose his scholarship, graduate together, go to Tech united, build a life, maybe adopt children, live long, and die in each other's arms, just as they were now. Of course, this assumed Jason wouldn't freak out when he woke up.

Kyle tried to think of a few comforting words to have ready. Maybe then Jason would feel okay. But before Kyle could conjure any sage phrases, Jason raised a sleepy hand to his nose. His eyes blinked open. Upon seeing Kyle, the eyes clouded for a moment, then cleared with recognition.

"You don't hate me, do you?" Kyle whispered.

Jason blinked again. "Huh?"

A car engine sounded in the driveway. "Shit!" Jason sprang up. "It's my mom!" He scrambled from beneath the covers and ran to close the door.

Kyle reached for the nightstand lamp. "I can't see anything."

The light turned on. There stood Jason, his lean, muscled body naked in front of Kyle. In that moment Kyle thought contact lenses were the greatest invention ever created. He stared breathlessly, beyond caring that Jason's mom was home, forgetting the outside world even existed.

"Come on!" Jason hopped into his underwear, tugging them on. "Get dressed!"

Mrs. Carrillo called from down the hall. "Jason?"

Kyle touched back down to Earth from Naked Jason Land, dressing speedier than he ever had in his life. Jason straightened the bedspread. Kyle jammed his shoes on, not bothering with the laces.

A knock came at the door. "Jason?"

"Your zipper," Jason whispered, and Kyle zipped it.

"Look normal," Jason ordered, opening the door cheerily. "Hi, Ma. We were just listening to music."

Mrs. Carrillo's eyes were red and puffy, as if she, too, had been crying that afternoon. Melissa lay asleep on her shoulder.

Kyle tried to ease his breathing and look natural. "Hi, Mrs. Carrillo." He wanted to say something sympathetic. "I'm sorry about what's happened."

"Thanks," she said, trying to smile, but her mouth didn't seem to cooperate. Her eyes moved between him and Jason. She shifted Melissa on her shoulder. "Don't stay up too late," she told Jason. "We have a busy day tomorrow."

After she left, Jason glanced down at his shirt. "Shit," he whispered, tucking it into his pants.

Kyle gritted his teeth. "Do you think she realized . . ."

"I don't know. You better go." He looked so worried that Kyle was sure he was going to say, "Look, sorry, it was all a mistake. Could we forget it ever happened?"

Kyle braced himself for the worst as they walked to the front door. Once there, he didn't want to say good-bye but was at a loss for what to say in its place.

Jason gave a shrug, as though he didn't know either. "Well, I better see how my mom's doing. See you at school," he whispered, and disappeared inside.

Kyle stood there a moment, wishing they had said more. He bit into his lip and could still taste the lingering salt from Jason's cheeks. The living room went dark, and the familiar sinking feeling came back—ditched once more. Kyle tried to reassure himself. Jason hadn't especially freaked out. Not yet, anyway.

He wandered home and stepped stealthily up the stairs to his room. His parents' door was ajar, the light on. Sneaking past would be impossible, so he leaned in to say hi.

His mom sat in bed, penciling a crossword, eyeglasses perched on her nose. His dad lay asleep beside her. "Did you have a nice time?" she whispered.

Kyle knew she hoped he had. She liked Jason, and he wished he could tell her, "He said he loves me back!" Instead, he shyly nodded.

"I'm glad." Then her face took on a puzzled look. "Honey, where's your cap?"

His cap. He'd left it behind. Wow. The last time he forgot his cap somewhere, he'd been a kid. He thought about that a minute. Maybe it had come time to stop wearing it.

CHAPTER 21

JASON

KYLE

NELSON

Sunday morning, Nelson bounded downstairs to the kitchen. He yanked the leash from its hook, announcing, "I'm taking Atticus for a walk."

His mom glanced up from her cup of decaf. "That's a rarity. Must've been quite a phone call."

Nelson smirked. "It was!" Jeremy had called. Not only that, he'd asked Nelson out on a real date.

Nelson ran down the block alongside Atticus, feeling elated. He just wished Jeremy weren't HIV positive. But wishing wasn't going to change that.

As he circled back home, he saw Kyle sitting on the front stoop, basking in the warm morning sunshine, his eyes blinking.

Nelson recalled Kyle's phone call the previous evening and knew what Kyle had come to tell him. "You and Jason did it, didn't you?"

"You can tell?" Kyle smiled and petted Atticus.

Nelson didn't think he'd ever fully get over wanting to be boyfriends with Kyle, but seeing him smile so genuinely, he couldn't help but feel happy for him. He sat down. "So?" He smiled coyly. "How was he?"

Kyle gave him a wallop. "Shut up."

Nelson punched him back. "Hey, you look great with your contacts."

"Thanks. My face feels so naked."

"What did Jason say about it?"

Kyle wrapped his arms around his legs and stared at the ground, in thought. "Nothing. He was kind of depressed. His dad walked out yesterday. I feel kind of guilty about how everything happened—like I took advantage of him."

"Get over it." Nelson reached over and clapped his shoulder. "You just got laid, man! You should celebrate."

"I just hope he doesn't get scared away off the face of the earth again."

"If he does," Nelson said, "we'll find him. Come on." He stood up, pulling mopey Kyle with him. "I'll make your favorite. Waffles. By the way, I'm glad you finally stopped wearing that stupid cap."

Nelson mixed the waffle batter. "I've got news for you, too. Remember Jeremy? He phoned and asked me out."

Kyle handed him the eggs. "That's great, isn't it?"

Nelson shrugged. "What if I'm not infected?" The doctor his mom had taken him to was monitoring him during weekly visits, ready to start medications the moment he tested positive. But what if he didn't test positive? Did he want to fall in love with someone who was?

"It's not like you have to sleep with him." Kyle said in a calm voice. "You can always be just friends, can't you?"

"Yeah," Nelson agreed. "Shit. He is so cute. You think I should go out with him?"

Kyle pulled plates from the cupboard. "It's up to you."

Nelson broke the eggs open. "Big fucking help you are."

"Hey, I forgot to tell you. Guess who cut my hair at the Hair Cuttery? Shea!"

The eggbeater slipped out of Nelson's hand. That was the last thing he expected to hear. "Really? How is she?"

Kyle grabbed a paper towel to wipe up the spill from the eggbeater. "She's excited. It's her first job. Did you know she broke up with Caitlin?"

"No way!" Nelson said. He remembered the messages from the week he'd been so depressed. She'd mentioned a fight with Caitlin, but he never imagined it was serious enough to break them up. He sat down, recalling how he'd hung up on her. He'd felt shitty about it then and even worse now.

"Kyle?" he asked. "Have you ever felt like I abandoned you?"

Kyle set the table. "Well, I wouldn't say you *abandoned* me. But sometimes you get angry and withdraw. I feel like you're punishing me. You don't do it a lot, but when you do, it feels pretty crappy."

Nelson scratched his forehead, feeling a little ashamed to hear Kyle saying basically the same thing as Shea. "Do you think I'm irresponsible?" he asked.

"Sometimes, but so am I."

"Kyle! When are you ever irresponsible?"

Kyle scrunched his eyebrows up, thinking. "Well, like when I forget to brush my teeth."

Oh, brother, Nelson thought.

Later that week, Nelson decided to surprise Shea at work. He needed to do something with his hair, and besides, that way she couldn't be too angry at him. He peered into the store window and watched her snip a woman's bangs. He cautiously entered, as it occurred to him he should've brought her flowers or hair gel or something. Shea spotted him immediately. He pulled his hand from his jacket, offering a wave. "Hi."

She gave him a frosty glance and kept cutting the woman's tresses. "What happened to your hair?" she asked him without expression. "You join the army?"

At least she was speaking to him. "It's a long story," he replied. He realized how much he'd missed her. "Think you can do anything with it?"

"Have a seat," she said. "I'll be done in a sec." She obviously wasn't ecstatic to see him. But she didn't seem too, too angry, either. At least that's what he told himself.

He grabbed a magazine and flipped through it, pretending not to watch her and trying to decide how to apologize.

"Shea?" he said as soon as she started shampooing his hair. "First of all, I'm sorry I hung up on you. And I'm sorry I didn't return your calls. I've thought a lot about what you said. You were right. I was irresponsible and I shouldn't have blown you off like that. Do you forgive me?"

She stopped shampooing, and her green eyes flashed him a harsh, not very forgiving look. "I forgive you . . ." She paused, as if about to add *but*.

He anxiously waited for her to continue. Instead she rinsed him off and led him over to her cutting chair. He nervously followed, bumping into a planter on the way.

Once he was in the chair, she draped him with her plastic cloth. "I'm not sure what to do with your hair."

Nelson nodded. "It looks like shit, I know." He ran a hand across it. "What about, you know, a marine cut?"

She raised an eyebrow. "*You* of all people, with a marine cut?"

"Yeah," Nelson said, forcing a laugh. "Pretty radical, huh?"

She didn't laugh. Instead she grabbed her clippers and started trimming.

He watched his hair tumble onto the drape. "Kyle told me about Caitlin. I'm sorry. Mind if I ask what happened?"

Shea snapped the clippers off. "I don't know. We went to Massachusetts over Christmas break to visit the college and meet some teachers. The school has an amazing lesbian community. Caitlin really liked it. But I felt out of place, like I'd just get in her way." She pressed a thumb and fingertip to her eyes. "It would be a big step for both of us, you know? And I'm not sure I want to move away." She turned the clippers back on.

Nelson breathed a huge sigh. "I'm sorry," he said consolingly.

"I'm okay. Besides, I like my new job." She switched the clippers off. "There, you're done."

Nelson stared at the marine cut. "That was fast." He ran his hand across the prickly hairs in back. It felt so butch.

Shea pulled the drape off him and gave it a shake. "There wasn't much to start with."

He laughed cheerily, as if she'd made a joke. She led him to the register and rang him up.

Their meeting seemed so cold compared with when she used to cut his hair at her house. "What time do you work till?" he asked, handing her his money. "I thought maybe we could hang out afterward and catch up . . . if you're not doing anything?"

She gazed over his shoulder, as if hoping a customer would come in. "Uh, actually, I have plans."

"Oh," Nelson said, disappointed. He glanced down at the scraps of hair scattered on the floor.

"Well, uh, when's your day off?" he asked.

"Look, Nelson. I do forgive you, I really do, but . . ."

There it was. Didn't he say the "but" was coming?

She sighed. "I think it's better if we move on. This has really hurt and I don't want to hang out anymore. I'm sorry, okay?" She looked away, wiping her face.

Nelson's nose started stopping up. He was starting to cry too. "Okay," he said, though he felt anything but okay.

When Nelson arrived home, the phone was ringing. He nudged Atticus out of the way and picked up the receiver, hoping it was Kyle. "Hello?"

"Nelson?" It was his father. Great, he told himself. Just what he needed. He dabbed his nose. "Yeah?"

He presumed the call was the result of his mom's insistence on telling his dad about the Brick episode. Nelson had told her it was none of his dad's business. "Besides, he won't care." But she had told the old goat anyway. Now he was calling. Maybe he did care after all.

"Your mom phoned. You really upset her. She's worried about you."

Typical, Nelson thought. His dad would never in a million years admit that *he* was worried. He'd never acknowledge that he felt anything at all.

Nelson shook a cigarette from his pack. "I know she's upset. I live with her, remember?"

"Well, then, why can't you learn to stay out of trouble? She told me about the fight."

Nelson lit up his cigarette. "We got jumped! The fight wasn't my fault."

"No," his dad said. "It's never your fault, is it?"

"Dad," Nelson said, choking up. "Stop blaming me!" He tried to swallow, but his rage wouldn't let him.

"Hold on a sec," his dad said.

Nelson puffed on his cigarette and waited, wishing he could tell his dad how he hated him, and how he needed him, and how he wished he would never call again, and how he still stupidly hoped that one day he'd come back and be a real dad. But he knew he couldn't say any of that. The thought of completely losing his dad was too much right now. Nelson hated the prick, but at least he was calling.

His dad came back on the line. "You need to start taking some responsibility."

Excuse me? Nelson thought. *Where do you get off lecturing me? As if you ever took any responsibility. Sure, you send child support, but that's it. I may be irresponsible, but it's obvious who I inherited it from.* God, he wished he could tell his dad that.

His dad blathered on, never even mentioning the HIV. His dad didn't care. His mom had wasted her breath telling him. He was probably hoping Nelson had it and would die, so he wouldn't have to deal with him anymore.

"Dad?" Nelson said, unable to tune him out any longer. "Can't you see my side of it for once? You never listen to me." His eyes grew moist. It made him furious that a call from his dad could do this to him. "As if everything's always my fault."

"Well," his dad said, "it usually is, isn't it? Why can't you just be normal, so your mom doesn't phone me all the time, worried about you?"

This is hopeless, Nelson thought, snubbing out his cigarette. He heard his dad's other line ring. "I've got to go now," his dad said. "Let your mother know I called." With that, he hung up.

Nelson listened to the dial tone, then banged the phone against the counter. "Fuck you! Fuck you! Fuck you!" The plastic cracked. He threw the receiver into its cradle. Atticus stared up at him.

KYLE JASON NELSON 221

Nelson's eyes drifted to the jumbo bag of potato chips on the counter. He unclipped the bag and started gobbling. Atticus licked his lips, begging. Nelson tossed him a chip. Only one, otherwise he'd get sick. Of course, Nelson would eat the whole bag and make himself sick. Then he'd hate himself afterward. He'd done it enough times to know that's what would happen. He was tired of it. So why did he keep doing it?

He stopped biting a chip and stared at the cracked phone receiver.

"Fuck him!" Nelson said, and closed the potato chips back up. Atticus stared up at him with pleading eyes. "No, boy," Nelson told him. "Let's go for a walk." He grabbed the leash off its hook.

Maybe his dad would never change, Nelson thought, but he could.

As his date with Jeremy approached, Nelson had more and more doubts about it. Maybe Jeremy would cancel. Of course, Nelson would be devastated if he did. After all, it was his first real date. And Jeremy was a hottie. Totally stressed, Nelson smoked one cigarette after another.

Saturday afternoon he tried on a dozen different shirts, hoping to get the right look. He showered and put on too much cologne and showered a second time to wash it off.

His mom watched him fret up and down the stairs. "How old is this boy?" she asked.

Nelson could tell she was worried. "He's nineteen, goes to college in Maryland, lives with his older brother. I don't know how old his brother is. Anything else you need to know?" Needless to say, he left out HIV status.

She gave him a motherly scowl. "Don't be sassy. Now, listen." She shifted uneasily. "I don't encourage you to have sex, but you do have condoms, right?"

"Mom!" How intrusive could you get? Nevertheless, he patted his pocket. "Yes."

She didn't seem very relieved. "And be home by midnight. Don't look at me that way. I mean it."

In his romantic daydreams, Nelson never imagined a date would be so nerve-racking. Now he knew why Kyle acted like such a spaz around Jason. It seemed like anything he could possibly do wrong, he did. He tripped on the sidewalk. He accidentally called him "Germy." His palms sweated like Niagara Falls. At dinner the chopsticks slipped from his fingers. He knocked over his water glass. And it didn't help that he refrained from smoking, since Jeremy didn't smoke. But in spite of it all, Jeremy complimented his new haircut, laughed at his jokes, and didn't ditch him.

When they left the movie, to Nelson's amazement, Jeremy was still smiling. "It's still early. You want to come over to my place?"

Nelson's stomach tightened. Should he? It might lead to you-know-what. But not necessarily. Maybe they'd simply talk, listen to music, just be friends. Sure, and maybe Jeremy would turn out to be Judy Garland, not really dead, but in boy drag. *Definitely say no,* Nelson told himself. *Make up some excuse. Say that you're asthmatic and have to go to your iron lung.* But he said: "Yes."

At the apartment, Jeremy told Nelson to make himself at home. "My brother's gone for the weekend."

That's mighty convenient, Nelson thought.

"What would you like to drink?" Jeremy asked.

"Got any beer?" Nelson hoped it might calm his nerves.

"ID, please?" Jeremy laughed. "We've got Coke and 7 Up."

Nelson forced a chuckle. "Coke, I guess."

Jeremy went to the kitchen. Nelson fidgeted with his earrings, trying to stay calm. He looked around the living room. On the wall were an Honor Society certificate, a bunch of Boy Scouts awards, and a track-team photo of Jeremy that revealed awesome legs.

When Jeremy returned, they sat on the couch, side by side. Nelson began to worry. The heat from Jeremy was having a noteworthy effect on him. He should never have come over. Why was he even on a date with a guy he knew was HIV positive? He should leave. Now. In record speed he gulped his drink.

"Nervous?" Jeremy asked.

"No," Nelson said, wiping his palm on his pant leg. "Well, maybe a little."

Jeremy smiled and slipped his soft hand into Nelson's. It embarrassed Nelson how clammy his own hand must feel, but he couldn't help it. He awkwardly smiled back.

Suddenly they were kissing. It no longer mattered that Jeremy was HIV positive—only that he was warm and sweet. Jeremy caressed his cheek, and Nelson moved his hand to Jeremy's lap.

Jeremy pulled away. "Whoa, slow down. There's no need to rush, is there?"

Nelson drew away, taken aback. Rush? Compared with Blake and Brick, he was already late. Besides, all the indecision about sex with an HIV-positive guy was making him crazy. Might as well get it over with.

Jeremy looked into his eyes. "We don't have to do it tonight, do we? I mean, I don't want it to be just sex. I hope we're going to have more than just one date."

Nelson bit into his lip, trying to make sense of the events. Why didn't Jeremy want to have sex? Couldn't they have sex and still have more than one date?

Jeremy sighed. He once again took Nelson's hand between his own. "Look, I'm sorry. It's just . . . I don't want to rush. That's how I got in this HIV mess in the first place."

Nelson wondered, could it be that Jeremy had his own anxiety about having sex with someone who might be HIV negative?

He wished that just once he could get laid without some complication. But that obviously wasn't going to happen—not that night, possibly not ever. Maybe sex was never simple, and he needed to stop expecting it to be. He pondered that a minute.

"What are you thinking?" Jeremy asked.

Nelson shook his head and smiled. "Can we at least go back to kissing?"

Jeremy smiled. "Yeah." Then he leaned over and kissed Nelson, long and tenderly. When he announced they'd better go, Nelson glanced at the clock and was stunned to discover an hour had gone by. He never knew kissing could be so much fun.

As Jeremy drove him back home, Nelson clutched his fingers anxiously. He'd enjoyed the evening a lot, a whole lot.

Jeremy parked the car in front of Nelson's. Nelson waited, fearing that Jeremy would now announce he'd had a rotten time and never wanted to see him again.

But after a few seconds that seemed like centuries, Jeremy said, "I had a real nice time."

"Yeah, but . . ."

"No buts. I'd like to do it again." He leaned across the seat and kissed him.

Nelson wished they could keep kissing all night. But the dashboard clock read 12:00, and the last thing he wanted was for his mom to blame Jeremy. "I'd like to do it again too," he said, kissing Jeremy one last time.

Then, with Herculean effort, he forced himself from the car.

On Monday, in MacTraugh's art class, Nelson told Kyle everything about the date. "The weird part is that even though we didn't have sex, I really like him. Now I understand why girls hold out when they're going with guys. It makes you want the other person even more."

He glanced toward the door and nudged Kyle.

Mueller had appeared, motioning for MacTraugh. He whispered to her, gesturing toward Nelson and Kyle. MacTraugh waved them forward. "Nelson? Kyle? Come here, please."

As they crossed the room, other students hooted and laughed. Nelson ignored them and walked out to the hall with Kyle. Mueller greeted them with a defeated nod. "Well, the school board approved your group."

MacTraugh beamed. "Unanimously!"

Nelson felt his heart soar. Mueller tried his best to dampen the mood. "But with conditions. I want to meet with the three of you this afternoon in my office. Set some ground rules. Understood?"

Nelson's excitement couldn't be quelled. "You're fabulous, sir!"

Mueller stepped backward, like he was terrified Nelson might kiss him, and strutted away.

MacTraugh, Kyle, and Nelson slapped high fives. They'd done it. Their school would have a GSA.

The following day, they began putting up flyers for the group. Kyle asked Nelson, "Do you think anyone will show up?"

Nelson knew what he really wondered: Would Jason?

CHAPTER 22

JASON

KYLE

NELSON

When Jason awoke the morning after making love with Kyle, he tried to put in order all that had transpired the past few days. For years he'd lived in dread of what would happen if he ever again touched another guy. Surely his dad would kill him. Or the police would whisk him to juvenile jail. Yet the moment had arrived, and he wasn't dead or in prison, but alive and free.

As sunshine streamed through the bedroom windows, his mind raced with thoughts. With his dad gone, he no longer feared losing his scholarship. He could always stay home and go to college. That was a relief. But what about Kyle and him? What if people at school found out? He definitely wasn't going to that stupid GSA group.

He climbed into the shower, questions swirling in his head. Were he and Kyle now "boyfriends"? What did that mean? Did Kyle even want to be boyfriends? Why was he even thinking about all this? All they'd done was have sex—that's all, just sex.

He turned the faucet off and vigorously rubbed his body with the towel, his thoughts pursuing him. What about Kyle telling him he loved him, and him saying it back? Wasn't that more than just sex? Well, yeah, but he didn't honestly mean it, or did he? He nearly tripped as he stepped out of the tub.

He wiped a circle of condensation from the mirror and attempted to shave but kept nicking himself. He recalled how everything had been so much simpler with Debra, at least at the beginning. When they first had sex, it was understood they were boyfriend and girlfriend—the rules were pretty much set. But with Kyle it was so different, so new.

Maybe he was in love with Kyle. Would that be such a bad thing? The idea made him want to go for a long, exhausting run. But that was crazy. He'd just taken a shower.

The following afternoon, he was snacking on a sandwich when the doorbell rang. Jason licked the mustard from his fingers and stepped into the living room, peering out the window. On the front step, patting one hand with the other, stood Debra.

Jason's pulse quickened. What was she doing here? It had been months since they last spoke—since she told him she hated him. He ran a hand through his hair and opened the door. Her clear blue eyes gleamed up at him. "Hi," she said.

Jason hesitated. She didn't seem angry.

"Can I come in?" she asked.

"Yeah. Sure. Sorry." He pulled the door open. "Come in."

She stepped inside and turned to face him, looking some-what anxious. "I was sorry to hear your dad moved out. I wanted to see if you're okay."

Jason nodded, still a little wary. "I'm all right."

She smiled, as if relieved. "Mind if I sit down?"

"Sure. Course." He gestured to the armchair. He sat on the sofa. "I just didn't expect . . . I mean, I'm glad you came over. So, how's everything with you?"

"I'm better. Jason, this has hurt a lot. What happened between us."

She sounded angry, after all. He looked down at the carpet, feeling bad.

She must've noticed. "Look, I'm not here to yell at you. What I want to say is, the reason this has all hurt so much is because I really love you."

Jason stared at his sneakers, not sure what she meant by that. Did she want to try to get back together? Is that what she was saying?

"What I mean is I'd like to be friends, Jason. It hurts too much to stay angry at you."

He brought his gaze up to her. Was she serious? Did she really want to be friends after all they'd been through? "Are you sure? You know I didn't mean to lie to you. I just hadn't figured things out."

Debra smoothed her hand across her slacks. "I think I understand that. At least I'm starting to."

Jason thought about it. "I don't think this is going to be easy. A lot has happened since we broke up." He wasn't ready to tell her about Kyle, but he knew he'd have to eventually, and he wanted to be sure she was prepared for it.

She nodded. "I know."

She's amazing, Jason thought. How could he not forgive her? She'd been his first love. He'd always treasure that. "I'd like to be friends too." His voice quavered.

She reached her hand out to him, and his eyes grew moist. Then he was hugging her and saying, "I've missed you too. I'm really sorry."

That evening, while doing homework, Jason searched his odds-and-ends drawer for an eraser. Instead he found the button Nelson had given him—NOBODY KNOWS I'M GAY.

He turned it over in his fingers, remembering how he'd wanted to cream Nelson that day.

Sitting down on his bed, Jason thought about how much had changed since then . . . about Kyle—and how he'd always been there to listen; how he'd held him while he cried the night his father left; what it felt like to wake in his arms after making love. . . . Maybe he and Kyle could be boyfriends after all. The thought startled him.

He wished Kyle were there now. He wished there were a second Kyle—a clone of whom he could ask advice about Kyle. Crazy.

At school the next morning, Jason passed the bulletin board and saw a notice announcing the Gay-Straight Alliance. Across the bottom of the flyer someone had scrawled, FREE HEAD. People were so immature, he thought.

Amid the clamor of students in the hall, he spotted Nelson coming toward him. Jason still felt nervous about being seen talking to him in public, but he could no longer ignore him. "Wha's up?" he said.

Nelson ripped down the GSA flyer. "I'm sorry your dad left. I feel kind of responsible."

"Don't," Jason said. "It was bound to happen sooner or later."

Nelson stapled a clean flyer on the bulletin board.

"You think anyone will show up?" Jason asked. "If they do, they'll get shit from everyone."

Nelson shrugged. "So?"

"Well"—Jason hooked his thumb through a belt loop—"I'm certainly not going."

Nelson gave him a quizzical look. "I've got to put the rest of the flyers up. See you later."

"Yeah, take it easy." Jason watched him disappear down the hall, then turned to see some stupid little freshman writing GET NAKED on the new flyer Nelson had stapled up.

"Hey." Jason pushed him away. "What are you doing?"

The freshman stumbled and glowered back. "What do you care?" He stepped away, muttering under his breath, "Faggot."

Jason grabbed the boy by the shoulder and spun him around. "What did you say?"

The freshman stared up at him, his lip quivering. "Nothing, I didn't say anything."

The students nearby turned to stare. Jason calmed down and released the twerp. The first bell rang, clearing the hallway, leaving Jason standing alone.

In homeroom, the teacher glanced at each desk and marked attendance. Over the loudspeaker, Mueller's voice droned out the usual list of announcements. Classmates finished homework and spoke in low, sleepy tones.

Thoughts collided in Jason's head about the flyer for the meeting, and Kyle, and the freshman calling him a faggot.

Abruptly the room became quiet. Mueller was saying something about the Gay-Straight Alliance. The homeroom teacher stared up at the loudspeaker, scratching her head. "The meeting," Mueller said, "will be held during lunch in the counselors' conference room."

One of the class clowns flailed his wrist in the air and lisped: "That soundth just fabulouth!" Everybody laughed.

Jason slinked down in his seat, thinking, *You'd have to be a fool to go to that meeting.*

The boy stood and pranced between the desks with his hands

on his hips. "I know where I'm going to thpend my lunch!"

It was too much for Jason. "Hey!" He sprang up. "Shut your face!"

Abruptly the laughing ceased, and everyone turned silent. The boy stopped prancing and returned to his seat. All eyes stared at Jason. He felt embarrassed but not sorry. He was sick of gay jokes.

At lunch he started toward the team table, then changed his mind. He would hang out in the hall for a minute, just to see who showed up for the meeting.

Outside the main offices, a group of boys watched. Even though Jack and José were no longer at school, some of their buddies had come forward in their place, obviously trying to figure out who was going to the meeting.

Corey walked up behind Jason. "Yo, what are you doing out here?"

Jason wasn't sure whether to lie or be honest. "I . . . I . . . ."

Corey glanced down the hall. "You thinking of going to that meeting?" he whispered. "What if Tech finds out? What do you think their coach would say?"

Corey's advice confused Jason, but only for a moment. "It's a gay *and* straight meeting," he said defensively. "Besides, it's nobody's business but mine."

"Whoa!" Corey motioned him to calm down. "I didn't say it wasn't."

Two basketball teammates came by, calling them into the cafeteria. Corey clapped Jason on the arm. "Hey, do what you need to do, man." He walked into the lunchroom.

Jason bit off a fingernail, uncertain. Through the cafeteria doors, he saw Nelson carrying his tray. Someone yelled, "Fucking queer," and a wad of crumpled paper hit Nelson on the shoulder. He bent over and threw it back at the boy who had pitched it. The boy sprang up, protesting, "Hey, I didn't do it."

Nelson walked away from him, approaching Jason. "This is it," he said. "Wish us luck."

"Yeah," Jason said. "Good luck."

He watched Nelson walk down the hall toward the main office. The group of boys outside the office door jeered him: "Hey, faggot!" "Homo!" "Queer!"

Jason started after Nelson, not with any intention of going to the meeting—just to help Nelson if the boys jumped him. But Mueller charged out of the office, yelling at the boys and spreading his arms, stopping any scuffle.

One boy noticed Jason and whispered something to another boy. Oh, shit, Jason thought. By fifth period it would be all over school.

He hesitated a moment, then continued past the boys, into the office, his heart beating wildly. He could always say he had an appointment with his counselor. But he wouldn't. He wouldn't lie. Not anymore.

He walked down the corridor to the counselors' conference room. Through the glass window he saw Kyle moving extra chairs over to the table. Some girls sat on one side, MacTraugh and a group of boys on the other. Quite a crowd of people— more than Jason had expected.

His hand hesitated on the doorknob. He could still turn around.

Then Kyle looked up at him and smiled. He motioned to the chair beside him.

Jason took a deep breath, opened the door, and stepped inside.

FOR MORE
INFORMATION
ABOUT . . .

ORGANIZING A PEER GROUP

GLSEN (Gay, Lesbian and Straight Education Network)

121 West 27th Street, Suite 804

New York, NY 10001-6207

Phone: (212) 727-0135

Fax: (212) 727-0245

www.glsen.org (Please visit this Web site to find the chapter in your region.)

The Gay, Lesbian and Straight Education Network strives to ensure that each member of every school community is valued and respected regardless of sexual orientation or gender identity/expression. GLSEN believes that such an atmosphere engenders a positive sense of self, which is the basis of educational achievement and personal growth. Since homophobia and heterosexism undermine a healthy school climate, we work to educate teachers, students, and the public at large about the damaging effects these forces have on youth and adults alike. GLSEN recognizes that forces such as racism and sexism have similarly adverse impacts on communities, and we support schools in seeking to redress all such inequities. GLSEN seeks to develop school climates where difference is valued for the positive contribution it makes in creating a more vibrant and diverse community. We welcome as members any and all individuals, regardless of sexual orientation, gender identity/expression, or occupation, who are committed to seeing this philosophy realized in K-12 schools.

GLSEN combats the harassment and discrimination leveled against students and school personnel. GLSEN creates learning environments that affirm the inherent dignity of all students, and, in so doing, teaches them to respect and accept all of their classmates—regardless of sexual orientation and gender identity/expression. GLSEN believes that the key to ending anti-gay prejudice and hate-motivated violence is education. And it's for this reason that GLSEN brings together students, educators, families, and other community members—of any sexual orientation or gender identity/expression—to reform America's educational system.

GLSEN's student organizing project provides support and resources to youth in even the most isolated of places, supporting students as they form and lead gay-straight alliances—helping them to change their own school environments from the inside out. A Gay-Straight Alliance (GSA) is a school-based, student-led, noncurricular club organized to end anti-gay bias and homophobia in schools and create positive change by making schools welcoming, supportive, and safe places for all students, regardless of sexual orientation or gender identity. GSAs help eliminate anti-gay bias, discrimination, harassment, and violence by educating school communities about homophobia and the lives of youth, and supporting lesbian, gay, bisexual, and transgender (LGBT) students and their heterosexual allies.

VIOLENCE AND HATE CRIMES AGAINST GAYS AND LESBIANS

The New York City Gay & Lesbian Anti-Violence Project and the
National Coalition of Anti-Violence Projects
240 West 35th Street, Suite 200
New York, NY 10001
Phone: (212) 714-1184
Fax: (212) 714-2627
Bilingual hotline based in the New York area: (212) 714-1141
www.avp.org (Please visit this Web site to find a branch and phone
contact for your region.)

The New York City Gay & Lesbian Anti-Violence Project (AVP) is the
nation's largest crime-victim service agency for the lesbian, gay, transgender, bisexual, and HIV-affected communities. For twenty years,
AVP has provided counseling and advocacy for thousands of victims of
bias-motivated violence, domestic violence, sexual assault, HIV-
related violence, and police misconduct. AVP educates the public
about violence against or within our communities and works to
reform public policies impacting all lesbian, gay, transgender, bisexual, and HIV-affected people. The NCAVP is the nationwide network
of anti-violence projects of which the New York's AVP is a part.

Human Rights Campaign
919 18th Street, NW, Suite 800
Washington, D.C. 20006
Phone: (202) 628-4160
Fax: (202) 347-5323
www.hrc.org

As America's largest gay and lesbian organization, the Human Rights Campaign provides a national voice on gay and lesbian issues. The Human Rights Campaign effectively lobbies Congress, mobilizes grassroots action in diverse communities, invests strategically to elect a fair-minded Congress, and increases public understanding through innovative education and communication strategies.

HRC is a bipartisan organization that works to advance equality based on sexual orientation and gender expression and identity, to ensure that gay, lesbian, bisexual, and transgender Americans can be open, honest, and safe at home, at work, and in the community.

ISSUES WITH PARENTS

PFLAG: Parents, Families and Friends of Lesbians and Gays

1726 M. Street, NW, Suite 400

Washington, DC 20036

Phone: (202) 467-8180

Fax: (202) 467-8194

www.pflag.org (Please visit this Web site to find the chapter in your region.)

Parents, Families and Friends of Lesbians and Gays promotes the health and well-being of gay, lesbian, bisexual, and transgendered persons and their families and friends through support, to cope with an adverse society; education, to enlighten an ill-informed public; and advocacy, to end discrimination and to secure equal civil rights. Parents, Families and Friends of Lesbians and Gays provides opportunity for dialogue about sexual orientation and gender identity, and acts to create a society that is healthy and respectful of human diversity. PFLAG is a national nonprofit organization with a membership of over 80,000 households and more than 440 affiliates worldwide. This vast grassroots network is developed, resourced, and serviced by the PFLAG national office, located in Washington, D.C., the national Board of Directors, and the Regional Directors' Council. The parents, families, and friends of lesbian, gay, bisexual, and transgendered persons celebrate diversity and envision a society that embraces everyone, including those of diverse sexual orientations and gender identities. Only with respect, dignity, and equality for all will we reach our full potential as human beings, individually and collectively. PFLAG welcomes the participation and support of all who share in, and hope to realize, this vision.

HIV (HUMAN IMMUNODEFICIENCY VIRUS) AND AIDS (ACQUIRED IMMUNE DEFICIENCY SYNDROME)

Centers for Disease Control

National AIDS Hotline: 1-800-342-2437

www.cdc.gov/hiv/hivinfo/nah.htm

The Centers for Disease Control and Prevention (CDC) is recognized as the lead federal agency for protecting the health and safety of people at home and abroad, providing credible information to enhance health decisions, and promoting health through strong partnerships. CDC serves as the national focus for developing and applying disease prevention and control, environmental health, and health promotion and education activities designed to improve the health of the people of the United States.

Behavioral science has shown that a balance of prevention messages is important for young people. Total abstinence from sexual activity is the only sure way to prevent sexual transmission of HIV infection. Despite all efforts, some young people may still engage in sexual intercourse that puts them at risk for HIV and other STDs. For these individuals, the correct and consistent use of latex condoms has been shown to be highly effective in preventing the transmission of HIV and other STDs. Data clearly show that many young people are sexually active and that they are placing themselves and their partners at risk for infection with HIV and other STDs. These young people must be provided with the skills and support they need to protect themselves.

TEEN SEXUALITY

Advocates for Youth
1025 Vermont Avenue, NW, Suite 200
Washington, DC 20005
Phone: (202) 347-5700
Fax: (202) 347-2263
www.advocatesforyouth.org

There is much to do to improve adolescent reproductive and sexual health in the United States and in the developing world. Recent declines in teenage pregnancy and childbearing are threatened by growing political battles over adolescent sexuality. Societal confusion over sex and a growing adult cynicism about youth culture further fuel the debate. To date, conservative forces have successfully censored sexuality education in over one-third of American schools, confidential access to contraception is under attack in the United States and routinely withheld from adolescents in the developing world, and adolescent access to abortion is almost a thing of the past. Concurrently, poverty, homophobia, and racism continue to confound the battle against HIV, leaving gay, lesbian, bisexual, and transgender (GLBT) youth, youth of color, and young people in the developing world particularly vulnerable to infection.

Advocates envisions a time when there is societal consensus that sexuality is a normal, positive, and healthy aspect of being human, of being a teen, of being alive. Advocates for Youth believes that a shift in the cultural environment in which adolescents live—from one that distrusts young people and their sexuality to one that embraces youth as partners and recognizes adolescent sexual development as normal and healthy—will yield significant public health outcomes for youth in the United States and in the developing world. To ultimately have the largest impact on improving adolescent sexual health, Advocates believes its role is to boldly advocate for changes in the environment that will improve the delivery of adolescent sexual health information and services.

GAY AND LESBIAN TEEN SUICIDES

The Trevor Helpline: 1-800-850-8078 and 1-866-488-7386

www.thetrevorproject.org

The Trevor Helpline is a national 24-hour toll-free suicide prevention hotline aimed at gay or questioning youth. The Trevor Helpline is geared toward helping those in crisis, or anyone wanting information on how to help someone in crisis. All calls are handled by trained counselors and are free and confidential.

The Trevor Helpline was established by the Trevor Project in August 1998 to coincide with the HBO airing of *Trevor*, hosted by Ellen DeGeneres. *Trevor* is the award-winning short film about a thirteen-year-old boy named Trevor who, when rejected by friends and peers as he begins to come to terms with his sexuality, makes an unsuccessful attempt at suicide.

When *Trevor* was scheduled to air on HBO, the film's creators began to realize that some of the program's teen viewers might be facing the same kind of crisis as Trevor, and they began to search for a support line to help them. When they discovered that no national twenty-four-hour toll-free suicide hotline existed that was geared toward gay youth, they decided to establish one and began the search for funding.

GAY AND LESBIAN TEEN SERVICES ON THE INTERNET

Youth Guardian Services, Inc.
101 E. State Street
Ithaca, NY 14850
Phone: 1-877-270-5152
Fax: (703) 783-0525
www.youth-guard.org

Youth Guardian Services is a youth-run, nonprofit organization that provides support services on the Internet to gay, lesbian, bisexual, transgendered, questioning, and straight supportive youth. At this time the organization operates solely on private donations from individuals.

The YOUTH e-mail lists are a group of three e-mail mailing lists separated by age groups (13-17, 17-21, 21-25). The goal of these lists is to provide gay, lesbian, bisexual, transgendered, and questioning youth an open forum to communicate with other youth. The content ranges from support topics in times of crisis to "chit-chat" and small talk. Each list is operated by a volunteer staff made up of members who are in the same age group as the list subscribers.

The newest addition to the YOUTH Lists is the STR8 List for straight and questioning youth aged twenty-five or younger who have friends or family members who are gay, lesbian, bisexual, transgendered, or questioning. The list provides a safe space and supportive environment to talk with other straight youth in similar situations about the unique issues facing straight youth who have friends or family members who are gay, lesbian, bisexual, transgendered, or questioning.

YOUTH ADVOCACY

National Youth Advocacy Coalition

1638 R Street, NW, Suite 300

Washington, DC 20009

Phone (202) 319-7596

Toll-Free (800) 541-6922

TTY (202) 319-9513

Fax (202) 319-7365

www.nyacyouth.org

The National Youth Advocacy Coalition (NYAC) is a social justice organization that advocates for and with young people who are lesbian, gay, bisexual, transgender, or questioning (LGBTQ) in an effort to end discrimination against these youth and to ensure their physical and emotional well being.

NYAC strongly believes that to be effective in creating change at the national level, focused, grassroots advocacy at the local level is critical. As a result, NYAC operates with a five region infrastructure through which member agencies can work on a local level to affect national policy.

Annually, with the support of NYAC, regional conferences provide the opportunity to hundreds of youth and adult allies in that region to share expertise, exchange resources, build support networks and shape policy in support of LGBTQ youth. Additionally, NYAC's Annual Summit, held each spring in Washington, DC, brings together more than 500 youth and adult allies.

Youth Activism

National Gay and Lesbian Task Force
1325 Massachusetts Avenue, NW, Suite 600
Washington, DC 20005
Phone: (202) 393-5177
Fax: (202) 393-2241
TTY: (202) 393-2284
www.ngltf.org

The National Gay and Lesbian Task Force (NGLTF) is the national progressive organization working for the civil rights of gay, lesbian, bisexual and transgender people, with the vision and commitment to building a powerful political movement.

GLBTQ youth are part of that movement. NGLTF operates four programs to nurture and support youth activism: Youth Leadership Development Training; Youth Organizing Intensive at Creating Change; Creating Change Youth Scholarship program; and Youth and Campus Field Organizing.

NGLTF views this work as a critical component to realizing its mission of advancing equality and civil rights of GLBT persons and raising public awareness about issues that affect GLBT communities. NGLTF recognizes the necessity to provide institutional support to young people, and is committed to supporting the needs of GLBTQ youth and youth activists.

Take a look at what's to come for
Kyle, Nelson, and Jason in

RAINBOW HIGH

Monday after school, Kyle offered to go with Nelson to his HIV test, hoping it would help calm his own worries. But as they pulled into the parking lot, a new unease came over Kyle. "You think I should get tested, too?"

He had, after all, made love with Jason. And Jason had made love with Debra.

"It depends," Nelson said. "What did you and Jason do together?"

Kyle shifted in his seat. Such detail made him uncomfortable, even if he and Nelson were best friends. "Well . . . we didn't exactly . . . you know . . . S or F."

Nelson's eyebrows arched. "S or F? Come on, Kyle, be a big boy. You're allowed to use grown-up words." He flicked his cigarette out the window. "Why don't you ask the doctor what he thinks?"

In the reception room, Kyle thought back to his night with Jason. They hadn't done anything truly unsafe—like Nelson had—but he'd read so many conflicting things about what really was safe. The more he thought back on it, the more he squirmed in his chair. When Nelson's name finally got called, Kyle whispered, "I want to go in with you."

Nelson's physician, Dr. Choudhury, was a wrinkly South Asian guy with glasses perched on the tip of his nose. "That's very interesting hair," he told Nelson in a high, cheery voice.

After studying Nelson's folder the doctor explained the test procedure. He placed a specially treated pad with a handle between Nelson's cheek and gum. "Now we leave it for two minutes."

While Nelson held the swab in his mouth, the doctor monitored the time on his watch.

Kyle wiped the sweat from his palms, debating whether to

speak up. The procedure looked painless. It wouldn't hurt to at least ask about it. He cleared his throat. "Um, Doctor? I was wondering? If I should get tested too?"

The doctor tilted his head back, squinting through his bifocals. "You too? Don't you boys know to use precautions?"

Kyle squirmed in his seat, wishing he'd kept his mouth shut.

"Tell me," Dr. Choudhury asked impatiently. "Did you engage in unprotected penetration?"

Kyle cringed, sinking into his chair. "Um, no."

"Any exchange of body fluids? Blood? Semen? Pre-ejaculatory secretions? Breast milk?"

Kyle slid further down in his seat. "Um, no, not really."

The doctor threw his hands up in exasperation. "If you want, I can test you. But my suggestion to both of you"—he pulled the handle of the pad from the inside of Nelson's cheek and sealed the swab into a plastic tube—"is to wait till you're older before you start fooling around with this sex business."

Kyle decided there wasn't much point in being tested now, though he should definitely ask Jason: Had he and Debra used condoms? Or was she on the pill?

But how could he ask Jason that?

Kyle's parents' cars were already in the driveway when he arrived home. He hadn't told his mom or dad he was taking Nelson to get tested. No sir. No way. When Kyle came out to them, one of their biggest concerns had been his health. Now that they'd calmed down some, he didn't want them getting hyper again.

Kyle kicked his shoes off in the foyer and followed his parents' voices to the kitchen. "Did Jason call?"

His dad glanced up from the tomatoes he was slicing. A

goofy smile lit up his face. "The future college student is home!" he sang out.

Kyle ignored his dad's goofiness, turning to his mom. "Did Jason call?"

"No, honey." She smiled, lifting a head of lettuce from the sink. "But you got a letter from Tech." She dried her hands on a washcloth and handed him an envelope.

At the sight of the letter, Kyle's heart jumped. The return address was from the admissions office. This was it—his acceptance to Tech; the start of his college life with Jason—unless . . .

"Come on," his dad encouraged him. "Open it."

"Honey," his mom chimed in. "With your grades I'm sure you got accepted. Go ahead."

Kyle turned the envelope over, his hand trembling as he ran his finger beneath the flap. Slowly, he unfolded the letter and quickly scanned the page. Halfway down, he looked up again.

His mom and dad were staring at him, their faces crinkled with worry and hope.

"I got accepted!" Kyle gasped.

"Honey, that's wonderful!" His mom wrapped her arms around him.

"That's great news, Son." His dad patted him on the back. "You should be hearing from Princeton next."

Kyle bristled. "Can't I just enjoy the fact that I was accepted to Tech?"

"Of course," his dad agreed. "Didn't I say it was great news?"

Yeah, but Kyle knew where his dad really wanted him to go— his *alma mater*.

Kyle gave a sigh, turning to his mom. "Can Jason come over?" Kyle wanted to share the news with him in person.

"All right," she said, "but—"

Before she could finish, Kyle was racing up the stairs. Grabbing the cordless phone, he speed-dialed Jason. "I've got a surprise," he said as soon as Jason answered. "Can you come over?"

"Um, I don't think so. My mom's going to a meeting, and I've got to watch Missy. What is it? Can you bring it here, or is it, like an elephant or something? Is it a car? Did you get us a car?"

Kyle smiled to himself, stretching out across the bed. Had Jason really said *us*? "It's better than a car," Kyle told him.

"Hmm," Jason said. "Better than a car? Can you give me a hint?"

"No hints," Kyle said as the phone's call-waiting beeped. "I gotta go. I'll be over soon as I eat, okay? Laters!" He pushed the flash key. "Hello?"

"Woo-hoo!" Nelson shouted, before announcing news of his own acceptance to Tech.

"Awesome!" Kyle leapt off the bed. Not only would he be going to college with Jason, but also Nelson.

"You got yours, too?" Nelson asked. "Of course *you* got accepted, but can you believe they accepted *moi*? This is going to be so cool!"

Nelson's dog started barking. "Uh-oh, Mom's home. She'll probably have a heart attack when I tell her I actually got—" His fingers snapped in the background. "Ac-cep-ted. Woo-hoo!" He hung up.

Eager to get to Jason's, Kyle wolfed down dinner, but slowed down for dessert. His mom had bought an awesome chocolate-raspberry cake. "Can I take a piece to Jason?"

"All right," his mom said, cutting a slice. "But remember it's a school night. Don't stay too—"

"And one for his sister?" Kyle asked before his mom could put the knife down. She cut another wedge.

"And one for his mom?" Kyle added. "And another piece for me later?"

"Why don't you just take the whole cake?" His dad laughed.

"Okay," Kyle said, pretending his dad was serious.

Melissa, Jason's six-year-old sister, answered the Carrillos' door. Behind her, the TV blared. Dolls and toys lay scattered before it. She grabbed Kyle's hand, pulling him in, her eyes opening wide at the box he carried. "What's that?"

"Mmm . . ." Kyle rubbed a circle on his stomach. "Cake!"

Jason strode in, wearing jeans and a flannel shirt that hung wide over his broad shoulders. A toothbrush handle protruded from his mouth, as he vigorously brushed up and down, causing his left cheek to bulge and jiggle.

At the sight of him, Kyle fell in love all over again.

"Wha's up?" Jason said, popping the brush out. A perfect circle of paste ringed his mouth.

"I like your green lipstick," Kyle said, kidding.

Jason looked in the wall mirror. "Whoa!" He jogged back toward the bathroom.

With Melissa's help, Kyle dished out cake and set the plates on the kitchen table.

"Oh, wow." Jason sauntered in. "You were right. This is better than a car."

"That's not the surprise," Kyle said, handing Jason the Tech letter. "This is."

Jason scanned the page, his lips moving to the words: ". . . pleased to inform you . . . you've been accepted for admission—"

He glanced up at Kyle, high-fiving him. "Awesome! Congratulations, man."

"Can I take my cake to watch TV?" Melissa asked.

"Sure. Wait. You want some milk?" Jason poured them each a cold glass. "Careful you don't spill."

While Kyle sat down, Jason held the door for Melissa, then he returned to Kyle. "Of course, did you ever really think you wouldn't be accepted? You've got a four-point-oh!"

"I don't have a four-point-oh," Kyle said in mock protest. "It's a three-point-nine."

"Oh, right. Ex-cuuuze me." Pulling out a chair, Jason sat down, his knee grazing Kyle's.

The touch sent a spark through Kyle's body. Two excruciatingly long weeks had passed since they'd been alone together. It wouldn't take much for Kyle to jump Jason's bones right then and there.

"Nelson got his letter too," Kyle said in an effort to calm himself down. "So we'll all three go to Tech. It's going to be such a blast."

Jason studied Kyle, then glanced down at his cake.

"What's the matter?" Kyle asked.

"I've been thinking"—Jason paused, gulping a swig of milk as if fortifying himself—"about coming out to Coach."

Kyle's throat clenched as he swallowed his cake. Had he heard right? He knew Jason's going to the Gay-Straight Alliance had been an enormous step toward coming out. Practically the whole school knew who went to the meeting, and even straight people who attended got crap for it. Jason telling his coach would be an even huger step for him.

And for Kyle, it would also be a tremendous relief. He hated pretending they were just friends. While Jason garnered praise on the court or got interviewed by press, Kyle had to stand by anonymous. When Jason jaunted off to some post-game party, Kyle trudged home alone. Unlike Jason's ex-girlfriend, Kyle couldn't receive public recognition.

But if Jason came out . . . Kyle reveled in visions of the prom, dancing arm-in-tuxedoed arm.

"Are you sure?" Kyle asked, not wanting to get his hopes up.

Jason gave a weary sigh. "I don't know. It's just . . ." His voice became agitated. "Sometimes I feel like I'm going to explode—or implode—if I keep hiding. It gets to where I just want to tell everyone and get it over with—not just Coach, the team, too. Does that sound crazy? What's happened with you and the swim team since the locker thing?"

The "locker thing" had happened after December break. Someone scratched QUEER on Kyle's hall locker. Kyle repeatedly asked the school administration to repaint it, and they did nothing. Finally, he got fed up. One morning, he marched to school, and beneath the word QUEER he spray-painted AND PROUD!

The news raced around school. The following day, his locker was repainted, but not before some teammates took notice.

"A few of the guys won't talk to me anymore, but they were never really friends to begin with. Besides, swimming is different from basketball. Except for relays, you're really on your own. In team sports, you're a lot more reliant on each other."

Jason nodded, slowly chewing a bite of cake. "So you don't think I should do it?"

Kyle immediately thought, *Of course you should do it!* He had always encouraged Jason to be honest and accepting of himself.

But before he could say anything, Jason confided, "I'm afraid I'll lose my scholarship."

Kyle set his fork down. "For coming out? They wouldn't

dare. Look at how we fought for a GSA and won. If they tried to take your scholarship, we'd fight that, too. You're not going to lose your scholarship. You'll come out, we'll go to Tech together, and graduate side-by-side."

He almost added how gay marriage would hopefully be legal by then, and about the kids they'd adopt and how they'd live happily ever after. But he decided he'd leave that discussion for later.

"Just suppose," said Jason, tapping his fork. "I did lose my scholarship—"

"Jason," Kyle interrupted. "I told you, you're not—"

"But just suppose," Jason insisted. "Would you still go to Tech?"

"Well . . . could you still go without a scholarship?" Kyle asked.

Jason shrugged. "I don't know how I'd pay for it. My mom can't afford it, especially with my dad gone. I could get loans, but not enough to go away. I'd probably stay home and go to a community college, then transfer later."

Kyle felt his heart sink. More than anything, he wanted to be with Jason. But did he want it enough to put aside his dream of going away to a university?

"I hate this!" Kyle blurted out. "Our society is crazy. Why should we even have to deal with this? Our whole future together shouldn't hinge on whether you're honest and come out. It's homophobic b.s."

Jason leaned back, looking a little blown away by Kyle's out-burst.

"I'm sorry." Kyle took a deep breath. "I didn't mean to go off like that."

"It's okay. I'm sorry I brought all this up. It isn't your problem."

"It is my problem," Kyle told him. "If you don't go to Tech, where would that leave me? What you decide affects both of us."

Jason looked back at him, a solemn look on his face. "Maybe I should forget all this," he said softly.

"How?" Kyle said. "It's not going to go away. Do you want to go through college like this? What happens if they find out after you're already there and take away your scholarship *then*?"

Jason bit into a fingernail. "I hadn't thought of that."

"At least," Kyle said soothingly, "if you come out now, you'd be, I don't know, like, a role model—someone people would look up to."

"Yeah, right," Jason said. "No one's going to look up to me."

"I do," Kyle said, staring deeply into Jason's brown eyes.

Jason pursed his lips into a little pout. "Yeah, well, you're biased. *You're* the role model, not me."

"Oh yeah?" Kyle asked. "And you're not biased?"

Jason's mouth opened in a wide show of teeth. "Maybe."

Kyle thought how much he loved those teeth, that mouth, this boy. He considered what he was about to say and, fighting all common sense, he said it: "If you feel like you need to come out to your coach, then I think you should do it."

Jason gazed back at him, sighing, and slumped down in his chair. In the process, his knee bumped against Kyle's.

Kyle let it rest there and reached across the table for Jason's hand.

Jason flashed a glance toward the door. An instant later they were on their feet, pressed against each other. Jason's lips devoured Kyle's, tasting of chocolate-raspberry cake, sweeter than the original.

As Kyle's tongue rolled across Jason's, he no longer cared about college next year. He only wanted to live this moment, forever. Except . . .

From the doorway came a giggle. Startled, the boys jumped apart.

Melissa stared at them, carrying her empty plate and milk glass. "Were you two kissing?"

Jason, bright red, darted a questioning glance at Kyle, but Kyle looked away, embarrassed. It was up to Jason what he told his sister, though Kyle hoped he'd be truthful.

Jason cleared his throat. "Um, yeah." He hurriedly took her plate and glass. "Don't tell Ma, okay?"

Melissa glanced at Kyle. "I won't." Giggling, she skipped out of the room.

"Oh, man!" Jason brought his fingers to his forehead. "I can't believe she saw us."

"At least you were honest with her," Kyle said, patting him on the shoulder. "That's great."

Jason rubbed his temples. "I'm glad you think so."

The front door sounded as Mrs. Carrillo came home. Fortunately, Melissa kept her word, not saying anything about the boys' kiss while Jason's mom chatted with them, thanking Kyle for the cake.

Before Kyle left, Jason handed him a pair of tickets for the game Friday. "For you and your dad. Can you come?"

"Of course!" Kyle beamed.

As he walked home through the cold, dark night, past brick houses with blue-hazed windows and dogs barking in yards, he thought how clear his life had seemed only two hours earlier.

Now everything seemed so uncertain. What if Jason did lose his scholarship? Would Kyle stick by him no matter what? Wasn't that part of loving someone?

Kyle felt the game tickets in his pocket, desperately hoping he wouldn't regret encouraging Jason to come out to his coach.

LIFE. LOVE. FRIENDSHIP.

From critically acclaimed author Ellen Wittlinger

Love & Lies

Hard Love

Parrotfish

Heart on My Sleeve

Blind Faith

Razzle

Sandpiper

SIMON & SCHUSTER | BFYR

TEEN.simonandschuster.com